Killer Heart

Cursed Hearts, Book 1

Rhys Lawless

Killer Heart, Cursed Hearts Book 1

Copyright © 2019 by Rhys Lawless

Cover Design by Ethereal Designs

Editing by Victoria Milne

Proofreading by Alphabitz Editing

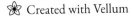 Created with Vellum

ONE

WADE

T his witch was going to be the death of me. Not only was she more elusive than a politician with a tendency for telling the truth, but she also had friends in high positions, which meant wherever she went on a daily basis usually involved high levels of security, and I doubted my sword would pass through their monitors.

Even if I retracted the blade into the hilt, the high levels of angel blood that were infused in the weapon would alert any guard's detectors.

Which meant that I had resolved to standing in the middle of a muddy puddle outside the pub she often visited, waiting for her to get out, drunk and with her guard down.

There was a skill in hunting a witch, one that I had perfected over my fourteen years in the BLADE force.

You weren't allowed out in the field until you had that skill.

Camille Matthews walked out of the pub with a little stumble in her step. Her blonde hair rested on her bare shoulders, and her red puckered lips looked kiss-able. It was a shame she was a witch, or I might have been tempted to hook up with her. But there was no chance in hell I'd let a witch anywhere near me.

I continued to admire her lithe body, hugged by an emerald dress. Her butt didn't look bad either. But then she turned around and I spotted her spellbook, an intri-cate, beautiful necklace around her neck, and any arousal I had allowed myself to feel was shot off the roof.

It had been a while since my last hit, and I could see the glow of her spells from the distance, calling out to me.

Fuck! Get your head straight, Wade. You can't go off the rails during a hunt.

I gave myself the mandatory slap in the head and followed Camille down the road. I knew I had a limited time to get her, as her house was only a couple of blocks down the street, and it was an absolute no-go. Not only had she placed very powerful spells around the house to ward off intruders, but there was also no need for me to leave my fingerprints every-where. If so much as a hair was found as evidence in a witch murder case by the human police, I was a goner.

Besides, I had to take her to Southwark, which was

the opposite way, so the less carrying I had to do, the better.

The witch turned right into another street, and I mimicked her.

This road was off the high street and, as such, less busy. A perfect place to initiate the plan.

I pulled my phone out and sent a quick text to Lloyd. He responded almost instantly. Well, he better have. I hadn't picked him to be my partner for his ability to buy a good muffin.

Just around the corner. Give me the thumbs up when you've got her, the reply said.

Good. Everything was in position. I wasn't sure why the last couple of cases had involved a different modus operandi than usual, but I trusted director Christian Marlowe and his system. Not only had he spent years studying the angel blood properties and how to best protect everyone from witches, but also, ever since he'd taken over, we had achieved the highest results in the history of the BLADE force.

Christian had given me a trial run of a new ritual to kill the witches, and while I wasn't entirely sure how the results were calculated, I wasn't going to go against my director's orders.

Camille was a few steps ahead of me, and with a last glance around, I quickened my pace and came right up behind her, extracting the blade of my sword from its hilt.

The witch turned around before I even managed to make any noise as if she could sense me.

"Who are you?" she said, but then she saw the sword and stepped back.

I didn't know if witches were trained about witch hunters or if it was a natural instinct, and to be frank, I didn't care to find out.

Her hand came up to her spellbook; the necklace had probably cost a few thousand pounds to be made and carried a selection of green gemstones. Gemstones that seemed to call my name the more I looked at them.

I was getting a boner over the crystals that matched the color of the witch's dress when Camille pulled one of them out and held it in her palm.

"*Vota*!" she shouted, and green dust erupted from the depths of the crystal and attacked me.

Before I could react, vines wrapped around my body, restricting any movement, which I wouldn't have minded—who didn't like a bit of bondage every now and again—but one particular goddamn vine was squeezing my balls and giving me a bitch of a pain.

"You shouldn't have come after me, witch hunter. Do you know who I am?" she asked me with a quirked grin on her face that I would soon wipe off.

The witch lifted her arms and the light in the street changed. The darkness became ominous and the shadows started closing in. This must have been her natural power. I couldn't see dust anywhere, which meant she hadn't used another spell. The shadows took slender human shapes all around me, which drew closer with each breath I took.

"Cool. Can you do this with clowns too? That would be a lot scarier," I said, despite the fear growing inside me with every step of the human shadows.

She laughed. I laughed. The shadows laughed. It was a good vibe. And while I was afraid of her natural power, it was time to take her down.

That was the worst part about witches. Their natural powers. While we could always more or less predict the spells they used in battle, it was impossible to tell their natural power unless you witnessed it first-hand. With spells, it was easy. Every witch had a fondness for a certain kind of spell. Some fancied elemental and usually leaned on one side of the four elements. Others liked trickster spells, which made sense. Trickster spells looked more like a trick of the light than supernatural forces. Easier to conceal once cast.

This particular witch had a thing for Mother Nature. I'd followed her long enough to know green was her color and vines were her kinky preference. Did I not hate witches, I would have let her take me for a ride tied up in leaves.

The shadows gave me a big hug that wasn't warm, which was upsetting, and washed me with their coolness, which was sort of welcome.

"Fancy power," I said, hoping she could hear me

because I couldn't hear myself. "I'm not here to hurt you. Can we talk?"

I pulled the blade back into its hilt and counted to three. I liked giving people a chance to make up for their mistakes, even if those people were witches.

That was not to say I wouldn't kill her. But if she pulled those shadows away from me, then I might at least give her a few seconds head start.

"I guess that's a no," I said, and my breath caught. The shadows were starting to drown me. The oxygen supply was decreasing, and the coolness of the dark was suffocating me, awakening my dick.

It truly was a shame she was a witch. She liked ropes and a bit of choking. Plus, she was smoking hot and knew how to get what she wanted. She wouldn't have made it as a COO in a male-dominated industry if she didn't. But as much as I was enjoying her company, I had work to do.

I tilted the hilt of my sword upwards and slightly inwards, then tugged the blade from it, and as it grew bigger along the side of my arm like an aroused penis, I sliced through the vines and pulled it back in position in front of me. Before the witch could react, I slashed at everything in front of me. A yelp permeated the silence and the shadows receded, bringing the witch, now with a sliced arm, back into my vision.

She looked at me, the creases on her face making her look even sexier, and she tried to stand straight, clutching at her spellbook. Before she could cast another spell at me, I cut the distance between us, and with the hilt of my sword, I hit her in the head with enough force to knock her unconscious.

I took my phone out of my pocket and looked at the screen. Lloyd was still waiting for my text. But there was just one thing I needed to do first.

I bent down and picked the beautiful green spells off her necklace. It was impossible sometimes to believe that such little gemstones could cause so much trouble. We had studied the whole science behind crystals and spells—some bullshit to do with alchemy and words—but it always confounded me how spells that could destroy the entire world were lying dormant inside the crystals witches used.

Feeling philosophical at moments like this was a common occurrence. It might have been the adrenaline, or I might have just been a clever asshole who liked to pretend I was more than my kills. Fuck knows. I stashed the crystals in the inside pocket of my jacket and sent a signal to Lloyd making sure to look around me for any witnesses.

Not that it mattered. Most of the time, the police wrote off those incidents as hallucinating loonies, and even when they didn't, they could never find criminal evidence. And that was solely because they didn't know what to look for.

If they had, they'd know the little blue or red stain on the ground wasn't paint or sand. It was magical dust, residue of spells used, and even that residue faded away after a while, depending on the strength of the spell.

Put it this way; the more powerful the spell, the longer the dust residue lingered where it was cast. The less powerful the incantation, the faster the residue faded.

Needless to say that with me, witches usually didn't get a chance to use their crystals, so one way or another, I was covered.

A black van screeched on the road and came to a halt by the pavement where I was standing with the unconscious Camille, who I hauled over my shoulder and then dumped unceremoniously in the back of the van.

"What took you so long?" Lloyd asked me with a perked-up eyebrow once I joined him in the front.

We'd been together for give or take five years now, and he was a friend as much as a colleague. So, I didn't take his arrogance personally. He was a prick with most people, and that's why we were a good fit.

"She tried some mumbo jumbo with shadows. Obviously, I showed her who's boss," I told him to put him in his place.

I didn't want him running around headquarters telling people I'd gone soft on witches, or that I'd grown weak. It didn't take much for a rumor to get someone dismissed. Which was why my brother Winston and I had kept our little problem to ourselves. No one at head office knew our hearts had been cursed by a witch, and we weren't planning on telling them, either.

"Man, why did they have to go and change things. Blades have been killing witches for centuries the good ol' fashioned way. A pentacle on the skin and off they go to hell. I don't understand this new shit," Lloyd grumbled as he sped through the streets of central London.

"I told you. Don't call us Blades. We're more than the sum of our weapons, asshole. Also, if Christian says this way is more effective, who are we to say he's wrong?" I said.

I really hated the slang term. A lot of witch hunters called themselves that, but I didn't like it. I was more than my job. That stupid term made me one with my sword. As if I was a weapon myself and not a human being. I already had my predicaments. I didn't need the objectification to make it worse.

———

Once the job was done and the witch was dead, finally, I left Lloyd to write the report and headed home.

It had been hours since my last dose, and the cravings were making me twitchy, which was the worst part of addiction.

My flat wasn't anything fancy even though the money from the job was more than generous. I hardly ever saw the inside, especially when I was on super-long missions like the last couple had been.

Camille was the third trial so far, and each witch had taken me about a week to monitor and kill. It had to be done. Once we got the names, we needed to know the effect of their reach. Who they'd influenced, who they met. It was all-important intel that led us to the next witch and the one after that.

The insides of my fridge proved futile, so I resorted to ordering takeaway. With a quick thumb through a restaurant delivery app, I had pizza on the way and a rumbling stomach until its arrival.

It didn't matter because I knew just the thing to keep me busy until it got here.

I opened the door to my bedroom and walked to my wardrobe. The mirror on the panels showed me my tired mug, and I didn't care for it, so I slid it open to reveal my clothes. I wasn't adventurous with my fashion choices, and most of my outfits were laced with angel blood to protect against witches. They didn't always work. Which meant the current jacket I was wearing could go in the laundry. I would have to take it back to headquarters to replenish the intricate lacing. Sliding away the hangers with shirts and T-shirts revealed the back panel of the wardrobe.

I fiddled with it until I found the grip I was looking for at the bottom and pulled the panel up to reveal the secret room behind it.

It wasn't big, but this space was definitely fancy. It

had to if I was going to store powerful spells some-where, especially in such large volumes. Spells couldn't be dumped anywhere. The energy lying dormant inside could play up if not placed properly either in a spellbook or a carefully created display.

Or that was the idea anyway. I always collected witch's spells. Been doing it since I was first sent out in the field, more or less. But my prized collection had now diminished to a handful of spells.

My addiction had grown out of hand. That much was true. But it wasn't my fault that their effects didn't last long anymore.

It all started with good intentions. If I could find a spell powerful enough to break the curse on my heart, why wouldn't I? So, I did just that and collected all the spells I could find. Sometimes, if the witches weren't that well off to afford security, I even raided their houses to find spells they hadn't carried with them when I killed them.

But I didn't think things through. Humans couldn't use spells, crystals—whatever you wanted to call it—so unless I found a witch to help me, I was doomed either way. But young me hadn't thought about that. See? Good intentions.

But those intentions had come to be my undoing. It had only taken one bitch of a witch to blow dust in my face, and I'm talking literal magical dust, to get me high as a kite, and that had been it.

To this day, I have no idea what the spell had been

for. All I can remember is the feeling of warmth when I inhaled it. It had taken all my strength to kill her. Not easy to fight off a witch when you're that high, but once I had, I'd tried it again with my collection of spells.

And what do you know? Spells can be addictive.

Here I am, two years later, and I'm a spell addict. If you want to judge me, be my guest, but wait your turn. I do enough self-judging as it is.

The crystals in my jacket were calling out to me, begging me to use. And I obliged, removing them from the insides of my garment and placing them on the little desk in front of me, and I took a seat.

The green of their magic was luminescent, and their texture was polished. I looked at them and it was like they were looking back at me. My hands twitched even more, and I had to use all my energy to grab the mortar and pestle and place all the spells inside.

I ground them until they were nothing but crystallized powder, and somehow, they looked more appealing in their current form than they had before.

I lined up the powder on the desktop, three perfect magical lines, and snorted them one by one.

Each managed to hit just the right spot between light-headedness and warmth. They were so warm, in fact, they made me sweat. The blood thumped inside my veins and my dick awakened. Everything was bright and time slowed down. And my boner was throbbing.

It'd be a shame not to.

I unzipped my pants and let my cock out of its fabric cage. The effects of the spells wouldn't last long, so I palmed my dick hard and fast. I could have waited it out but coming while high on magic was the best drug of them all.

My breath caught and sweat trickled down my back. A soft moan escaped my lips as I let loose. Cum shot out of me and dribbled down my fist.

As if on cue, the high wore off, and I was left there, sitting in a tiny red room with my dick in my hand and feeling like a washed-up whore.

I'm fucked up. I've got eyes and I can see it. But it's all a witch's fault for casting a curse on my brother and me.

And because of them, neither one of us can ever feel love.

Two
Caleb

I couldn't take any more of this shit. Graham had pulled me out of bed at an ungodly hour. Again. And I already woke up at ungodly hours for work. Third time in a month, and I was not liking it one bit. And he knew that the wee hours of the next day was the one time I actually got some rest.

And what did he do? Give me a crime scene to investigate at four in the bloody morning.

I looked at my watch and the numbers changed from 4:09 to 4:10. Yep, still an ungodly hour, just like it had been two seconds ago when I last checked. And Lorelai was taking her jolly good time as usual.

I mean, how long did it take to sniff around a churchyard for a filthy witch hunter anyway? She needed some more training on how to be a better familiar, or as they were more widely known, shifter, because I was still not convinced.

Yes, I was cranky. How could I not be? It was so irritating to be dragged out of the nice warmth of my bed into the cold and rainy streets of London before a soul, human or otherwise, arose. All I wanted was to investigate the crime scene, report back to Graham, and go back to bed. Hopefully, *hopefully*, I could sneak in another hour of dreamless bliss.

Knowing my luck, there was a fat chance of that happening. So, I was stuck with Lorelai for the rest of the morning. And as if she could read my mind, she appeared. A big red fox with shiny black eyes and a menacing look on her face.

I placed my hands on my hips to show her my annoyance, and with a flash of light and a puff of smoke, the red fox disappeared and, in its place, a tall white woman with long, sleek red hair and an ample body appeared in front of me.

"You're so impatient, Caleb." She chuckled.

I rolled my eyes as a further indication that at this time of day she would not get friendly Caleb any time soon.

"And?" I asked.

Lorelai relented and pointed behind her with the confidence of a rugby player during a bar brawl.

"All clear. No witch hunters in the vicinity," she said.

"Finally," I grumbled and walked into the Christ Church Southwark churchyard with Lorelai on my tail.

"Excuse you, douchebag. It takes time, you know. I don't just have to sniff everywhere; I also have to differentiate between trump smells and pigeon shit. It's not easy."

"Yeah, yeah, yeah, I bet it's horrible." I cut her off and approached the clearing in front of the stairs that led to the main building.

Lorelai was a friend, and if the way I treated her rubbed anyone the wrong way, they should wait and see how I treated my enemies. Like the people that did these horrible things that made my high priest drag me out of bed at this ungodly hour.

An intricate pentacle was drawn on the ground, and in the middle of it, the limp and lifeless body of Camille Matthews, high council member and an acquaintance of mine.

Graham had taken me under the wing of the coven when he'd found me, lost, heartbroken, and empty, and he'd given me a life. Camille had been there to help me adjust and learn the ways of both the coven and the high council. And while it had been a while since I'd seen her last, her death hurt as much as the rest of them.

Camille's green dress was drenched in blood from the big stab wound in the middle of her chest. Another gash on her arm told me she had not been ambushed here, but they had planted her body on this ground on purpose.

But why on earth there was a pentacle on the

ground and not on her skin, I did not know. The way witch hunters operated was that they hunted witches down, and once they'd killed them, they drew pentacles on their skin with angel-blood laced blades, exterminating the witches' souls. It was a fucking cruel thing to do to a soul, witch or otherwise, and I hated it with all my being. Being dead was no fun as it was. You didn't need asshole hunters messing with your afterlife.

I got my phone camera out and took pictures of Camille and her surroundings before I took my gloves off—leather and magic sewn together to protect me from the rest of the world—and touched Camille's body.

A rush of adrenaline took over me as I relived her emotions from her last moments on this plane of existence.

There was anger, making my head pound. The limited lights around us blurred as I tried to soothe the pain, but the fear emanating from Camille's dead body made my heart beat wild in my chest, and any sort of restraint I had was gone in an instant. Acid burned my throat as the hatred she'd felt before she'd died left a bad taste in my mouth.

You shouldn't have come after me, witch hunter. Do you know who I am?

Camille's thoughts rang in my head.

Fuck! Fuck! Fuck! I need to get away. Why did I leave my best spells at home? Stupid, stupid Camille.

The thoughts associated with her emotions were

strong, otherwise I wouldn't be able to hear them. But they were on a loop. And that's how much I was going to get out of her. I wasn't surprised. None of the others had much more to say about their assailant. All of them had been too terrified to think about anything else.

I mean, it would help if their stubbornness to live had taken over them and they started describing the hunter that had killed them, but that would make my job easy, and I didn't do easy. Apparently.

As much as I tried to navigate through Camille's feelings, nothing else showed up. The whole point of being an empath was that I got an imprint of people's emotions just as they'd felt them. Even with dead bodies. And boy did dead bodies have a lot of emotions lingering. But Camille, and the others before her, could only give so much away.

I removed my hand and stood. Lorelai was looking at me, waiting for answers, and I had none. We were no closer to getting any sort of resolution than we had been yesterday or the day before.

I reached out to my bracer, a plain black bracelet that held my spells, and took a red ruby off it. Placing it on top of Camille's chest, I whispered the words to activate it and quickly took a step back as the blue spirit flames burned her body and made all traces of it vanish into thin air. If she'd still had her soul, the flames would have guided it to the afterlife, but as it was, they'd do nothing to get her to rest in peace.

"What did you feel?" Lorelai asked.

"Nothing new," I said.

"I'm sorry, hon."

We stood there for a few moments as if that was going to change the situation or give us any more clues, but it was pointless.

"Shall we head? Got to open the cafe in a few."

I would have loved to ask her to cover for me so I could go back to bed and wallow for a bit longer before I made my appearance, but I wasn't one to bail out on a friend. She turned around, and I followed her as we walked out of the churchyard and headed for the bus stop.

Yes, we live a fancy life us witches. We live in creaky old houses and take the bus to work. We even work two jobs to make a living. Lorelai and I run the cafe in the front and the spell shop at the back, for those witches that know how to find us.

Despite the fact that Lorelai wasn't a witch, we made a good team. One of the reasons Graham gave us the odd jobs for the high council. And as their only empath, I was very handy to them.

None of it mattered to me. I was just going through the motions, and I was fully aware of that. It was hard to care about anything when you'd lost so much and life kept hitting back at you again. And again. And again.

We got on the bus and sat on the bottom floor as hcights made Lorelai sick.

The bus was deathly quiet, as there were just a couple of drunk people sleeping in the front seats, stinking of booze and dancing. As the driver took us the scenic morning route, I took my mobile phone out of my jacket and dialed home.

"Hello," came the almost immediate reply from my roommate and co-parent, Annabel.

"Hey, Ann," I said. "How are things at home?"

Nora had woken up when Graham had called, and Annabel had had to literally yank her away from me to let me go. I hated it when she got like that. It was becoming harder to leave behind.

"She's fine. I read her a story and it knocked her out like a log."

"Let me guess. Pixie and the Firestarters?" I asked.

It was her favorite story. Both Annabel and I had read it to her hundreds of times, and we even knew the words by heart. I was bored as fuck of it and couldn't wait until she got a bit older and could read more middle-grade stuff. For the moment, we were stuck with pyromaniac pixies.

"What else?" Annabel answered. "How are things your end?"

"I'd rather not talk about it."

I wouldn't know where to start. None of us had any idea how high council members were being tracked and killed. And not only that, but their spell-books completely empty of crystals when it was clear they hadn't used any.

Things were getting curiouser and curiouser, and I didn't even know what to do next. Not that I had to worry about it too much. It was Graham's and the high council's job to connect the dots and find out what the hell was going on. But in my boring-as-fuck routine, curiosity was leading me down a dangerous path of caring.

When we got to the cafe, it was five-thirty, and we still had another hour and a half before we opened. Despite this, Lorelai started setting everything up, and first business was turning on the coffee machine.

"What do you think those hunters are playing at? Do you think they've gone rogue?" she asked as she whipped up filter coffees for both of us.

I shrugged. It was the only response I could give that made any sense. Witches and witch hunters and bullshit politics that I had no interest in. I was sure the high council had its ideas of what was going on, but they weren't very forthcoming with the information they let out. Not that I could blame them.

But life had been simpler when I had been just a vampire and all I'd had to worry about was getting my blood supply from my allocated dealer and trying to explain to employers why I couldn't do any interviews before the sun set. See? It sounded so much simpler than all this shit.

I wasn't ungrateful. I swear. Despite the simpler times, life hadn't resisted taking its punches at me. First, they'd taken my Jin from me. And when I say "they," I mean the Nightcrawlers. The creatures of the night. I had been one of them, of course, at the time. And so was Jin. An incubus with a heart of gold. The "mine is bigger than yours" mentality of the paranormal world was unbelievable. Everyone fighting to come out on top. Everyone except for my Jin.

And trolls. Trolls didn't care for any of that shit. Probably because they could knock anyone that came close out cold for good, which probably also meant they were the clear winners. Maybe if trolls acted like the powerful beings they were, elves wouldn't go rampant killing incubi to prove something. But they didn't because they hated humans and preferred to stay with their own kind.

"Hey." Lorelai waved her hand in front of me and took me out of the depths of my head. "Are you okay?"

I nodded and took the cup she was offering. The smell of coffee alone was enough to set my cranky straight and help me focus on the here and now.

"Do you want to take the till today? I can tell you won't be a hundred percent. I've told Graham to avoid waking you up at ungodly hours."

And there it was, the reason why Lorelai was my best friend. Regardless of the fact the high council had forced us together. Who better to look after the galore of spells at the backroom than a witch with nothing left to lose and a familiar with a bubbly personality that could cut you in half at the mere sniff of a threat?

After our heart-to-heart over coffee, which meant

quiet stares and the occasional sigh, I went to the back office to get the tills up and running and, of course, report back to Graham.

I removed my pencil-thin crystal from my bracer and drew a square with it on the mirror.

"Call Graham," I said, and in a puff of dust and smoke, the white drawn square rippled. I waited until it cleared again, and an older man with white hair, a beard, and striking green eyes appeared inside the mirror.

"You look like shit," was the first thing he said to me.

I opened my mouth to respond, but he raised his hand and stopped me.

"Before you say about me waking you up at ungodly hours, I just have to say I don't keep a roster of witch hunters and their hits. I will call you when I need you."

Fair enough. He had a point there. It didn't change the fact that I looked like shit, and it was his fault.

"It was Camille. Same as the other two. Pentacle on the ground, no crystals, and they were all mighty terrified when they died."

"Poor Camille. She deserved better," he said.

I bit the back of my lip. "They all did, Graham."

He nodded and looked away from me at something I couldn't see.

"What are you doing?"

Graham didn't reply.

"If you're watching porn, I'm going to cast a spell on your dick and turn it into a fucking worm," I told him while trying to look inside the mirror, but the communication spell didn't work that way, so I couldn't dig my head inside and reach him on the other end.

The high priest snapped his attention back to me and frowned.

"That potty mouth of yours is getting tiring," he said.

I laughed.

"You've been saying that since you met me. When are you going to realize I'm never going to change?"

Graham looked off mirror again.

"Are you going to tell me what's going on or are we going to keep sitting in silence when I could be doing better things?"

My high priest had always been secretive since I'd met him. To this day, I did not know what the fuck had happened to me before he'd found me and told me I was a witch. The year after I lost Jin—and almost lost my life trying to avenge him—all of a sudden another year had suddenly passed; Nora was two years old, and I was standing in front of Graham being told I was a witch.

Graham had given me a gift. Access to a different world. A part of the world where I could make a differ-ence. Because as fun as being a vampire had been, it was quite useless. He'd also given me a semblance of family and normality. One I hadn't felt since the army.

Graham turned to me and grimaced.

"What do you think I'm looking at? The pictures of all the crime scenes, you doofus. Third high council witch to die in a month. When was the last time a high council witch was killed? Huh?"

I opened my mouth to reply, but Graham slammed his fist on the desk again.

"Over a decade, Caleb. Over a decade. You know why? Because the high council members have the highest protection and security protocols of all. Our names aren't even on public record to protect our identities," he shouted.

I narrowed my eyes and watched him try to compose himself again, an idea crossing my mind.

"You know what that means, right?" I said. "There's a mole in the council."

Graham pursed his lips and nodded.

"We need to test that theory. Can you tell me what Camille and the other two had in common other than their status? There's, what, a hundred or so high council members. Why target these particular witches?"

"I know what they have in common," Graham replied flatly, his face blank of emotions. "They're all part of a very special mission. And before you ask, I can't tell you about it."

I rolled my eyes and made a point of showing how stupid this secrecy thing was.

"I don't give a shit about it," I said. "I'm fully aware you are not the sharing type. What I want to know is can you get me into that special mission team?"

"What part of secret did you not understand?"

"Calm your knickers, Gray. I mean on paper."

"I don't follow," he said.

There was a knock at the door, and Lorelai peaked her head in.

"Sorry to interrupt, but I'm about to open the doors, and there's already a queue of witches outside."

"I'll be right out," I told her, and she closed the door again. Once I'd made sure she was out of earshot —and not because I didn't trust her, but because this was delicate shit, and I didn't want her involved in what I was about to get myself into—I asked Graham, "How big is the team that is working on this super-secret project?"

"There's three of them running the operation."

"Great. You need to make me the fourth member in that operation. On paper. And let that intel leak. I'll take care of the rest."

Graham nodded in understanding.

"You'd be putting yourself in a lot of danger, Caleb."

"I can take care of myself. If a witch is working with the witch hunters, we've got far bigger problems."

"I'll get it done and get you an update ASAP," Graham said. "Caleb? Be careful, son."

And with that, he disconnected the call, leaving me alone to handle a flurry of witches in need of spells.

Just another day in my life.

THREE

WADE

L ater that same morning, I left home and walked along the Southbank in Westminster. The place had only just started filling up with morning office workers rushing to work or the nearest underground station, and I pushed past several of them to get clear and continue my journey.

I wasn't walking about aimlessly. I, too, had work to do, which was why I tapped my Oyster card at the entrance of the Westminster tube station and climbed down the stairs, two at a time. While most people continued their trail down the second set of escalators that took them even deeper underground, I took a left turn and walked to a simple silver door.

Like most things in London, people wouldn't know it was there unless they saw something major happen outside it, and even then, only a handful would notice. The fact that it also had tape stuck at the top that said "private" helped with the whole cover-out-in-the-open thing.

I placed my hand on the door handle and pulled it outwards. The door swung open, and I let myself inside a dark room. I was used to the mechanics by now. The door closed and sealed up behind me, then one bright spotlight came on, blinding me, and once that was over, the ground I was standing on shook, and my trip continued farther down the depths of the earth.

Once the lift arrived at level -3, I stepped out and thumbed through the security checks that had been put into place since I'd joined the force. Before that, it had been scanning plain white cards that everyone kept losing.

The main area of the force was open plan. Several rows of desks and chairs adorned the space, and daylight bulbs placed behind glass panels and wallpapers of scenic views made the office look less claustrophobic and more like another spacious room on top of a skyscraper. To the right was the training room where every witch hunter performed their mandatory five-hour weekly sword fighting and angel rituals.

On the left were the labs where our experts replicated angel blood and laced our swords and clothes with it.

As usual, the office was a bustle of activity. Some hunters were already sparring in the training room, while others typed away on their computers, researching their next case. It was life as normal for everyone, myself included.

I walked to my desk and sat down, throwing my jacket onto Lloyd's, which woke him from his mesmerizing screen.

"Have you slept at all?" I asked him.

He shook his head.

"Of course not. I've been trying to write that report," he said.

I chuckled. Lloyd was not a guy of the written word which had become blatantly obvious by how long it took him to write those reports. But practice makes perfect.

My brother approached behind me and attempted to get one on me by slapping my head, but all the years in the force had done wonders for my reflexes. I turned and grabbed his wrist before it landed a blow.

"You all right, bro?" He laughed. "Took you long enough to get that last witch."

I squeezed my hand on his wrist as I felt the temper boil inside me.

Uh-oh.

I hated it when that happened.

"The fuck did you just say?" I growled between my teeth.

Lloyd pushed his chair back and stood up. He placed a hand on my other arm, but I batted it away and brought it up to Winston's neck, who took my anger like the man he was.

He didn't have much of an option. When either of us got into the heat of it all, nothing the other would do could stop us. And we'd both rather take each other's punches than let them loose around the force and get detained.

Most of our colleagues knew us anyway. And they all thought that's what our playful, brotherly love was like. If only they knew how real the pain we inflicted on each other was. Hopefully, no one would ever have to find out.

My hand tightened around his throat and my heart palpitated so fast that I had to take deep breaths to keep up with it. Winston's neck was red, and I could see his struggle under my strength.

But as quickly as my temper had risen, so quickly it also evaporated, and I was left weak and yet more broken. There was no time to run through my emotions and the memories of Sarah that always haunted me after these breakouts because Director Marlowe appeared from his office at the other end and shouted my name.

"Rawthorne, in my office. Now," he hissed.

He always hisses, so that wasn't a sign of trouble. It's just the nature of his voice. What told me I was, in fact, in trouble was the bloodshot eyes as I approached him.

He quickly looked away from me and rushed through the double oak doors that led to his office, and

I followed him inside, closing the door behind me carefully.

It hadn't ended well for the last witch that had slammed those doors without much consideration. According to Marlowe, the doors were hundreds of years old.

When I turned around to look at Director Marlowe, he was already sitting behind his desk looking pissed off. No one in the force liked to upset him. He had a short temper, and everyone knew better than to get on his wrong side.

Hesitantly, I approached the table, sat down, and waited for my boss to reprimand me. It wouldn't be the first time, and it certainly wouldn't be the last. My curse had got me in a lot of trouble, and it would for a long time still. That was the whole point of the curse. It was with me for life unless I found a way to break it. It's a good thing I was one of Marlowe's favorites. My brother and I had worked for him for many years. He'd known us since we were just starting out as witch hunters, and while that said fuck all about anything else in life, in the BLADE force it meant a lot.

Of course, it also meant that a lot of people didn't like us because of that relationship with the director, but I cared very little about other people's opinions. Since friendships and any sort of relationships were out of the question for the rest of my life, my rank and my job were all I could fight for. So what if my boss liked me more than the others? That was a win.

"Listen, Rawthorne, I have a new witch for you," Marlowe said.

I was surprised to not hear a reprimand about what had just happened outside and that he, instead, went straight to the next subject. Maybe he was finally getting used to the relationship Winston and I had. Or maybe we were both going to get it really bad later.

"Is there a problem?" Marlowe asked.

I shook my head, maybe a bit more frantically than I'd intended to, but the message was received.

"Good. Now, this witch is very important. I've just got the information, but he's one of the leaders of the witch community, and who better to send after him than my best witch hunter? The problem is, all I've got is a name. No photos or further information. Are you up to the task?" Marlowe's eyes pierced me as if they could read my soul. And the more I looked at them, the more I felt like they actually could.

"Of course I can. I will not let you down, sir."

Marlowe rolled his eyes and let out a big sigh.

"All these formalities mean nothing to me, Rawthorne. Besides, I wasn't asking. I need results with this one," Marlowe said, and his eyes seemed to glimmer.

A chill ran through my body. That wasn't uncommon with a cursed, frozen heart, but this particular one made me shudder. Christian Marlowe was serious about this witch. I had to find him and terminate him fast. There was no letting my boss down on this. Not that I ever could. I was the best in the field with the biggest success rate. That wasn't a coincidence.

"Message received."

Director Marlowe nodded ever so slightly. If I'd blinked, I could have missed it. I got up, turned around, and was heading for the door when something occurred to me, and while I wasn't sure about asking him, it would bug me if I didn't.

"Sir? A lot of the hunters have been asking me about this new trial..."

"Yes?" he said, narrowing his eyes.

"Is this new ritual going to go wide if it's successful? You know how people are with traditions. A lot of them are scared they won't be able to sustain the high success rate if this is introduced."

The truth was the witch hunters were talking about it, but I was more concerned about myself. It was taking me longer to track the witches than ever before. And also, something felt off about these rituals, but I just couldn't put my finger on it. Maybe I was just missing something. Maybe I was doing something wrong. And I didn't want to fail, especially on a trial run.

"The chatter of the witch hunters concerns me not. And neither should you be concerned about what they think. Habits are hard to break, I am well aware, but if we have to, we will," Marlowe said.

His words did nothing to appease my curiosity.

"And how are the results measured exactly? You've never explained, and I was just—" A slam on the desk stopped me.

Marlowe stood, his blood-red face a contrast to his usual milky-white complexion.

"This does not concern you, Rawthorne. If I want to make announcements, I will. Now you may leave. I need to pray," he said, and there was no way I was disobeying his order this time.

I left the office carrying the new witch file. Winston tried to find out what happened, but I wasn't in the sharing mood after my meeting with Marlowe. Instead, I retreated to my desk and opened the file to read the witch's name. Robert Jones.

A male witch, huh? Hadn't had one of those in a while.

———

How did this always happen to me? How come I always ended up in a dark, dirty alley looking for witches? It was becoming a bit of a joke, honestly. And as if that wasn't enough, rain decided to happen too. So, there I was, in the middle of a stinking fucking alley, waiting for the witch to come out of the bloody pub. I had only been following him for a day, and I'd already had enough of his bullshit. This guy didn't stop moving. He went from one place to another like his pants were on fire.

If Marlowe was correct and he was an important witch, I could at least go after his network, and let me tell you, it was quite extended. It was the only saving grace of this mission, because, frankly, everything else about it was fucking shit.

But while I'd been chasing him around town all day, strangely, he had been in the pub for over two hours, and I had no idea when he was bound to leave. He had also gone in alone, and I didn't know what he was up to. When people drank in groups, they were predictable. They hopped from bar to bar until they ended up either home or passed out in the street. When they were out drinking on their own though? That was a different beast.

The rain was starting to get on my nerves, and so did the wait. The pub had gotten much busier, so keeping my distance would be easy without getting detected. Even if he saw me and knew what I was, he wouldn't dare cause a scene in front of humans. But that was unlikely to happen because I had tucked my sword away in my pants, along with any other indication that I was a witch hunter.

I went inside the pub. It was a center of loud-mouthed drunks and sexy women doing shots. Had I not been on a mission, I would have loved to join the girls and buy them some more drinks. If one of them woke up in my bed, it wouldn't be the end of the world. But that's as far as I could go with women. Just a one-time fuck and out the door. I couldn't risk becoming attached to anyone. If anyone stayed close to me long enough, my wrath could kill them. Because that's what my curse was about. It's not that I couldn't feel love necessarily, it's that if I began to feel it, my killer instinct took over.

One-night stands were the only thing that could offer some sort of normality most days. On the days it didn't, it was a tough one. Thankfully, I always had the crystals at the back of my closet.

I scanned the room, trying to find the witch I had been stalking today. He wasn't difficult to spot. He had wild, white hair and an attitude to kill. A goth a needle away from overdosing. Which was why when I'd found him, I'd been surprised he was the mastermind behind witches. Surely a person like this was a mastermind of nothing.

I spotted him at the back of the room. His back was turned, but he wasn't talking to anyone. No one was engaging with him, but he did have a drink in his hand. I decided to keep a close eye on him. He was an unusual creature, and there was no place for error on this mission.

I squeezed past the crowd, even got some angry looks from punters, but I got closer to the witch while still keeping a safe distance so I wasn't spotted. It was best to keep my face hidden because if I kept following him for the rest of the week, he would grow suspicious. I had to be cautious and methodic.

The witch turned around, and with only a few feet

separating us, I got a glimpse of his eyes. A conniving silver-gray that complemented his hair color. He also had a few piercings, one on his eyebrow, one in his nostril, and two in his ear. This kid was a punk. A pretty punk, but still. He was a weirdo. I have nothing against weirdos—or pretty people for that matter—but I did when those descriptions were mixed with the word *witch*. I could appreciate a handsome man and while this witch was anything but, I couldn't keep my eyes off him. Partly because he was my mission. But partly because there was something about him.

The witch waded through the crowd, and I realized too late that he was edging closer to me. I tried to turn and engage with the people behind me, but there was no time. The witch stared me right down before I could react.

"Hello, witch hunter. We need to talk," he said to me, and I froze.

What the actual fuck? This had never happened before. Had I just been caught by a witch?

Four

Caleb

The hunter looked at me as if he had seen a ghost. It was fun to watch his reaction to my words, even though only a few seconds passed before he responded. It felt like I had been studying his face for hours. And damn, was he hot. No one had warned me that the hunter would be hot. How annoying was that? I just wanted to get my job done and get back home to my family. But from the looks of it, this wasn't going to happen any time soon.

"Excuse me? Do I know you?" the hunter asked.

It was cute. Trying to play all innocent in front of me. Pretend that he didn't know anything about witches and hunters. But neither of us was born yesterday.

Before I thought too much about it, I grabbed his crotch. However, instead of his dick, my hand found the hilt of his sword.

"Are you just happy to see me or do you wanna talk?" I asked him.

The hunter furrowed his brows and his nostrils flared as he let out a defiant breath, piercing me with pure hatred. That was more like it. That, I was used to. He pushed my hand away from him and nodded.

"What do I have to talk about with you?" he asked.

The loud music of the pub was enough cover for a witch and a witch hunter to have a conversation, so I wasn't planning on moving any time soon, but it did mean that we had to shout to be heard.

I gave him the come-hither gesture with my index finger and then approached the top corner of the bar. There was a table for two and a sofa occupied by two lovebirds. Not for long.

"Hey, you two! Move it," I shouted at them and kicked the guy's feet to get their attention.

Both stopped kissing and turned. The girl looked dazed, and the guy pissed. He tried to get up and come at me, but I wasn't having any of his bullshit. I had a hunter to negotiate with and very thin patience.

"What did you say, bro? What the fuck did you say to me?" he barked.

"Firstly, I spoke to both of you, not just you, you self-absorbed dickhead. And secondly, you need to move. Before I move you." I finished with a smile. They told me that smiles won people over. It hadn't happened to me yet, but I still held hope.

It seemed I would have to keep on hoping because

the guy tried to throw a punch my way. But there was no punching an ex-vampire. My blood thirst and my sensitivity to light might have vanished when I was healed, but my natural reflexes were still alive and kicking. I ducked away from his punch and came up to his side, blocked his hand, then lifted my elbow hard on his chin. The guy stumbled back but attempted to have another go at me.

Before I could react, a hand was placed on his chest and the hunter pushed him back. He was trying to protect me. How quaint. The man that had come here to kill me edged closer to the douchebag with a sudden wooden move and whispered something in his ear. The red in the guy's face told me he had not just been told a bedtime story. Whatever it was the witch hunter had told him worked because he dragged his girlfriend off the couch and allowed us some relative privacy at last.

We sat next to each other but not close. I didn't want to give anyone the impression that I was with a witch hunter. I didn't need any Nightcrawlers around spreading word on the street about me. There was enough of it as it was.

"So, what does a witch have to tell me? What does a witch have to talk to me about? And most importantly, why should I listen to you?" the hunter asked me.

I smiled at him. He was so innocent. I could tell from the way he spoke. Yes, he had killed loads of witches, but he knew nothing about this world—as much as he thought he did. I felt sorry for him in a way. I had once been in his shoes. Maybe not the same ones since I had never been a witch hunter, but similar ones, anyway.

"We both have a problem that needs fixing. You have a witch in your force, and we have a mole in our midst," I said.

I waited for the effect of my words, but it didn't seem to reach him.

"Do you understand what I just said?" I asked him.

The hunter seemed to be contemplating my words, and when he spoke next, it was all but a grumble of hatred.

"We would never work with witches, so don't try and mess with me, witch. Whatever it is you want to tell me, tell me now before I terminate you."

"God! Does someone write your lines for you? Do you have, like, a screenwriter in that empty space between your shoulders feeding you lines, because I'll tell you now, they are fucking cliché."

The hunter responded only with a pair of evil eyes until he spoke again.

"I have nothing to discuss with you. So, say your last graces, if you have any, and say goodbye to this world."

The laughter that escaped me was uncontrollable. I tried to tame it, I really did, but it was impossible. I'd met my fair share of witch hunters before, none that lived to tell the tale of course, but none had been so far up their own ass as he was. It certainly made for interesting conversation.

"Steve? Can I call you Steve?" I said, not caring much for his actual name. "There's a misunderstanding here. You're not the one calling the shots. I got you here, and you're going to listen to me because we both have a problem. Like I said, you have a witch working for the BLADE force, and I have a mole I need to deal with myself. So, we're gonna make ourselves a deal, okay? You can find out who that witch is, and I will let you live."

It's not that I'd practiced this whole spiel in front of the mirror for hours, but yes, yes I had. It had been a while since I'd last hunted witch hunters, and if I was being honest, I was a bit rusty with the talk. Because you have to have a talk when you hunt a witch hunter. They are bigoted assassins, the worst of assassins if there was one, and you've got to have the banter. Otherwise, it's just senseless killing.

"There is no witch working for the BLADE force. We don't work with filth," was his only reply.

I turned around and looked him square in the eyes. The blue of his irises was distracting, but I forced myself to focus.

"You see, Steve, if there wasn't a witch working in the BLADE force, then you wouldn't have found me. I made this name known on purpose. Which means one of my own has betrayed us and has come running to you filthy assassins. So, I'll ask again, what do you want to do about that?"

The hunter betrayed no emotion and continued staring me down, not even getting distracted by the partying crowd or the discomfort of looking a stranger in the eyes.

"We are fully capable of hunting witches ourselves. So excuse me, but I am not buying any of your shit," he said.

I sighed.

"I know not all witch hunters are as exhausting, but do you have to be? Do you try? Is that your thing in the office? Do you try to bore everyone to death with the same dialogue?" I asked.

The hunter turned his head to scan the room as if to process what I'd just told him and what to do next. Had I been in his position, I probably wouldn't have believed me, either, but we'd get there. Rome wasn't built in a day, and I had all the patience in the world. For now.

"If we're done here, I'll go back to my job," the hunter said.

"What? Are you going to kill me? I'd love to see you try. But we're not done here, as a matter of fact," I said as he tried to get up. I grabbed his arm and stopped him from going. I didn't like people blanking me. And neither did the witch hunter like to be touched from what I gathered because he turned around and grabbed my throat with his bare hands.

How sweet. I had taken all the precautions, but he went and touched my bare skin. Willingly.

Anger and frustration knotted up my stomach.

I hate witches. The thoughts associated with the emotions were not surprising to me at all.

Neither was the rest of the stream of consciousness that was linked to his feelings. Naw, he was a real puppy. He believed blindly everything the hunters had taught him.

Never trust witches. Witches only put curses on people.

I was tempted to laugh, but then another emotion tugged at the back of his emotional spectrum. He wasn't letting it out, so with an extra push of attention, I urged it out into the open.

Let's see what secrets this hunter was hiding.

If only I could find a witch to break the curse of my frozen heart.

This confused me. Did he just say he had a frozen heart? What did that even mean? I dug deeper, looking for the answers. His frustration was feeding me more of his inner thoughts. And boy, was it an essay in and of itself.

I can't believe I can never fall in love because of a witch. I need to thaw my frozen heart. I need to collect all the spells I can get and break this curse. I need to. I need to.

The hand on my neck was getting a bit tighter than I preferred, so I removed a glove and wrapped my hand around his wrist. Not only did my hands give me better access to other people's emotions, they also allowed me to overpower them.

I shot back all his emotions at him. Made him kneel. Tears ran down both our faces before he understood what was happening to him.

"Now, let's see what the fuck you're hiding," I whispered and let my head loose inside his.

Stillness came over my entire body and nothingness surrounded me. With every breath, the emptier my body felt. As if I'd once had meaning and I'd lost it all at once. Depression.

I just want to feel something. Anything. Some sort of warmth in the heart that's been cursed to never love.

Had I just discovered a treasure trove of a witch hunter? I usually hated complicated people because it meant I had to go through their entire emotional range before I could actually do anything. This dude was different. If he really had a frozen heart, I was intrigued.

"So, a witch has cursed your heart," I said to him, and he looked at me full of horror, his face white from the empathic drain I was causing him.

I let him go and he crumpled on the sofa next to me, trying to catch his breath.

"What the-fuck did-you-just-do to me?"

I cocked my head and looked at him as if I'd just found a lucky penny.

"I gave you a taste of your own medicine," I said to

him. "Is it true that a witch has cursed your heart so you can never fall in love?"

The hunter growled at me like a rabid dog. He pulled away from me, still too weak to do anything to hurt me.

"How do you know?"

"Oh, I don't tend to reveal my secrets, but I do have my way of getting into people's heads."

"Yes, it's true. One of your kind has cursed me," he admitted.

It must have taken a lot of balls for him to do that to someone who he absolutely hated. Someone who he'd been raised to despise.

"Interesting. I have never heard of a curse of the frozen heart."

Was it possible? Was it true? My powers only gave me access to how he was feeling. And his feelings told me he didn't have any love left inside of him. That didn't necessarily mean it was true. That was the thing about emotions. They weren't factual.

Of course it was true. Why on earth would his entire inner monologue be about a curse if it wasn't real? Which meant, that if he had a frozen heart, I could possibly...

No, that was risky.

I couldn't possibly do that, could I? If I did, though, life would be so much better. No more sleepless nights, no more grumpy Caleb in the morning if he did manage to get some sleep. And I would never have to worry about falling in love again. All it took was a simple exchange.

Before I could think too much about it, I spilled it out.

"I will make you a deal. I will take away your frozen heart if you help me get the mole."

"I don't trust witches," the hunter said.

"Yes, so I've heard many, many times in your head. I get that. But you want to break your curse more than you hate witches, so hopefully, we can come to an arrangement."

"I. Don't. Do. Deals. With. Witches," he repeated, and I was starting to get frustrated. And bored. He was lucky I was interested in his affliction, or I would have walked out of there.

"Not even if it means you can fall in love and not hurt anyone ever again?"

The witch hunter seemed to contemplate my offer for a few moments before he turned around to me.

"I'm telling you, there is no witch working in the BLADE force."

"And if there is?"

"If there is," the witch hunter said, and he seemed to be making a decision right on the spot. "If there is, you got yourself a deal. But what do you get out of it?"

Well, he was good, wasn't he?

"Why I want to do this is my business," I replied. "Go to your boss. Find out where he's getting his information. You know how to track witches. I'm sure you can spot one in your headquarters."

And when he found the witch, he would come running to me. And then all we'd need would be a transference spell to give me his heart along with the curse. I might have never heard of a frozen heart curse before, but I needed it. I needed it more than anything in the world.

The hunter reluctantly offered me his hand to shake.

"You've got yourself a strange deal, witch. But I'm warning you. If you cross me, you will die," the witch hunter said and stood up.

"Likewise." He started to walk away when I shouted at him. "Meet me here tomorrow at nine. Alone."

And he would.

FIVE
WADE

I wanted to stay on the witch's tail, but his power had weakened me. Besides, I wasn't a fan of the way he had ambushed me. It had made me feel all broken inside. All... wrong.

Where had I gone wrong? How had I given myself away? As I walked from the pub back home, all of these thoughts circled my head, and the only thing keeping me from having an angry fit was focusing on the one thing I needed that I knew would make me feel better. I just needed to get home. By the time I got there, it had become my mantra.

That witch was cunning, for sure. Maybe he wasn't smart, or not smarter than me anyway, but he had somehow managed to not only locate me but also lure me into the pub and weaken me.

And as if that wasn't enough, he had also got into

my head and found out about my curse. How was this possible? But most importantly, was his offer real?

I shook the thought off immediately. Never trust a witch. Never.

But what if he was telling the truth and he could save me?

Witches might not have been trustworthy, that much I was crystal clear on, but I also had a curse on my back I needed to get rid of. What if his offer was real? What if he could give me what I'd always wanted?

Bursting through the door, I stumbled into my bedroom and opened my wardrobe. I quickly pulled up the panel and ducked inside my little red room. I looked around me, trying to find a crystal big and strong enough to take the edge off.

I knew I was running low, but I didn't realize how low until I started rummaging through cupboards and countertops and found nothing. Even the locked drawers, the ones I had purposefully made less accessible, were empty. Despite the frustration, I managed to find one tucked away at the back of a drawer, and I quickly grabbed it and smashed it inside the mortar, but it only yielded one line.

One line was not good enough after everything that had happened today. I probably needed ten to make me feel normal again. Well, whatever normal was for me. A normal that I was being offered to change.

I snorted the line and waited for the effects to kick in. It didn't take long. My heart pounded faster, and my lids became heavy. This particular one didn't give me an erection, which only meant it wasn't strong enough. Five seconds later, the high vanished. And I was back to my shitty old self with no means of escape.

Except for one. But putting my faith and trust into a witch would take all my strength. What if he made it worse? Why would he help a witch hunter? What would he get out of it?

I looked for another crystal, but my search yielded no results. As much as I needed another hit, it wasn't going to happen tonight, or anytime soon, unless I hunted a new witch. I left the room and returned to my kitchen where I slapped up a couple of sandwiches to drown out the cravings.

It turned out to be a long night, and I could not get any rest. No matter how much I tried it was impossible. Not two hours after I arrived home, my phone rang.

"Where are you, man? What happened in that pub?" Lloyd shouted in my ear.

Fuck. I'd forgotten all about Lloyd. I hadn't even told him I was leaving. How the hell did I explain that I had been ambushed by a witch and I had abandoned my mission for the night?

"I'm sorry, Lloyd. I wasn't feeling very well, and I lost track of the witch. I will pick up where we left off tomorrow."

Waiting for his response was like waiting for the judge's verdict on a murder case. Lloyd wasn't stupid, and he didn't fall for bullshit, just like me. Which was why I had chosen him as my partner. I fully expected him to call me out on my crap.

"Okay. You gonna be okay for tomorrow? I've never heard you take a day off, so it must be serious," he finally said.

A small breath of relief escaped me. At least there was one less thing to deal with tomorrow.

"Yes, I should be okay. It must be some food poisoning, but I am already starting to feel better," I replied and hung up.

I plugged my phone into the charger and paced around my living room. It was all I could do to try to calm myself down, and guess what? It wasn't working.

No matter what I tried, I couldn't dismiss the witch's words. It all kept coming back to me. Marlowe would never work with a witch. He was a deeply religious man, and he was renowned worldwide as the expert on angel blood. He had monthly meetings with the heads of other forces abroad and shared his knowledge about witches' weaknesses.

On the other hand, I couldn't believe those gray eyes of the witch could ever lie. Despite the guy's attitude, I knew his eyes had been telling the truth. I'd seen humans and witches lie for years. I could tell the signs. And those beautiful gray eyes had been telling the truth.

What's wrong with you, Wade? Now you're thinking that a witch is telling you the truth?

They were born and raised to lie. That's all they ever knew. What would the repercussions be if the witch was telling the truth? Would Marlowe be dismissed? What would the other witch hunters do? What would I do?

There was only one way to put a witch's words to the test. Confront the truth. I could just go to Marlowe and ask him. He might have been a difficult man, but he hated witches just as much as any other hunter, and besides, all I needed was to ask him where he was getting his information. How he'd been tracking them down.

There must be a perfect explanation that doesn't involve the director of the force betraying everyone and working with witches.

The touch of the witch came back to me. When my hands had curled around his neck and all my strength had seemed to have been suspended between us, the rush of emotions had been nauseating.

The look on the witch. Somehow, he had managed to find out about my frozen heart. The way he had looked at me when he'd realized. It hadn't been pity. It had been interest and maybe a little sadness.

But why would a witch feel sorry for me? Why would he want to help me?

I decided sleep was going to be a no-go, so I grabbed my jacket and walked along the bankside to the headquarters. Director Marlowe was always in his office, so what better time to talk to him than in the middle of the night when most witch hunters were either home or on a mission? I walked a few blocks to Westminster, but since the tube station was closed, I went the other secret way.

I walked across the bridge and underneath it where I found an old rusty door. I wedged it open and behind it a more advanced, newer door appeared. I scanned my thumb and the new door opened, letting me in the lift which took me underground.

This particular elevator took me to the other side of the headquarters, and I had to walk through the canteen, the arsenal, and the doctor's quarters, then climb up the stairs to the main office.

I only spotted two hunters at their desks religiously typing on their computers. With barely a nod of acknowledgment, I walked past them and aimed for the oak double doors that belonged to director Marlowe.

When I got there, I took a deep breath and knocked. I didn't know how to tell him a witch had overpowered me, so instead, I would ask how he got his leads. There was no reason why he couldn't be honest with me.

"Come in," a voice hissed.

I pushed one door open and let myself in. Director Marlowe was sitting behind his desk on his comfy armchair with a tall brunette woman in a red dress standing beside him.

She looked up when I entered and smiled at me.

Christian, on the other hand, narrowed his eyes and stared me down as I approached him.

"How can I help you, Mr. Rawthorne," Marlowe asked.

I'd never seen this woman before, but something was off about her. I stole glances at her, but I couldn't spot a spellbook. Surely if she was a witch, she'd be carrying a spellbook. No, this was a mistake. I'd let the witch get to me. I was such an idiot. How could I doubt my own job? My own boss? My own family? Marlowe had taken us in when our mother had died and gave us a home and a purpose. And all of a sudden, a witch had managed to make me doubt my entire existence.

"Sir, I wanted to ask you how we are... locating the... witches because I've been unable to find... the last one. Are we using some new angel blood technology, or is someone giving you the information?" I asked Christian, fully aware that it wouldn't go down well with him.

———

Everything was blurry and dark. I blinked and rubbed my eyes until they adjusted, and the familiarity of my bedroom greeted me. The sheets underneath me were wet, and my head was pounding.

How on earth did I get here? The last thing I

remembered was standing in front of Marlowe and this woman asking questions and then...

What even was the time? I looked at my watch and realized it was five in the afternoon. I had been out for more than fourteen hours? What the fuck had just happened in that office? Why did I not remember anything?

As I rose from the bed and switched the lamp on, the witch's words hit me. The BLADE force was working with a witch. Maybe he was right. How else could I explain waking up in bed having missed half the day? The woman sitting next to Marlowe must have been a witch. I hadn't seen a spellbook on her, but if witches were known for something, it was their ability to blend in. She must have put me to sleep, cast a spell on me. Whatever it was she had done, Marlowe had allowed it.

I did not like doubting the director and the BLADE force, but there was definitely some suspicious shit going on down there, and I needed to find out what. That witch could potentially help me find out.

Before I could act on my thoughts, my stomach complained, and I couldn't blame it. I hadn't eaten since last night, and I was running on low. Low on all accounts.

A shower proved mandatory after sweating all over my bedding, and a frozen meal did wonders to appease the hunger crawling on my insides. I opened the blinds so I could have a full view of the setting sun behind the city I had always called home, and as the limited sunlight disappeared behind the skyline, so did my resistance.

I needed a spell. I needed a hit. But there was nothing in the back room. And I needed to be in top shape to meet with the witch. But I couldn't do anything about it now. Perhaps I'd be able to sneak a spell off his spellbook while he wasn't paying attention, but that was highly unlikely.

At eight, I made my way to the pub and got there half an hour early, my feet shaking to the rhythm of the ambient music only more frantically. If this was an ambush, I was going to be pissed. But I was nothing if not resilient. If it was an ambush, I could escape it.

The pub was quieter today with far fewer people than the day before. At nine o'clock sharp, the silver-haired witch showed up, entering the pub and drawing all eyes on him as he walked through the bar. There was something about him, something about the way he moved and his presence, and I could see why people were staring at him. It wasn't just because he looked unconventional. He felt unconventional too. His energy... there was something about it.

"So, you changed your mind," the witch said as soon as he came up to me. This time, he took a seat opposite me instead of next to me.

I couldn't say I minded the distance, although my

hands were itching to touch him again and relive the events from yesterday.

What was wrong with me? Why was I fantasizing about a witch? And more specifically, why was I even having these thoughts about a man? What the fuck had happened to me? Was this part of Marlowe's witch's spell? Had she done more to me than just make me forget half a day? Was this whole thing a setup?

Oh crap! Maybe this was all a test and I was failing it miserably.

"I went to see my director. There was a woman there," I said.

It was too late to step back down now. If this was a test and I was failing, I might as well fail with flying colors.

"I've never seen her before. I tried to question him about the way he located the witches, and the next thing I know, I'm waking up in bed fourteen hours later. Does that sound right?"

The witch put his hands together and played with his thumbs. His eyes settled on me. Unmoving, unyielding, unnerving. His energy was palpitating. It was as if I'd taken another hit of a spell and I was intoxicated, high on magic.

I looked away from him. There was something seriously wrong with me if I was thinking about this witch in that way. All this bullshit was what was causing the crumbling of humanity. All those spells the witches cast on humans, and all the things they made them feel and see to bring them to their undoing. I was being foolish like the rest of them. As if I didn't know better.

"That certainly sounds like the workings of a witch. Do you believe me now?" he asked.

I leaned forward.

"I don't know what to believe anymore. There might be a different explanation for why I can't remember the last fourteen hours. It doesn't mean that the BLADE force is compromised."

"Believe what you want, but the question is, do you want to find out what's going on?"

I couldn't lie to myself anymore. Whether this was a witch working with Marlowe or not, there was something weird going on, and I needed to find out what. If that also meant my curse was lifted, that was an added bonus.

"I do. What do we do next?" I asked.

The witch's lips twisted up into a smirk I wanted to wipe off his face as soon as it appeared.

"Well, we have a deal to uphold, don't we? You just need to find out who that witch is, and then we will switch hearts."

"You've got yourself a deal," I said, and the witch extended his hand to shake mine.

I didn't know if I wanted to touch him again. On one hand, he had made me feel all these strange things last time he'd touched me, yet on the other hand, he had also weakened me. I looked at his gloved hand and hesitated.

"Don't worry. These won't let my powers through," he said, pinching the fabric of his gloves.

I took his hand, and I knew right there and then that my life was about to change in the biggest possible way.

A burly man slammed his hand on the table right where our hands were linked, and the table broke in two.

Both the witch and I jumped up and stepped back. The burly man followed me with his gaze. He had a bald head and tattoos etched all over his scalp and the rest of his body. He was wearing a T-shirt that was far too tight for his huge, muscly arms. And he looked pissed. I had no idea what I had done to upset him.

"Your kind are not welcome here," he told me, and before I could ask what he meant, he turned around to the witch and spoke to him. "And you should know better than to bring a witch hunter in here."

"Step back, cyclops. I'm here to do business, and what I do and who I do it with is none of yours," the witch said.

Had I heard right? Was his name Cyclops? And what did he mean by my kind?

A beautiful girl in a leather jacket and a high pony-tail stepped forward and caressed the burly man's big arm. She looked at the witch and spoke to him.

"You are doing business with a witch hunter, Caleb? Really? The beasts that hunt us and kill us? I would love to hear what the high council has to say about that."

I watched the witch I knew as Robert Jones as his dark eyebrows creased where they met. Was his real name Caleb? He was staring at the two people in front of us, but I could still not understand what was happening.

"Like I said to your Nightcrawler boyfriend, my business is my business," he said.

I assumed she was also a witch, but I couldn't be sure. I couldn't see a spellbook anywhere. That was until she pulled one of her jacket buttons out and held it in her hand, ready to target Caleb.

"Are you sure you want to do this, Stef?" Caleb said.

I felt for my hilt in my pocket and pulled it out, but before I could extend the blade, Robert, Caleb, whatever his name, shouted at me.

"Don't you dare get that out in here. I've got this." While I wouldn't normally obey a witch's orders, I did this time, at least until I understood the situation we were in.

The girl said a word I couldn't understand, and smoke appeared in front of her. A purple intoxicating smoke that encapsulated Caleb. But the purple smoke was eaten by a green spurt of dust that came from Caleb's hands. Then another spell erupted, and dust wrapped around both the woman and the guy, and when it cleared, they looked stuck where they stood.

Unable to move their feet, they tried to grasp at Robert and myself, but I walked around them and came shoulder to shoulder with the witch that was going to change my life.

"How long is that going to last? I asked him.

"Not that long," he replied and grabbed his jacket off the chair that he had occupied only moments ago. "Let's get out of here."

I nodded.

"What's your name by the way?"

"Wade."

"Well, I guess now that my cover is blown you know my name is Caleb."

Six
Caleb

I took the witch hunter out of the pub immediately even though he looked like he was enjoying the attention more than he should.

When the door closed behind us, he turned to me with curiosity written across his face.

"That was weird. What the hell just happened in there?" he said, his voice a mix of bewilderment and curiosity.

I took in our surroundings. We needed to go somewhere away from the prying eyes of the Nightcrawler world. I didn't need any more interference. I needed to discover who the witch was that was working with the hunters, perform the ritual between us, and go our separate ways before my reputation was completely ruined.

"That was the witch community looking out for me. It's not common for us to hang out with hunters, you know." My tone came out toxic despite my best effort to keep myself tame.

"It's not common for the BLADE force to work with witches, either," he bit back.

"Exactly," I said and pointed my finger at him. "Which is why we need to find out who the hell this witch is who's working for your boss. And most importantly, why."

"You and me both, pal. You and me both. So where are we heading now?" he asked.

"As far away from there as possible." I pointed at the bar behind us and turned left into an alley. The Green Mile pub was starting to get too popular with Nightcrawlers and witches lately, and I wasn't sure I liked it.

A, because it wasn't ideal in situations like these where prying eyes were unwanted and unwelcome, and B, because if I wanted to hook up with anyone other than a human, I had a hundred or so applicants on my Mated app, both a bespoke and secret app used by the Nightcrawler world to connect, make friends, and fulfill one's booty call quota. It was mainly used for the latter.

No, going into the Green Mile had been a mistake. Turning the corner proved to be mistake number two.

Wade froze in his position, and so did I, taking my time to assess the situation. There were three hunters standing in front of us, all of them with swords drawn and their faces unreadable.

"Lloyd? What are you doing here?" Wade asked one of them, and I looked at Wade. Was this a trap? Being surrounded by four witch hunters could never be fun. Unless it involved a disguise, a lot of alcohol, and lots of lube. Now that was a get together I could get behind. Not that I knew from experience, but a girl could dream. It wasn't my fault witch porn was twisted like that and planted stupid seeds in young impressionable fledglings' minds.

"The question is, what are *you* doing here, Wade? Working with witches now?" the guy in the middle said.

I masked my sigh of relief with a deep breath. Not a trap then. I tried to make out the guy Wade had called Lloyd's features. His face was too square and asymmetrical to be considered attractive, or maybe he just wasn't my cup of tea. He definitely did not look happy to see us. The feeling was mutual.

"Lloyd, I can explain. You don't understand what's going on," Wade tried to say, but Lloyd raised his hand to make him stop.

"Save it for Marlowe," he said.

All three witch hunters lifted their swords en garde, tempting fate. Wade tried to plead with them, but they didn't listen.

"Lloyd, you don't want to do this," he said. "We're partners."

"It looks like you found another one," Lloyd said, and he was the first to lunge towards us.

From the corner of my eye, I saw Wade draw his sword, the blade illuminating the street as it extended from the hilt. I reached for the bracer on my wrist and pulled a green crystal from one of the notches. This guy might have been Wade's partner, but he was attacking us, so I was hoping he wouldn't mind a little distraction spell.

"Repel," I shouted, and the green crystal burst a puff of dust that attacked Lloyd, and he was thrown across the street in the opposite direction.

"Hey, be careful. He's my partner. Don't hurt him," Wade shouted, grabbing my wrist and squeezing it until his thumb met his finger, which, granted, didn't take much considering my size, but it still hurt like a motherfucker.

"Then tell him to stop attacking us," I growled and pulled my hand away.

Who the fuck did he think he was, telling me what to do? I distracted myself with another spell, biting down the urge to rub my wrist where he had grabbed me.

I aimed another spell at the two hunters that Wade was now fighting, but the spell caught the edge of a blade and evaporated before it had a chance to work.

"Fuck," I spat.

I looked at both bracers I was wearing and at all my options. I tried to remove a distraction spell, but before I could use it, a blade hacked in front of me, and

I stumbled as I stepped back, trying to avoid its murderous point.

"Your time is up, witch," Lloyd said, and a grin sported his face.

I desperately wanted to wipe that grin off his face.

"So they *do* give you a script. What's it called? I'd like to go through it and give it an update," I mumbled, but I didn't think Lloyd heard me.

I grabbed the first crystal my fingers found, one settled on the notch close to the center of my wrist, and threw it at him, shouting the word "fire."

Yellow dust and smoke enveloped him, which soon turned into flames that started to burn his body.

"Stop it. I told you..." Wade shouted at me, but before he could finish his sentence, a sword grazed his thigh.

"That was a warning shot," one of the witch hunters that had managed to get one up on Wade said.

Wade screamed in pain but turned to the witch hunter that had hurt him.

"No, that was a lucky shot," he growled.

The flames that enveloped Lloyd died down, helped by the angel blood lacing his clothing. It was all the distraction I needed to get us out of there. There was no point fighting all three of them, especially if my witch hunter friend was going to get all sentimental about his colleagues who were obviously trying to kill us.

I grabbed a black crystal and tried to get close to Wade.

"We need to go. Now," I said, and he turned to me.

"I'm trying," he said, the strain in his voice clear as he swung his sword at his opponents.

Lloyd, who had dropped his sword while he'd battled with the flames, fell on his knees and tried to retrieve it. I ran towards it and kicked it away from him. The sword knocked against one of the other witch hunter's shoes. Wade had pushed both of them to the ground, and they were holding back his sword with their own.

It all happened in a flash of a second before I could do anything to help him out.

The witch hunter closest to the fallen sword grabbed it and pierced it through Wade's ribs, and it jutted out of his back.

Wade fell on his knees, and the witch hunters found their footing.

I ran to him and activated the black crystal that was already resting in my hand.

"Chaos," I whispered, and the crystal spurted with black dust that enveloped the entire street, and with it, the three witch hunters.

That should keep them distracted for a little while.

I took Wade's arm and put it around my neck, helping him off the street. His skin on my nape meant that I could feel his pain as if it were mine, which probably wasn't wise. The sword was still wedged in his body, and the blood had soaked his clothes.

I couldn't believe he'd just cost me a very expensive spell to save his ass, and now he was going to bleed to death before I could find out who the mole was, and especially before I could swap his heart with mine.

"Shit," I spat, thinking of the consequences of what I was about to do.

I couldn't possibly take him home to Nora, could I? Annabel would never forgive me, and I wouldn't forgive myself if Nora gave a part of herself for him.

"Everything okay," Wade grumbled and clutched just below his wound. My empathy told me he was biting down a lot of pain to sound normal.

"Going to have to take care of this," I said and pointed at the sword. "But you have to promise me you're not going to hurt her."

"Hurt who? What are you talking about?"

"Promise me." I was losing my patience, and I was upset with myself for not having seen the setup earlier. Of course there would have been witch hunters after him. He had gone to his director and had woken up hours later without remembering a bloody thing. Who the fuck knew what had happened and what kind of questions had been asked?

Thankfully, I also had a memory-erasing spell handy. And maybe I'd have to use it on him earlier than I'd intended to.

Because, of course, I was going to erase his memories as soon as the transference spell was done and I'd found out who the witch was that had turned on our kind. I was not stupid. I knew what kind of man I was working with, and while I was prepared to kill Wade, I really had put that kind of life behind me. Besides, a simple memory spell could do the work and there was much less blood involved.

"I promise," Wade said and closed his eyes for a second as he recomposed himself.

I nodded in thanks and pulled a red crystal from the top of my spellbook.

"First things first," I said and gave him the crystal to hold. He flinched, and I couldn't blame him. His eyes seemed to glint, and his Adam's apple bobbed at the sight of the spell.

"What is this?" he drawled.

It was understandable that he didn't trust me. I wouldn't trust me either in his situation. Hell, I didn't trust him in our situation, but there was a certain amount of give and take that had to happen if we were going to work together.

"It's a disguise spell. Will you relax? I want to get rid of your cursed heart just as much as you do. Until then, I'm not planning on hurting you as long as you don't hurt me."

He took a moment to think through my words, but the gushing blood from his ribcage was making it hard to argue.

"Okay," he said, and I put my palm over his

hand, speaking the words to activate the spell. A cloud of smoke instantly transformed him into a blond college boy. The traces of his wound and the blood disappeared. Even the sword had been taken care of, although he would have to be careful who he came into contact with because it could still hurt people.

"Now you need to pretend... No actually, you look drunk already," I said, and he grimaced.

I took hold of him again and we went down to platform level on the underground.

It was probably a big mistake to take him home. But right now, Nora was the only one who could fix him.

———

We got to Brick Lane and I could sense the disguise spell wearing off when Wade started shedding the dust that was keeping him glamoured. That was one of the things about magic that always baffled me. The physical evidence that we left behind. And while humans weren't versed on crystal dust and its meaning, a witch worth her buck could drill down to even find out what the spell that was cast was.

Thankfully, disguise spells, tailor-made by Graham himself, weren't potent so didn't leave residue behind for too long. As soon as Wade's dust hit the floor, it disappeared, so hopefully, even if we were being followed, no one could track us by following the spell residue.

To be on the cautious side, I used a distraction spell that would make it easy for us to go unnoticed as soon as we got off the train.

Wade was getting weaker by the minute. I was doing most of the lifting, as he barely had any strength left. I could only imagine the bloodbath underneath the disguise.

"Just a couple more minutes, buddy. You will be fine in two minutes," I kept saying to him, but every two minutes turned into five and five into ten. I knew the longer we took, the weaker he would get, and the more it would take out of her to heal him. And I didn't want her to sacrifice herself again.

We finally got to my porch and a big red door with a number thirteen on it. I inserted my key and turned the knob to open it and carried Wade up the stairs.

Well, I tried.

Somewhere along the third troubled ascend, Wade missed a step, and he went tumbling down into the corridor.

"Fuck! Annabel!" I shouted the troll's name and dove down to get him.

"Who's Annabel?" Wade barely managed to say.

"You'll meet her soon enough," I said, and he tried to nod in a slow movement while the spell expired and gave me a view of his beautiful blue eyes that were losing all of their light.

It was hard not to admire his sleek features, even in pain. The high cheekbones and the beautiful kissable lips. If only he wasn't a witch hunter.

No.

Even if he wasn't, I was done with love. So fucking done with it. Yes, Wade would be good for a shag, but no more falling in love for me. There was a reason I needed that transference spell, and it wasn't because I wanted Wade to have his full emotional range back. It was because I wanted to stop mine from making me fall hard again, and again, and again, and only ever getting hurt and pain along the way. I was done with that stupid emotion.

So fucking done.

"Did you call me?" Annabel whispered from the top, but when she saw us at the bottom, she bounced down the stairs to get to us.

"What happened? Are you okay?" she asked.

I nodded. "I'm fine, but he needs her help."

"I've just put her to sleep."

"Annabel, this is important."

"Okay, but you can stay up with her all night because you know she'll be grumpy, and I'm not having it," Annabel said, and without me asking her, she put one hand under Wade's knees, and the other one under his neck, and lifted him in one swift movement as if he weighed nothing. Some days I was jealous of her super-strength. Mainly, I was jealous of her uneventful life. She didn't have to deal with rampant

Nightcrawlers, murderous witch hunters, or asshole lovers. She was content with her life and looking after Nora was one of her joys. On most days anyway.

I followed her up and ran into Nora's bedroom.

Her vibrant ginger hair illuminated the room, even without any lights on, and her freckled face looked so peaceful and serene it was almost sacrilegious of me to rouse her.

Settling down on her bed, I caressed her hair and called her name. She had grown so much in the last few years, she was starting to remind me of the woman she had once been. She had done so much for me since I'd met her, and all I did for her was use her. I'd made a promise to look after her, and a pang of guilt came over me by the fact that I had not kept my promise. She was more than happy to help heal the odd wound, but it always took a little bit out of her. She was a sweet kid, but she needed to become a sweet woman, and that would never happen if I kept using her. Just this one last time, I promised myself. I just needed this one and then I was done. Then we could be a happy family.

"Nora, sweetheart, wake up," I said.

Nora opened her eyes slowly, tiny little fingers rubbing the sleep off them.

"Daddy," she shouted and wrapped her hands around my neck.

"I'm here, sweetheart. I'm sorry I missed bedtime. But I need you to do something for Daddy. Can you do me a favor?" I asked her, and she nodded her head in a dizzying manner.

"What is it, Daddy?" she asked and removed her hands from my neck, looking for a wound on my body.

"I'm not the one who's hurt. It's...my friend. He needs your help," I said to her, and she jumped out of bed before I could ease her into it.

"Where is he? What's his name?" she asked, walking into the living room.

I followed her and found Annabel had placed him on the sofa. Needless to say, it would need some serious cleaning. I tried to remember why for the love of all that was good and sacred I got a white sofa. I'd have to add the cleaning spell to Graham's bill as part of my payment for doing this shit for the high council.

Nora ran to Wade and touched his forehead. I was getting a glimpse of the woman she had once been, the nurse who had helped me when no one else could. When my first thirst for blood had hit and I hadn't known what to do, she had been there for me to give me my first supply and had talked me through living life as a vampire. She'd shown me the ropes in the Nightcrawler world, and without her, I wouldn't have been here today.

Annabel pulled the sword out of Wade and snapped his shirt in half to give Nora access to his ribcage.

Wade stared at her, unable to say anything.

Whether from the shock of seeing Nora in front of him or from the sheer pain, I didn't know.

"It's not a big wound, it hit a vein, but he'll be fine," Nora said, and she sounded almost like the adult I had known once.

She was only six for fuck's sake. She shouldn't have been seeing blood. Dear Lord, I was a terrible father to her.

"Who is this?" Wade muttered, unable to take his eyes off Nora.

She turned to him and caressed his cheek.

"I'm Nora, and you are?" she said.

"Uhm-I'm Wade..."

When Nora told him how pleased she was to meet him and gave her undivided attention to his wound, he turned and looked at me.

"She's... my daughter. Sort of." I tried to explain. It didn't matter. Once we were done, he would forget everything about her, Annabel, and me. "She can help you. She can heal you."

He looked puzzled.

"How can a kid heal me?" he asked.

"I'm a phoenix, silly. Phoenices heal people." Nora put her tiny palms over his wound.

"A what?" he asked, but before he could utter anything further, Nora's hands glowed with green fire. Wade panicked and tried to move away from them, but his lack of strength made him take a tumble and introduce himself to the floor. Problem was, he also knocked Nora off her feet.

"Stop being stupid. She's trying to heal you, for fuck's sake," I shouted at him.

Nora chuckled as she sat up on her knees. "It's okay. That was funny. And Daddy needs to put a pound in the swear jar." She chuckled.

My head dropped, and I searched my pockets for change. I didn't find any, but I had a five-pound note that I made a point of showing to her before it went into the jar on top of the mantelpiece.

It was my last note but screw it. She needed it for her life fund, an initiative I'd started with Annabel when Nora became a baby. We'd taken hold of her credit cards and every month made a deposit from the swear jar into her account. By the time she was a woman again, she'd have a healthy fund to start her life over. Not that she didn't already have one. Last time we'd checked, there was more in her account than any sort of money Annabel and I would ever make in our lives.

The benefits of being an ancient creature, I guess. Savings interest.

Nora rubbed her hands together and again settled them on top of Wade's wound. The green flames appeared and burned bright over the two injuries, although, thankfully, his thigh wound was just a graze. Nora's lips were shut, but that didn't stop the beautiful humming, the phoenix lullaby, that serenaded the entire room. It was a hypnotic song. It always changed, never stayed the same, but was always as graceful as the last.

If we had been normal human beings, Nora would have been taken away from me a long time ago. I knew that. Annabel was doing her best to raise her, but I took advantage of my daughter. My friend. I hoped one day she would find it in her heart to forgive me.

The green flames now burned through Nora entirely and ashes fell from her fingertips onto Wade's lesions. Wade cried out, but his skin grafted back together, leaving no trace of the deadly injury that had been there only moments before.

The flames evaporated, and Nora fell back onto her bottom with a little chuckle.

Annabel went to her and helped her up.

"Are you okay, sweet pea?" she asked.

Nora's fingertips were a baby pink, different to the darker color of the rest of her body.

"I'm okay, Mommy. I just need to sit down," Nora said and took a seat on the couch.

Wade helped himself up and settled on the other end, his eyes trained on her.

"What just happened? Because if I know one thing, that's that this wasn't a spell," he said.

"It wasn't. It was a phoenix's healing force," I told him.

"What does that even mean? And what do you mean she is a phoenix?"

I went and sat next to Nora who rested her head on my chest.

"Have you heard of the myth of the beautiful birds that are reborn from their ashes?" I asked him.

Wade nodded slowly.

"That's what I am. But I am not a bird. I'm a person," Nora said.

"But she's a witch?"

I shook my head.

"No, she's a Nightcrawler. A phoenix more specifically."

"You've said that word before. When we were at the pub. What does it mean?"

Wade looked confused, and I wasn't sure why.

"Nightcrawlers, creatures of the night. Vampires, trolls, phoenices, incubi," I said, and the last word took a bit of effort to pronounce. Incubi. Jin. Our time together rushed back to me. Goddess, I really needed this spell. I had to swap with Wade and put an end to this heartbreak and this pain. It had been six years for crying out loud. And it still hurt like yesterday.

"Vampires are not real. What are you talking about?" Wade said.

His objection brought me back to my senses, and I turned to Nora. "Pixie-pie, do you wanna go back to bed? Daddy's still got work to do."

I ignored Annabel's huff and knew I'd have to deal with it later. Nora lifted her head from my chest, but she didn't move.

"I can help you."

She didn't say it to me, but Wade. Wade stared into her eyes and asked her what she meant.

"You've got a funny aura around you. It's like there's some beautiful orange that wants to come out and play, but the black is not letting it. But I know someone who can help you shoo the black aura away."

"Really? Aren't you, like, five?"

Nora giggled and looked at me.

"Six, actually. But I've been six before many times. And in one of those many times, I knew a witch. A witch who helps lost people," Nora said.

It was my turn to be shocked and curious.

"What witch? And how do you remember her? Are you starting to remember people from your past life?"

Nora had once told me that this would happen if she ever rebirthed, but up until now, we hadn't seen a trace of her remembering her old life.

"A little bit. It's just flashes. Nothing really solid. But she can help you," she said and turned to Wade again.

"Who is she?" I asked her.

Nora squeezed her eyebrows and hummed to herself. She tended to do that when she was stressed, which prompted Annabel to step forward.

"Nora, I think you've had enough. It's time to have some rest," she said and then she turned to me. "And you need to stop this. She is weak and she needs to go back to bed."

Nora shook her head and refused Annabel.

"I've got it here." She pointed to her mouth.

"You've got it on the tip of your tongue," I explained to her. Just because she didn't know all the words all the time didn't mean I couldn't at least teach her some.

Nora giggled.

"Daddy, you're being funny."

"Needless to say, I'm very confused," Wade said.

I ignored him and focused on Nora. If she knew a witch, she would be powerful. And if she was powerful, she could help with a transference spell because I highly doubted Graham would approve of my plan. Until I found the mole, he didn't need to get involved in what I had to do to get to them.

"Her name is...Mother Red Cap."

With that, she jumped off my lap and grabbed one of her sketchbooks and her crayons and put them on the table. Then she started sketching like a maniac, and she didn't stop until she had given us a colorful map of Camden.

"You can find her here. When you get there, you need to sacrifice a spell in exchange for her help and make a pact with her. She will only appear to you if she wants to help you," she said.

"If?" Wade asked.

"She's very weird about who she helps. But that's

why she survived from your kind for all those years," Nora said to Wade.

"You-you know what I am?" he asked.

"Yes, you're a witch hunter, and you've killed lots of witches."

I would have wondered how she knew that, but I gave up. Nora was always secretive about her powers, so if she had the ability to read minds as well, then I had no idea.

"And you're not scared of me?" Wade asked.

Nora got up and approached Wade, who stood still as if making any sort of rapid movement would scare her away. She placed her hand on his heart.

"No. I know you would never hurt me. And I know those you've hurt, you've only hurt them because of the blackness inside. You can't control it."

What did she mean the blackness inside he couldn't control? Did she mean the curse on his heart?

"All right, missy, time for bed. Enough chit-chat," Annabel shouted, and Nora got to her feet.

"Okay, Mommy, I'm coming," she said and then turned to Wade. "Take care of my daddy, will you? He needs you."

Wade stared at her, and I stared at him. He didn't flinch when he said, "I will."

Nora leaned in and gave him a kiss on the cheek, then gave me a hug, and finally followed Annabel, who was getting impatient, into her bedroom.

"She's an interesting girl," Wade said. "And I've got so many questions."

I stood up. "I'm sure you do. They can wait for now. Let's go find this Mother Red Cap."

"Why do we need her?"

"Because if Nora is right, she is a very powerful witch, and she can help us with a transference spell. And considering my coven's witches have just tried to attack us, I don't trust anyone else with this."

"I thought you wanted to find out who is working with my boss." He perked up his eyebrow when he said it, and I shot him down straight away.

"Look, mate. My witches are after us and your hunters are after us. If you even try to go back to your quarters, they will kill you. Let's deal with the problem that's less deadly first, and then we can figure out what the fuck to do about the rest."

On that note, Wade's phone pinged, and he took it out of his pocket, which was soaked with his blood.

"Fuck, fuck, fuck!" he shouted, and when I shushed him, he apologized. I liked that he was a cruel assassin but still respected a kid's bedtime.

"What?"

"That was my brother. He just sent me a message that there's a bounty for my head at the force."

Great. My witch hunter friend had turned useless for the mission I was being paid for.

Well, there was still one thing I could use him for.

SEVEN

WADE

The day had been a never-ending mess, and I most definitely needed to get my head straight.

For starters, what the fuck was going on with the BLADE force. What was going on with the witches? Were they really working with the force? What was a cyclops and why had Lloyd come after me? Most importantly, who was the fucker witch hunter that had stabbed me, and how soon could I kill him?

And how the hell had I ended up with a bounty on my head? Did we even do bounties on non-witches?

I needed a shower and fresh clothes and a good slam in the head to wake me up from whatever nightmare I was living through.

After having woken up and realized I had lost an entire day and trying to wrap my head around that confusion, more and more shit had kept on getting added.

There was a thing called a Nightcrawler? And vampires were real? What the fuck was that all about? And I knew Caleb had tried to explain it, but what the fuck was Nora, and how could she heal me with a simple touch?

Okay, I'd be the first to admit she was a sweet girl, albeit slightly creepy with her whole "other lives" and "the blackness" spiels, but she was an adorable kid. She had also healed me, so in my eyes, she was a superstar.

"Ready?" the witch asked, grabbing his keys off the floor. He was a superstar, too, even if he was a witch. Not only had he saved my life with that spell he'd cast back in that alley when we'd been ambushed—and what a spell that was, complete darkness and all—but he had also trusted me with his daughter. Or whatever Nora was to him.

I knew if I'd been in his shoes, I would not have brought me home. Maybe there was such a thing such as a trustworthy witch.

Not that I was letting my guard down any time soon. Things had gone south since I'd met him. And I expected them to go even more so.

"Ready for what?" I asked him.

"Another round of weird." He smirked.

Had he been holding on to that joke since Nora had gone to bed? How lame. And even more lame was the fact he thought he was funny.

"I need to change. I can't go out looking like this."
I held the hem of my T-shirt and inspected the
damage. It was as good as gone.

Caleb huffed.

"Wait here," he said and twisted around on the
spot, disappearing behind a door the opposite direction from where Nora's room was.

Annabel came out from Nora's room and nodded.

"Is she asleep already?" I asked her.

She walked to the kitchen counter and grabbed a
mug.

"Yeah, she goes out like a light when she uses her
powers," she replied and made herself some tea.

It hit me right then. I had been too busy, or
wounded, to notice earlier, but Nora had called her
Mom and Caleb Dad. Did that mean the two of them
were an item?

She was rather short with a mousy wave of hair,
probably half my size, and a little on the chunky side,
but she had a pretty smile. Maybe the witch had a
thing for her type. Earthly and butch. I didn't know.
And I didn't care. The question still remained. How
on earth had she lifted me and got me up all those
stairs? Was she a witch too? And if so, why couldn't I
locate her spellbook anywhere?

"Here," I heard, and before I had time to turn, I
was flailing, trying to catch the clothes the witch had
thrown at me.

I'd dropped the T-shirt, so I picked it up and

excused myself to the bathroom, which Annabel showed me to promptly.

As soon as the door was locked behind me, I pressed my ear against it.

"What the fuck is wrong with you, Caleb? Bringing a witch hunter home for Nora to heal? You need to stop doing this to her. She's not your personal first aid kit. And what if he wants to use her too? Do you ever think with your brain and not your dick?" I heard Annabel say. She wasn't exactly muttering to herself.

"Will you keep it down, Ann? I know it's shit. But this shit is important. We need to find out who's working with the hunters so we can protect ourselves. As for Wade? Don't worry. I'll take care of him when it's time."

It shouldn't have come as a shock, but it surely hit me like one. I needed to keep an eye on the witch if I was to continue working with him. I was fully aware of how stupid that sounded. Why would I work with a witch who obviously wanted me gone and was planning on hurting me?

Because he held the key to taking my curse away. Besides, I could take care of him, too, if the need arose. I wasn't scared of him.

What was there to be scared of? The gray eyes that cut through me every time I looked at them or the confidence he showed around me even though I could tell he only had half as much?

We were both in this shit together, whether we liked each other or not, and I was planning on sticking through with this to the end. Maybe get a promotion out of it too. Because surely there would be a promotion for the guy who exposed Marlowe working with the witches. Right?

I pulled my top off and bundled it up in my fist and threw it in the sink. I used a towel to rub my body clean of all the blood, and that alone took some effort. Blood was messy. Too messy. And not just in a physical way. How was I still okay despite losing so much? Did Nora regenerate my blood as well as growing new skin? Because I checked and there was no scar anywhere where there should have been a laceration or bruising even.

I didn't think I could make any sense of how this shit worked, so I gave up.

The T-shirt Caleb gave me was on the small side. Not that I was surprised. He was shorter and much skinnier than me. But it would have to do even if it was a bit tight around the ribs. The ribs that had only a few minutes ago almost bled me to death.

Weird night.

The T-shirt smelled of something I couldn't quite put my finger on, but it was the witch's smell for sure. A mix of roses and spice. I couldn't tell whether it was his fragrance or fabric softener. Maybe a little bit of both. It was a pleasant smell, and my nose tingled, my lips curled at the whiffs.

I tried the jeans, but couldn't even get them past my knees, so I gave up. I cracked the door open and whisper-shouted for help. Caleb appeared in front of me with a frown.

"What?"

I threw his jeans at him and told him they wouldn't fit.

"Hang on," he growled and stomped away. He returned a few seconds later with a bigger pair.

"Make sure not to fuck them up. They're important. 'Kay? They belonged to someone important," he said and handed them to me carefully.

I had no idea how a pair of jeans could be important, but I slipped them on anyway. If anything happened to them, I'd replace them. Whatever.

When I came out of the bathroom a few moments later, I found Annabel and Caleb hunched in the corner of the kitchen, and as soon as Annabel saw me, she stopped talking and turned around, disappearing behind one of the many doors in the apartment.

It wasn't exactly clear to me how a witch and whatever Annabel was could afford a place like this, in Brick Lane of all places, but it didn't take a genius to guess a lot of spells had been used to make that happen. Maybe there were some lying around. If I could get my hands on one, I could give so much more to this mission. Be a little bit more powerful. Not a weak-ass hunter that got stabbed by one of his own.

There wasn't any time to look elsewhere, and the

bathroom had proved futile. Caleb sprinted for the front door as soon as I came out, and soon we were back out in the dark streets of London.

He walked around the corner and stopped by the bus stop.

"Are we actually taking the bus?" I asked him.

In my head, I had this idea of witches using magic for everything, so I wasn't exactly sure why Caleb decided to take the bus to Camden.

"Yes. We are," he replied as if it was the only logical way.

"Why don't you just use one of your crystals to take us there?"

"Do you know how expensive that would be? If I used magic to go everywhere?" he said and put his hand out to stop the oncoming bus.

Money? Magic was all about money? I'd thought witches had unlimited access to spells and magic. It was one of the things we were taught in the BLADE force. We were taught that witches made their own magic using ingredients of all kinds to create their spells. What did money have to do with it? I followed Caleb onto the bus and tapped my Oyster card, then we sat down next to each other.

"You mean you have to pay to use magic?" I asked him. I couldn't resist it. I had access to a witch for a limited time before I had to kill him, something that was bound to happen, and he was an opportunity to get more information about them.

"Of course. How else would we use magic?"

None of this made any sense, and I told him so. I explained to him what they'd told me in the force training program, all the while Caleb was shaking his head with disapproval.

"I don't know if they've got it wrong on purpose, but not everyone can create spells. Yes, something simple like a lighting-a-candle spell we can create with a few ingredients, but to create spells of the caliber we use on a daily basis you need proper alchemy training and knowledge, which the majority of witches don't have."

"So how do you get your spells?" I asked him. I was so confused. And I didn't know if it was because the BLADE force had lied to me, or the fact that they didn't have all the information they said they did. In all my years in the force, I'd never had any reason to doubt anything. Now, after today...I wasn't so sure.

"Market. We have markets for that. Shops and traders," he said with a little hesitation, or at least, that's what I gathered from the way his voice broke after every word.

"You're trying not to tell me too much. I under-stand. I probably wouldn't trust me, either, in your situation. It's just that all my life I've been told things are a certain way, and now I'm starting to feel like that's not the case."

Caleb turned to look me in the eyes and bit his

lower lip as he seemed to ponder something that I wasn't privy to.

"I know how that feels. It might surprise you, but when I turned into a vampire I... My whole world changed. I had to learn everything from scratch," he started, but I couldn't concentrate on anything other than the word *vampire*.

"Are you trying to tell me you're a vampire as well as a witch?" I asked.

Caleb shrugged. "I was. Not anymore. It's a long story."

I looked outside the window and found we'd only moved two stops, so I turned back to Caleb and addressed him.

"We've got a journey ahead of us," I said.

Again, the witch seemed to contemplate something because he didn't start straight away.

"I guess it can't hurt," Caleb murmured and readjusted himself on the seat.

"Once upon a lifetime, I was in the British Army. I was deployed to Iraq straight after school. There was this operation, and I was there just to keep watch. You know, stand outside and make sure to signal if the enemy approached. But I was young and stupid, and I got distracted. There was this medallion on the ground, and I picked it up to inspect, but then my squad came out with the intel we needed, so I dropped it without giving it much thought and followed my team back to base. Then I got sick."

"Because of the medallion?" I asked, not entirely clear how that related to his alleged vampirism.

"Yep. Turns out the medallion was infected. And I grew weaker. I couldn't go out in the sunlight without feeling lightheaded, couldn't eat anything. One of the doctors saw me, but he couldn't understand what was wrong with me. According to him, I was healthy as could be. But my light sensitivity grew stronger, and I was getting burns if I had any sunlight on me, and I had lost a lot of weight. I was also getting this craving for iron, and I didn't know how I had it, I just knew that I needed something, and I couldn't explain it. But because I wasn't healthy enough to be on the battle-field, they sent me back home on an overnight flight. And there at the hospital, there was this woman that approached me and told me she could help me. I laughed it off because if the doctors didn't know what was wrong with me, how the fuck would a nurse know, right?" Caleb turned to me and laughed, the little laugh lines around the edges of his mouth creased as his lips twitched, giving me a little pinch in the chest. I didn't know what it was, so I shook it off.

"She took me out back, and I honestly thought she was going to murder me or snog me or something, but instead she threw a pack of blood on my lap. Needless to say, I thought she was crazy. But she pierced the bag before I could protest, and the smell just made me hungry as fuck. I couldn't control it. I grabbed the bag and drank someone else's blood, blood that had generously been donated to save a life. And it did. Although in a different manner than was probably intended.

"After drinking my first blood, the nurse sat me down and told me what I was and how I got it, and I had no choice but to believe her because, let's face it, I had just drunk human blood. She introduced me to Nightcrawlers and their world. See, the vampires used to bite each other to create another one until some very clever vampire developed this virus which he then released to the general public, and those who are susceptible to it, turn. That's how they grew their population until a witch put a stop to that. She altered the virus as much as she could so the vampire population would stop growing any further. But it was too late by that point. These things are really hard to contain. Which is how I contracted the virus from that bloody medallion. Which probably belonged to another vampire or was planted there by someone who wanted to turn some British soldiers into monsters.

"Regardless of the how, I was one at that point, and I had to get a new life. I had to find a night job because being a vampire doesn't pay the bills, and considering I couldn't be out in sunlight, my options were very limited, so I got a job as a bartender. And since then, I've met the craziest amount of people that were not very human at all."

I could hardly believe any of his words were real. But the fact that he was describing everything with so much detail and so much passion, and, if I was right, a little sadness, was proof to the contrary. This night wasn't getting any easier. And why did the BLADE force know nothing about vampires or any of the other creatures?

"How does being a witch play into that?" I asked.

"It doesn't."

Caleb was looking in front of him again, staring out into the street as the bus bolted through sleepy London.

"I found out I was a witch after I was no longer a vampire."

"So it can be healed?" I asked.

Caleb shook his head.

"No, not normally. But I was. And that ruffled a few feathers, I'll tell you that, but it all worked out in the end."

"But how? And I thought you people were born witches."

Caleb laughed but didn't look at me. Was he repulsed by me? And why did I care if he was?

"There's so much they don't teach you at BLADE force. You've got a lot to learn, witch hunter. I hope when our business together is finished you find the right path," was all Caleb said, and before I could prod for more information about the witch world, Caleb pressed the button to stop the bus, and before long, we were back on the streets again. Only this time, we were in Camden in pursuit of the very secretive witch his daughter had sent us to.

Had I been on a mission, this would have been a successful, promotion-worthy discovery. But I needed these witch's help, as well as Caleb's, more than any promotion. Besides, was it even worth getting a promotion with the BLADE force if they had lied to us? Had they lied to us? Or were the bosses more ignorant than they made out to be?

Caleb retrieved Nora's drawing and navigated the streets according to it. He turned left at the World's End pub, and then right, and continued up the road until we reached the canal. The majority of people were gathered around the hub of Camden back at the station where all the bars were, but the high street still had people going about their business even in the middle of the night.

We stood by the railing, under the bridge. The witch took a crystal out of his spellbook and threw it in the water.

"What did you do that for?" I asked, and he ignored me, choosing instead to stare at the water, which was flat and quiet except for the ripples his crystal had caused.

"It's her prize for appearing to us. A spell for a spell," he said.

"Is that it?" I asked when nothing happened.

"No. Now we wait."

Like him, I stared at the water, watching at nothing for a good five minutes, or what felt like five minutes, before anything of interest happened. Firstly, a drunk hipster stumbled into us and threw up in the water right in front of us. He hung about after he'd emptied the contents of his stomach, and I had to make the executive decision to pull him away from us and set him back on his path towards the next pub stop, and he drunkenly obeyed.

"Are you okay? Did he get you?" I asked Caleb, who was staring at me.

What had I just said to him? Why did I care? I didn't care about witches. Was my entire philosophy in life changing just because of one witch's words against an entire army of witch hunters? Was I going to believe this silver-haired man with the piercing gray eyes and his stories about vampires and Nightcrawlers over my director, and the lineage of hunters that came before us?

"No, he—" He was cut short when the water in the canal bubbled as if someone had turned on the kettle and it had just come to the boil.

We both turned to watch it, and it only became worse.

"What do we do now?" I asked him.

Caleb ignored me and leaned forward, grabbing the railings. He studied the water with a calculating look before he spoke.

"We come seeking the guidance of Mother Red Cap. We promise to uphold our end of the bargain and do no harm upon the mother witch. If we bring her harm in any capacity, we shall suffer the consequences for the rest of our lives."

"Wait, what?" I shouted. It was the only way to be heard over the boiling water.

Caleb let go of the railing and looked at me.

"Yeah, witches have to make a magical deal if they wanna visit her. I guess that's how she keeps her existence a secret," Caleb explained.

"And your daughter knows about her how exactly?" I asked.

Caleb shrugged.

"Nora is a complicated creature. She's had many reincarnations and helped hundreds of people, if not thousands. I'm sure they're friends from a different lifetime. Don't think too much about it. Trying to make sense of the Nightcrawler world sometimes is a bitch."

When he mentioned Nora's reincarnations, it hit me.

"Wait, is Nora the nurse that helped you when you turned into a vampire?" I asked.

I knew I was right before he nodded at me. It took a few moments to do so, but eventually, he admitted it.

"That's so weird, my friend," I said, realizing too late that I'd called him a friend when he wasn't. He wasn't even an acquaintance. He was a business deal and that was it. I still hated witches with all my being, and that wasn't going to change any time soon.

The water calmed and everything around us became normal again. I did a quick scan around the perimeter, but no witch had appeared. Maybe Nora had remembered wrong and had sent us on a wild goose chase. Maybe Mother Red Cap didn't want to see a witch hunter. Or maybe this was all bullshit, and I had fallen for it.

"Come in." We heard a whisper behind us, and when we turned, we saw the brick wall of the bridge had a crack on it, and from the crack, a light came through.

Caleb approach and gently pushed the brick wall, which popped open like a door, and we stepped inside. I followed behind him, and once we were both in, the door closed, leaving us in a corridor lit by torches hanging on the walls.

Caleb walked down the long stretch in absolute silence, and I couldn't blame him. It was not time for chit-chat when you were in a claustrophobic tunnel on your way to a powerful witch with no clear way of escape.

When we came to the end, there was an aged door with an iron handle. Caleb pushed the door open, and we came into a round stone chamber lined with doors all around, surely leading to other tunnels. A large bookcase decorated the other side of the room with books that looked ancient. The center of the room was tiered, with a few steps leading down towards a big bonfire in the middle.

A red-cloaked figure was sitting by the fire, completely unaffected by the heat of the flames.

"You must be this mother red witch," I said.

Caleb shushed me and watched the hooded figure as if he was face to face with a saint.

And that's where the differences between him and me started. He saw bigger, older witches as something to admire and respect, when I just saw her for what she was. A witch. In my experience, witches were all the same. They brought pain and torture into the human world and they didn't deserve to be in it. Except maybe for Caleb. He wasn't that bad.

I shook my head. What the hell was wrong with me?

"You've been hanging out with a witch all day, and you still can't get over your hang-ups and your lies, can you?" I heard a loud voice echo across the room.

Who had spoken? Surely, a frail person like the witch in front of me couldn't speak with such intensity. Had I imagined it? And if it was the cloaked woman, how did she know what I was thinking?

"Mother Red Cap can read your thoughts, witch hunter, so be careful what you think of," she said, and the hooded figure stood, giving us a view of her face.

While her hands had looked frail in front of the fire, her face looked middle-aged. Her eyes were green like emeralds, and her hair was a beautiful shade of chocolate curls that spilled to the sides of her face. She pulled the hood of her cloak back and stretched out a hand, inviting us both down to her level.

Caleb went down the steps and took her hand, kissing the back of it.

"Thank you for seeing us, Mother Red Cap," he said.

"Don't try to access my emotions, witch. That doesn't work with me. Has no one ever told you that? Us empaths can't use our powers against each other," she told him.

"I-I've never met one before," Caleb said.

Mother Red Cap pulled her hand back and quirked her mouth into a grin.

"We are indeed the rarer kind, aren't we?"

So that's what his power was. Empathy. I didn't know exactly what it meant, but it gave me more insight into what had happened the first night we'd met.

"On the other hand, this handsome witch hunter's brain is free for all," she said.

"I don't appreciate anyone invading my privacy," I told her as I came down the steps.

"Said the witch hunter who invaded the privacy of dozens of witches only to kill them, isn't that right?"

Why did I feel guilty in her presence? I'd never felt guilty about my job before, but standing in front of her right now, my heart beat frantically as if about to be squashed in her palm. She must have been doing something to my head to make me feel like that.

"Or it might be that you're seeing a different side to the witch world than what you were taught. And there's still so much to learn, my darling boy," she said.

Damn. I needed to keep my thoughts in check in front of this woman.

"No need. As long as you do me no harm, I will stop reading your thoughts. Besides, we are here for business, not pleasure," she said and gestured for me to sit down. Both Caleb and I sat on the steps, on one of the many cushions in front of the fire, and Mother Red Cap mimicked us. When she did, she threw a small pebble in the fire and it died down to a normal, tolerable level.

"Who has sent you my way? I don't get a lot of new visitors nowadays, which means someone old has sent you here."

I looked to Caleb who hesitantly offered his daughter's name.

"Oh, my darling Nora. It's been a while since I last saw her. How is she? How old is she?"

"She's only six at the moment. She…" he turned to look at me and with hesitation finished his sentence. "She saved my life when I was dying, and she rebirthed. So, we took her in. Annabel and me," he said.

"I remember her. The troll that she was best friends with. How is she doing?"

Did she just say troll? Had she called Annabel a troll? Like those online things that people hated?

"I'm sorry," Mother Red said to me, "I know I said

I wouldn't do it, but I can see you're struggling here. Of course I don't mean an online troll. I mean a real troll. Don't they teach you Nightcrawler history in the BLADE force?"

I shook my head, still trying to wrap my head around all these creatures that I apparently had no clue existed.

"Yup, that's the same Annabel. Although now she's Mom and I'm Dad, and it's all a bit...weird." Caleb continued the conversation, ignoring my interruption as if it hadn't even happened. It hadn't really been my interruption, had it? It was that sneaky old witch sitting across the fire from me.

"Who did you call old? I'll have you know I'm only three hundred."

I must've looked terrified because she burst into laughter.

"You had me there for a second." I cackled.

She stopped laughing for a moment and pierced me with her gaze.

"I am actually three hundred and fifty," she said.

How was this even possible? Were all witches able to live this long, or was she special? There were so many questions.

"We have a different lifespan than humans, it's true. But not every witch can live this long. You have to work hard for it, and I have. Hence the protections inside...and outside," she said, and with a flare of her hand pointed to where we'd just come from.

"You promised you would stay out of my head, so I would appreciate it if you kept that promise like I'm keeping mine," I told her. She knew what promise I was talking about. I wasn't gonna tell anyone about her existence if it meant I was going to suffer from another curse, so she'd better stay out of my head.

I said that with extra vigor in my head, knowing fully well that she would hear it.

"Very well, my apologies, witch hunter. I don't often interact with people, and sometimes I can be a little over the top, I will admit," she said, bringing her hands together. "Besides, you are here for business, not a history lesson. But tell me, witch, what is your name? I like to know the names of those I do business with."

"I'm Caleb. Caleb Carlyle, and I'm a member of the London Coven," he said.

I wouldn't have expected him to reveal his real name in my presence, or the name of his coven, but he'd done just that.

"A pleasure to meet you, Caleb Carlyle. And Wade Rawthorne," she said, and I flinched. Of course she would know my full name. Which made me curious how much more of my mind she could read without directly asking me something. "Tell me, why are you here?" she addressed Caleb.

I appreciated her effort to turn the attention away from me and back to Caleb, whose thoughts she couldn't read. She could have easily asked me to find out the answer, but she knew she had overstepped her boundaries. I could respect that.

"We need a transference spell. I want his frozen heart switched with mine," he told her.

"You what?" I asked turning to Caleb. "You never told me that."

Mother Red Cap looked from Caleb to me and back to Caleb, her eyes not giving away any of her thoughts.

"Are you sure you want to do something like that? Why would you want to curse your own heart?" she asked him.

"Wouldn't we all like to know that?" I said.

"That is for me to know. Can you do it?"

"What curse has been afflicted on you?" Mother Red asked me.

"A witch has cursed my brother and me with frozen hearts. We can never fall in love. And when we start to feel the emotions that should lead to love, it turns us into killers instead." It was hard to admit that I was not just a witch killer as part of my job. There was a natural killer not so deep inside, ready to come out at every opportunity. Memories of Sarah hit me, and I did my best to push them away.

"I—" the witch started, and I knew she had heard Sarah's name in my head. She drilled down to my soul with her green eyes, and I nodded at her in approval. If she wanted to reveal everything there was no stopping her. And if she knew, Caleb might as well know what he was in for if he switched with me. Give him a chance to change his mind. Because as much as I hated it, no one deserved our curse. Not even a witch.

"Who was Sarah, my dear boy?" I felt all eyes on me, and the flames made me sweat despite their very low intensity.

"She was a girl I liked. I tried to do the one-night-stand thing, and when I started feeling closer to someone, I would just ditch them because I could feel the anger and the hatred creeping in. I lashed out at one, actually, and they reported me to the police. My brother and I did our best to fight this in court, and there was a lot of shit that went down to get the charges dropped, but when we returned to our lives, we promised ourselves we would not get attached to anyone so that we didn't get ourselves into more trouble.

"But Sarah was...different. I don't know how or why, but she got through, and I didn't want to kill her. At least, not at first. We'd been dating for three months, and everything was fine. I was starting to think that the curse was not real. Maybe I had been cursed to not fall for anyone other than the one I was meant to be with, you know? I thought Sarah was my one."

Mother Red Cap watched me with sad eyes, surely familiar with the story already.

"But she wasn't," she muttered.

I took a big gulp and looked away from her and

stared into the fire. It was the only thing that couldn't judge me.

"She was. I really think I did love her, but the curse still triggered, even if massively delayed, and it made me lash out at her. I was unable to stop myself. I killed her," I admitted, and I could feel my eyes twitching, begging me to let the tears come out, but I wasn't about to do that in front of two witches.

"And the first thing I did was call my brother to help me figure this crap out. He helped me get rid of her body, but it annoys me, you know? Her family will never know what happened to her. They don't even have a body to bury. I took all that away from them and instead gave them nightmares."

It was all a nightmare. This wasn't living. This wasn't a way to live your life. I was sick of it, and I wanted to get rid of it.

I turned to Caleb and saw tears in his eyes.

"Are you sure you want to do this? Are you sure you want to be a killer?" I asked him.

He stared at me for a few moments before he brought his forearm to his face and wiped his eyes.

"Yes. Yes, I do," he said.

"What is wrong with you? Why would you want this? I know you're a witch, but why would you want to become a killer who can never fall in love?" I asked him. "I'm sure she has ways to just remove my curse without inflicting it on you."

"I actually don't. I've heard of broken heart curses

before, but never a curse that reacts like that. Unless I knew the witch that had cast this spell on you and the details of her curse, I can't fix it. But a transference spell? That I can do," the witch said.

If witches had a soul, and my entire life I'd believed they hadn't, it was time for Caleb to prove his now.

"Listen, I want to get rid of this more than you can ever imagine," I said, "but if you've changed your mind and you wanna break the deal, I'm fine with that. I'll just walk away, and we'd never have to speak of this again."

Caleb turned to the other witch and ignored me.

"What do we need for the spell?" he asked her.

I looked at Mother Red Cap, and with another glance drifting from Caleb to me, she stood and went to her bookcase. She returned moments later with a book in her hand.

"Once it's done, there is no way back," she warned Caleb.

I gazed at Caleb, but his eyes were settled on the book Mother Red Cap was holding.

"Good."

What nightmares had he gone through to make him want this so bad even after hearing my story? What was wrong with him? And did I really want to inflict my curse on someone else, even if they were a witch?

EIGHT
CALEB

When I was agreeing to help the witch hunter, I didn't think I would get no sleep. To be honest, I shouldn't really be sleeping in the presence of a witch hunter anyway, but I was hoping to at least get some rest before we continued our mission. But with hunters after us, and the threat of more witches dying, there was no rest for the wicked.

When Mother Red Cap gave us the list of the three ingredients that she needed for a potion, I knew exactly where to get all three. And if everything went well, we would both have what we needed before the next sunset.

Hearing Wade share his story of how he'd killed his only potential love had reminded me of Jin and our time together. It reminded me of everything I'd loved about him and everything I had lost. When he was killed, I must've felt something like Wade, although mine was even more intense. Having the blood of my lover smeared all over my skin, a vampire in mourning while also thinking how thirsty it was making me was a sick, disturbing feeling.

One I never wanted to experience again.

Yes, I was no longer a vampire, that much was true, but I was something worse now. I was an empath and these powers, as much good as they could do, could make things a lot harder too.

It was dawn when we came out of Mother Red Cap's sanctum, and the streets of Camden were eerily quiet before the hectic morning commute began. I turned to Wade to see how he was holding up. Mother Red Cap had done a number on him.

I hadn't known empaths couldn't read one another since she was the only other empath I had met, but she had infiltrated his mind over and over without even needing to touch him, and I could only imagine how intense that must have felt, having to control every single thought so as not to reveal everything about yourself. It was still admirable what he had done. Share his very personal story with two strangers —to witches, nonetheless. He had been trained to hate us and to kill us, so for him to put his trust in me, I didn't know what to make of that.

"How are you doing?" I asked him.

He turned to look at me and a smirk appeared on

his face, but it never quite reached his eyes, so I knew it wasn't real.

"I'm doing good. You? Tired yet?" he asked.

"Me? Tired? You gotta be kidding me," I said and responded with my own fake smirk.

The morning chill reached my bones, and I hugged my jacket tighter. It would be fine once the sun had settled in the sky, but for now, I had to suppress my weakness.

"So, where to next?" Wade asked.

"We're going shopping."

I sped up, hoping it would warm me up and leaving Wade to catch up with me.

"I have to say, I didn't expect a list of plants from her. Maybe a list of jewelry or other expensive things, but plants?" he said, pointing at the piece of paper in my hands.

"What? Do you think spells are just diamonds that have been magically inclined?"

I wouldn't blame him if he did. That's what I had thought in the beginning before Graham had shown me how spells were made. He wasn't proficient, either. Due to his power, he barely needed any ingredients to make spells, but the majority of his work was simple household spells. The good ones, those we bought from outside the coven, were American, mainly. I knew if I had asked him, he could probably make a transference spell for me. Maybe he already had one. But I didn't want to report back to him until I had more to go on. Also, the fact that we were attacked by witches didn't bode well. If someone hadn't reported it to him yet, they would do soon enough, and he would be furious.

"I don't know what I thought. I really just know what we learned at the force," Wade replied.

He was sweet. He was trying to be more than his job, but I didn't know what it was, whether it was the curse or growing up to be a hunter, that just made the attempt look sad. I could tell he was trying. I had brushed hands with him regardless of whether he knew it or not.

I knew he was trying to understand my world and make sense of it and what it meant for him, but I also knew he still had the same preconceptions that he'd had before he'd found out everything about Night-crawlers. The least I could do was give him an A for effort. We would only have to tolerate each other for a little while longer until we sorted the curse and managed to find out who the mole-witch was.

Did they even know they were responsible for these murders? Or did they not care about the death of their kind? It made me so upset thinking that one of our own was helping get rid of us.

"Alchemy is...it's the study of the arcane, but it's also the study of everything in this world that has a magical property. Plants, flowers, colors, everything has a meaning, and everything has a magical quality. What alchemists do is take those properties and infuse them in such a way so as to create the magical spell. It's a real art, and not everyone can do it," I told him.

He deserved to be treated kindly by a witch. I couldn't overlook the deaths of many witches, and his count was high, but perhaps if one witch was good to him, even for a little while, it would change him, and he would try to be different. Maybe not a witch hunter anymore.

Then I reminded myself that I was going to erase his memories anyway, so I didn't know why I bothered. Thinking about him that much and the effect I could have on him was an unnecessary attachment I was creating. And that was exactly why I needed this spell to work. I was sick of getting attached to people so easily, so quickly, and so foolishly.

Even before I was an empath, I got attached to people way too fast, but as an empath, that feeling was now tenfold. Because I could always see the motivation and meaning behind every action, every word, and I guess that's what being an empath was, but all I ever got from it was hurt.

"Where are we going now?" Wade asked.

I looked at the piece of paper and read the three ingredients on the list.

"First up, Old Spitalfields Market."

Wade nodded and followed me to the tube station, where we rode the underground for a few stops to Whitechapel. By the time we got there, the morning rush had started, so we had to fight our way through suits and stressed, grumpy shop assistants.

We walked up the street and closer to the market which was heaving with life. Old Spitalfields Market was a big thing in London, and there were hundreds of stalls selling all kinds of wares. It was the perfect hiding place for witches to trade from. One just needed to know where to look for them.

I'd come here more times than I cared for to find ingredients for Graham and his high council. So, when I saw the familiar face of Grace, she gave me a big smile and came round for a hug.

She was a hugger. I wasn't. She couldn't get it, and it was annoying. You would think a witch would understand that an empath would want to avoid touch as much as possible, yet she persisted. Probably because of her earthly, nurturing powers, she tried to sneak in as much human contact as possible. I couldn't blame her, but I could be quietly mad at her.

"Caleb, how are you, my darling? You didn't swing by yesterday, and I was getting worried. Everything okay?" she asked and let me go. Finally.

I forced a smile to appease her and then turned towards her stall. There no point making small talk with Grace because I could be there for hours.

"I just got busy with work. Can I have a root of mandrake please?" I said, looking at the flower pots that decorated her stall.

"I think I sold the last one yesterday," she said and started going through her merchandise.

Please, Goddess, tell me we didn't make all this effort for nothing. The only other witch that had root of mandrake was on the other side of London, and I was already getting drained. I needed to rest and the sooner we got this spell over and done with, the sooner I could get back in my bed.

"I really need it. Tell me you have some."

I knew sometimes she played up about her availability to push the prices a bit, and I was hoping that was the case right now. I didn't mind paying extra on this occasion, although I would hate to spoil her. Her prices were always unstable, and if I continued to go along with her games, our ingredients would cost more than the spells themselves.

"Oh, wait. No. There's one more left. Today's your lucky day," she said, turning around to wink at me.

I didn't know what part of my life she had found to be lucky, but I wasn't going to argue with her now. Instead, I smiled and got my wallet out.

"How much?" I asked her. "It's fifteen pounds, right?"

"Well, actually, it's thirty pounds."

I held my tongue, but I was sure my face said something along the lines of what the actual fuck are you talking about because she creased her eyebrows and scolded me.

"Don't look at me like that, mister. This is pure

root of mandrake. The stuff you got before was shavings. This is the price, take it or leave it. I can't make a loss because you don't wanna pay up."

Wade pushed me to the side and retrieved his wallet.

"That's fine. We can pay," he said and passed her a fifty-pound note.

What an idiot! Why did he think he knew better than me? Now she was going to hike up her prices to an extortionate amount. I would have to have a talk with Graham when all this was finished to get Grace appeased and her prices stable.

"See, your friend appreciates a good plant. It's worth taking a lesson or two from him," she said and smiled flirtatiously at Wade.

If only she knew who he was and what he did for a living. For the moment, it didn't matter anyway. Grace gave us the plant, wrapped in a medium-sized box, and we were on our way.

"Make sure to tell Graham I miss him," she said as we left.

Couldn't keep her mouth shut, could she?

"Who is Graham?" Wade asked.

I continued walking, ignoring his questions. By the time he asked again, I had started to notice a few heads floating around us that looked familiar. They weren't hard to locate, discreetness and disguise were not their forte from what I could gather, and I stared directly at the witch hunter we had fought yesterday. The one

Wade had called Lloyd. The other witch hunters that were surrounding us did not look familiar.

"Forget about Graham now. We've got company," I told him, and his head snapped in Lloyd's direction.

"Fuck. I knew this would happen."

Lloyd waded through the crowd and approached us as we tried to make our way out of the market. I needed to find a way to escape them without attracting any attention from the public.

"Wade, what the fuck you think you're doing? Have you lost your mind? Why are you under the witch's spell?" Lloyd grumbled when he got closer.

We were heading north of the market, and Lloyd was following us. I couldn't use a chaos spell again, partially because I had run out and partially because of how many people we were surrounded by. A chaos spell cast in such a public area would cause a huge problem. And if there was one thing they taught you in Beginner Witches 101, it was to keep the witches away from the media.

"Don't engage him. The less he knows, the better," I told Wade.

"You don't tell me what to do, witch," he replied, and I wished I had the energy at that moment to slap his face. But I had more important things to do, and a witch hunter reverting to his witch hunter ways was not priority at the moment.

It was now way past nine, and the market was crammed with people. But as soon as we came out of the market our problems would start. I didn't know how many hunters were stationed around, and I didn't know which areas they covered. A teleportation spell would have been ideal right now, but fuck were they expensive, and Graham would have never approved of me using one.

How had they found us? When did witch hunters become that good? I'd been a witch for a little over five years, and I knew hunters were terrible at tracking us down. So no, this was not it. There was another way they were able to find us, and I didn't understand.

"Hold up," I said and turned on my heel.

Wade almost bumped into me, but I put my hand on his chest and stopped him. Damn, those were some good pecs he was packing under there. If only he wasn't a hunter. And if only I was on the lookout for a new addiction.

"Do you guys have trackers so you can trace each other?" Wade shook his head. "Then how the fuck are they finding us?"

He shrugged with the naughty smirk on his face that I wanted to wipe off so desperately. Whether that was with my hands or my lips that was a different kind of question. One I wasn't sure I knew the answer to.

"Because we're good," he said.

I laughed. Lloyd was standing next to us now, and all I could do was laugh. Because the situation was so surreal, so unreal even, that laughing was the only thing I could do without freaking out.

"Have you gone soft for a witch, Wade? Is that why you betrayed your family. Is that why you betrayed your duty?" Lloyd asked.

"Shut up, Lloyd," both Wade and I turned around to shout at him.

Well, that was interesting. When that happened, however uncommon it was, it was usually because I was touching the other person. But my gloves were still on, and I wasn't touching Wade. This shit was getting weirder and weirder.

Focus, Caleb. Exit strategy. Now.

Lloyd attempted to get closer, and I turned around and stopped him.

"One more step and he's toast," I said, grabbing for a crystal around my bracer. Staring at my spellbook, Lloyd froze, unable to do anything.

Maybe that was it. Maybe all I had to do was pretend Wade was my hostage. However unbelievable that was, considering he had fought his own colleagues last night, I could certainly play up to it. This guy obviously cared about Wade and didn't want him to get hurt, or else he wouldn't care about my threat.

"You, follow me," I told Wade, then to Lloyd: "You, go to hell. If I see you following us, you'll get his balls delivered in a box with a pretty bow." I grabbed Wade's thick arm and pushed him forward. Boy, was it big and strong.

Focus, Caleb. Stop getting distracted by an attractive man. What the hell was wrong with me? My life was at risk, and all I could think about was Wade's thick arms, impeccable pecs, and beautiful blue eyes. For fuck's sake.

I was pleasantly surprised when Wade allowed himself to be pushed aside to make for a convincing abductee. Again, I wasn't sure how much of this the hunters were buying, but if it would allow us to put some distance between us, that was just fine by me. All we needed was a bit of distance.

"You know this won't work, right?" Wade muttered under his breath.

"Aren't you Professor Einstein? I know that. Which is why we need to run."

Call it a stroke of inspiration, or a stroke of brilliance even, but being around the farmer's market, surrounded by all the flowers and pots, I had found just the right spell. It was over my wrist bone on the spellbook, and I didn't even know why I carried it around. But I was about to find out.

I fiddled with the bracer and removed the yellow crystal that had been there since the beginning. It had been one of the first spells I could afford when I'd officially become a witch. The reason it was sitting there wasn't because of its value. It was a cheap-ass spell, and I'd bought it to make me feel better. Even witches make impulse buys to make themselves feel better.

"How many of them are there? I asked him.

"Eight. One stationed at each corner, and four rotating around us."

"Hm, so we've got the cavalry. I feel honored."

"You should feel scared," Wade replied and tried to turn around to look at me, but I grabbed his arm again, a bit harder this time, and pushed him.

"I told you, I need to put some distance between us and them, and then we'll be fine." I hoped at least.

That was the tricky part with spells. Because you'd never used them, and most of them you could only use once, you didn't know if they would work for what you wanted unless you tried them. Which wasn't really a problem when you used them in the conventional way, but when you tried to use them for a different purpose? That's when it was trial and error at best. And witches could die from trial and error. At least, if all else failed, I had a witch hunter at my side. Even if it was only for the moment and only a means to an end.

"See that side street?" Wade asked and turned his head slightly to the side to point at it but without making it obvious.

Straight ahead, out of the market, the road curved onto a narrow street.

"We can lose the four on the corners through there, but we won't lose Lloyd and the other three," Wade said.

I tried to assess the situation. I didn't want to leave my fate in the hands of a witch hunter. But why would he be lying to me? If all this went pear-shaped, he'd be the one stuck with the frozen heart or dead.

"Okay. When we come out turn left, pretend we're going around. Then, we'll run for the alley."

It wasn't a long stretch to walk, but for some reason, it felt like it. When we got to the end of the market, it felt like it'd taken forever, and we were still being chased. As instructed, Wade turned left, and I followed him, using the exit to our advantage. Lloyd and the three hunters behind us lost sight of us for the moment, but it wouldn't be for long.

We had to act now or risk being ambushed.

"Run," I barked, and Wade and I barreled across the street as a bus was driving through, giving us an added momentary block from our pursuers. We ran into the alley, and I squeezed the crystal in my hands, familiarizing myself with the spellword.

I opened my eyes and stared at the hunters who were catching up.

"What are you waiting for?" Wade asked, but I ignored him.

The spell was only a small one, so I had to wait for the last possible moment to make it count. And that was if it worked in the way I wanted it to. For all I knew, this would end up in a bust, and we'd be fighting for our lives in a few moments.

"Now would be a good time to do whatever it is you're planning to do," Wade muttered.

Lloyd smirked as he approached us with his lackeys.

"Tired of running already?" he said. "I like

running."

Ah, now it made sense why he'd made us believe he'd fallen for the hostage thing. He was a sick bastard who liked chasing his prey before eating it. Metaphorically speaking. I hoped.

"Lloyd, you don't understand. I can explain—" Wade started, but before I could stop him, Lloyd did.

"I can't believe you would let all those years of service go down the toilet. And for what? What's the reason for betraying us?" He attempted to step closer.

Great. Time for the show.

I turned to Wade and whispered.

"Look around for our escape route. You've got five seconds."

He nodded, and I let him do his job while I distracted the hunters. I opened my palm to reveal my spell to them.

"I wouldn't come any closer if I were you."

Lloyd perked one cocky eyebrow and crossed his arms in front of his chest.

"You think I'm scared of you?"

I knew it was a rhetorical question, but I couldn't resist.

"You should," I replied. "Lux," I shouted and with a quick motion, I threw the spell towards the hunters.

It exploded into dust mid-air, and right before the spell took effect, I turned around and yelled at Wade to shut his eyes. Thankfully, he turned his back to me and covered his eyes with his forearm.

I squeezed mine shut as hard as possible just at the right time, and I heard the screams of the witch hunters as the light spell blinded them. After a few moments, I turned around and inspected the situation. That was a sight to behold. Four witch hunters in the middle of the road, stumbling into anything and everything like brainless zombies while rubbing their eyes, trying to get them open again.

I hadn't expected a photosynthesis spell to work this well. Maybe it would be something to discuss with Graham, about increasing its price. Especially if it could be used in combat. Who knew a spell made to help plants grow faster and stronger could be used as tear gas against witch hunters?

"Your escape. Where?" I pulled Wade to the side and waited for him to open his eyes, take a quick glance behind him at his colleagues, and point at a door to the side.

We ran towards it and Wade, mandrake box under one arm, kicked it open. Any other time, I would have taken a moment or two to appreciate the sheer strength of my companion, but right now, all I could think about was escaping.

Oh, who was I kidding?

His ass was also imprinted on my mind. And who could blame me? With butt cheeks as tight as his, anyone would have been distracted.

We ducked inside, and Wade shut the door behind us and looked around him for something to block it.

"How much time have we got?"

I shrugged.

"I've not used that spell before. I got no idea."

He picked up a box and pushed it against the door and then propped a mop against the handle.

I inspected the building we had just entered. There was a corridor leading to the front of a business building, or that was my guess, and a staircase on the left that led up. From our position, we could see the front of the building and the street it was on, and when a couple of people wearing leather jackets and with hilts in their hands appeared, we turned to look at each other.

"Up," we said in unison.

Wade ran up the staircase. I wasn't really digging this whole twin's telepathy thing we had going on today. It was creepy as fuck, albeit a little bit of a turn on. Perhaps we were more alike than we thought.

When we got to the top of the building, Wade used his strength again to open the door to the rooftop, and we walked out to it.

"This way." Wade ran to the edge of the building where it was semi-connected to another one.

He helped me up the parapet, and I jumped onto the roof of the building next door, then he jumped around it himself, and we ran for the next one.

The buildings from across the street met at a corner in front of us, which we used to our advantage and got farther away from the hunters. When our escape route turned into gable roofs, we had to get back on the ground.

There was an open door that took us back inside, and we climbed down the stairs of the last industrial building, passing a vintage clothing store that was situated on the first floor.

"We need a disguise," I said, and we walked inside.

A change of clothes later and properly disguised, we returned to street level and blended in with the crowd in Brick Lane. We walked up towards the high street, planning on taking the underground to our next destination.

"You know this box is getting really heavy," Wade said when we reached the main street.

"Let's get a taxi then," I said, but his posture changed.

"No. We haven't lost our tail yet."

"What do we do now?"

I had picked up all the spells I could find while at home, but none were any good for combat. Those were expensive and were kept at the shop. The best I could do to get the hunters off our back was to send a lick of flames their way, but without knowing where they were, that would be a waste.

Man, I really needed to stock up with some useful spells again. Graham's allowance was not just restrictive, but downright dangerous if our current situation was anything to go by.

"When I say so, run," Wade said and pointed to the street opposite.

I nodded. We crossed the road and once our feet hit the pavement, Wade grunted, and we broke into a run down another street.

I turned around to check who was after us. It was Lloyd. Of course it was. The only obstacle between us and him was the busy London traffic, which was relentless at the best of times.

By the time we got to the end of the street, he was after us again, but too far away to catch up. We took a left turn and then a right one and came up against a little chapel.

"Get inside," Wade said.

"Oh, Mr. Darcy. Is that a way to propose to a lady," I swooned at him.

He shook his head in disgust and ducked inside the chapel. It was a small church of an indiscriminate denomination, and there was no service going on at this time, although there were a few people in prayer.

We walked around them and stood in front of a door that led to the chancel and the private quarters of the pastors. Wade gently pushed me in and closed the door back up, turning to look through the floral designs carved on the wooden panel, which had small holes in them allowing full view of the nave of the church.

"He's here," he whispered, and I joined him to watch what was going on.

Lloyd had entered the church and was looking around at all the people in prayer.

He was careful not to make any noise, and he walked down the middle, inspecting all the faces.

"He won't hesitate coming back here," I whispered.

Wade nodded. His gaze darted behind us, looking for an escape route. He must have found one because he got me off my knees, and we walked to the back where another door was. He tried to open it, but it wouldn't budge.

"It's locked," he muttered.

I pushed him aside and got back on my knees, pulling out a small knife from my back pocket.

"Witches know how to pick locks without magic?" Wade asked.

I looked up at him, making sure to give him the same arrogant smile he gave me when he answered my questions.

"Only the good ones," I said and returned my attention to the lock.

Wade approached the front panel to check on Lloyd's progress. Then he came back to me.

"Any luck? He's getting close," he said.

Instead of a response, I gave him the click of the opening door, and with a creak, we opened it and ducked inside. I clicked the lock back into place, and we turned to look at what we were dealing with. There was a staircase descending to the pits of the church.

Wade rushed down, and as I put my foot on the first step, I remembered a simple illusion spell I had on me. It would never have worked out on the street with so much light and distractions, but here? It should work like a charm.

Retrieving the blue stone, I whispered the spell-word as I set it down on the ground, picturing what I wanted Lloyd to see. Dust exploded in the room and a wall with some boxes and a lot of dust appeared where the stairs should be.

I ran through it and made my way downstairs into a storage room that stunk of mold.

There was no way of knowing if it would fool him, so we canvassed the room and found a hiding spot behind some old furniture. We both sat down on the ground and waited. I told him about the spell I cast.

"Lloyd won't be fooled," he said.

"Great. So now what?"

"We wait," Wade replied and put the box of mandrake down beside him. "What is this thing meant to do anyway?"

"I told you—"

"I meant as a plant, not as a spell ingredient."

I shook my head.

"What do you mean what does a plant do? It grows out of the ground. Blossoms on this side and then roots grow in the ground. Are you serious?"

Before I'd even finished my sentence, Wade started

chuckling as if he'd accomplished something incredible.

"Are you messing with me? Do you think this is funny? Is this whole situation a joke to you?"

He shook his head like a maniac trying to calm himself down.

"No, I wasn't...I just-I just heard it," he managed to say.

"Has the running got into your head?"

Honestly, I preferred him like this than the blood-thirsty witch hunter that he made himself out to be, and that he most likely was. I'd rather have a laughing man than a murderous hunter. It looked cute on him. Made me wonder how it was that he had the cursed heart because he didn't look anything like someone who couldn't feel love. Not how I would have expected someone to be like anyway. It only gave me hope that when I swapped hearts with him, old Caleb would still be there, he just wouldn't have his heart ripped to shreds from love ever again.

So, the waiting game began. If Wade was right and Lloyd would not give up that easily, it meant we had to stay in the church basement until the coast was clear. Until we found an alternative.

Wade tried to explain to me how Lloyd operated out in the field and what kind of person he was. I could imagine how it must have felt for him to be up against his partner, the one that was meant to be by his side, every step of the hunt.

Don't get me wrong. I wasn't feeling sorry for him. Being a murderer is not something I excuse that easily. But I knew how it was. Having a partner sticking up for you, being your backup and your shoulder to cry on.

I'd had to give all that up when I'd contracted the vampire virus. It still hurt that I'd had to leave my friends behind. The people I'd gone to school with. The people that I had fought hard to take me seriously.

As a foster kid, you move so often that kids start to sense it. They can tell you won't be there for long. So having friends is hard. Harder than making enemies.

I shook off the thoughts and focused on Wade, who seemed to be lost in his own.

He had bags under his eyes, and his skin glistened where he had sweated. But it wasn't just his physical appearance. It was his glazed eyes that screamed defeat. Granted, I probably didn't look much better, but he looked like he was suffering from more than just exhaustion.

Was it the curse? Was it making him feel exasperated? How did it even feel to have that kind of burden inside you? Did he even feel at all?

Sure he did. He had been nice to Nora. He had even been nice to me, in his own special witch hunter way. He wasn't a bad apple. He'd just fallen from a bad tree. He'd been taught the wrong things. Lies and deception were the only things he knew. Couldn't blame him for being unable to catch up with it all. It had only been a day since he had discovered his entire world had been a lie. How did anyone even deal with that?

"Are you okay?" I asked him before I could stop myself.

I didn't want to show him that I had any compassion for him, but, call it the empath in me, or the witch in me, but I couldn't be mad at him for his heritage and his background.

His eyes, those gorgeous blue eyes, looked up at and stayed on me for a few moments before he responded. I wished I was like Mother Red Cap and could read his thoughts without touching him. I wished I could let myself inside his mind, freely, and find out everything about him. What made him tick. What made him break. He was an enigma to me, and I wasn't so sure that it was all because of the curse.

"Fine. You?" he said.

Look at that. We hadn't even been together for that long, and he was already making progress. Caring about someone, a witch nonetheless, other than himself.

"Fine." Minutes flew by like seconds in the eerie basement. "This place is really quiet, isn't it?" I said after a long time.

If I could have slapped my forehead, I would have, but since that wasn't an option, I just reprimanded myself inside my head.

"That's the whole point of a hiding place." He smirked.

I grimaced. "All right, Mr. Smartass. I'm just trying to make conversation."

Wade smiled. It was a cute little curve of his lips, but I could imagine girls falling for it.

Before I could stop myself, I started leaning towards him, aiming for those beautiful lips with my own, unable to think about anything else.

But before our lips could make impact, I was pushed to the floor, pinned down by an angry Wade. His face was red, as if it was about to go off. What had I just done?

"What the fuck do you think you're doing?" he growled.

I tried to get him off me, but his arm on my chest only pushed harder.

He had me pinned to the ground with his forearm blocking my chest and with his other hand holding one of mine down. One of his legs pressed on my feet and I couldn't move.

"You got me. Now let me go."

He didn't budge. I tried to use my free hand to push him off me, but it seemed that he was a solid rock on top of me. Completely unmoving.

The more I tried to free myself, the more his forearm pushed off my chest to my throat, making me angrier and more desperate to save myself.

Had all of this been a ruse? Had he gone for our

deal just to get more information out of me and then get me in a church basement and kill me? Had I fallen for a trap? When I'd thought I'd had the upper hand, and I'd actually been played?

"Stop...moving," he hissed, but I didn't listen.

He dipped his head to meet my eyes.

"I said—" he started, and I could feel his warm breath on my face. It made my skin crawl. Goosebumps on the back of my neck that I could not control.

Before I could stop myself, again I closed the distance between us and took a taste of those lips.

His lips were dry, but thirsty because he kissed me back, and it was as if we were fighting for air, trying to find it in each other's mouth's.

One might think this would be weird for me. Kissing the man who was sent to kill me. But it wasn't. I was an empath. Also, a hopeless empath. I fell far too easily, and far too quickly, and I couldn't always blame my empathy for this. This had been happening to me long before I had been a witch, and it was happening to me now.

Because I didn't care that he was a killer. I didn't care about his past. All I cared about was his mouth. His hands on me. The eyes that could cut through glass.

Fuck!

I was falling for a witch hunter.

NINE
WADE

His lips were a sweet juice I couldn't stop drinking. Every one of his breaths made things happen down there, and his touch, dangerous as it could be, was a burn I couldn't stop enjoying.

What was I doing? What was happening? Why was I kissing a man? I forced myself off the witch and put some distance between us.

"What the fuck did you just do to me?" I shouted.

No, this couldn't be happening. I hadn't just kissed a witch. A male witch too. This was bullshit. It must have been some mind-control shit, and I had to stop it. Whatever it was he was doing to me had to stop.

"I didn't do anything to you. Nothing you didn't enjoy anyway," he replied, and that tipped me over the edge. How could he say that? How could he say I had enjoyed that? I hadn't. It wasn't even me who had kissed him. He was the one that had done it.

"I don't like men. I don't kiss men. Whatever it is you did to me, you better stop it," I said.

He laughed, a bit too loudly for my liking. Despite what had happened, I didn't want Lloyd to find us.

"What is it you think I did to you?"

"Use those fucking natural powers of yours to lure me. I don't know. I don't know witchcraft like you do. But whatever it is, don't try it again."

"I didn't do anything to you. I didn't use my natural powers on you. It was just a kiss, and one that you enjoyed more than you care to admit, if I might add."

His words only made me more furious. "Would you stop saying that?"

I was trying to control myself. I was trying to put everything in order, but it was impossible. The more he talked, the angrier it made me. It wasn't true. I wasn't gay. I didn't like men. And most of all, I didn't like witches. There had to have been something he had done to me, otherwise, why would I find his kiss so damn irresistible? Even when I was mad as hell, I was picturing it in my head and needing more.

Those were the consequences when a human meddled with witches. If they got too close, they could get burned. Tale as old as time. I had spoken to way too many victims of witches, and they had all said the same thing: the witch made me do it. That's what this witch had done to me. He'd made me do it.

How could I have been so stupid? How could I have let him take over like this? It was my fault in a way. I should have killed him when I'd had the chance. Now I was stuck with a witch and his sinful tantalizing nature.

"Listen, dude," he said, "whatever just happened, can we please calm down? We're still being chased by your friend, and unless you wanna be killed by him, we need to keep it down, 'kay?"

He was right. Lloyd might still be out there, and we needed to stay low. Which involved me sticking to my indoors voice. Although, knowing Lloyd, he had probably lost interest in the hunt the moment lunchtime struck.

"What's the time?" I asked him.

"It's past two," he replied, and when he realized what he'd said he looked at the watch again. "What the fuck? Where did all this time go?"

"Lost track of time with all the spells you're casting on me?"

He attempted to bite back, but I put my hand up.

"Lloyd is gone. He probably gave up hours ago. I think we can go now," I said, and he seemed to breathe a sigh of relief.

"Finally. I need to call Nora. See if she's okay."

He started moving towards the stairs, but my mind was still clinging to the moment our lips had met.

How intoxicating it had been, being in his thrall, having him kiss me like he felt something for me. This was why it had to have been witchcraft. No one could love anyone like me.

"Seriously, what did you do to make me kiss you?" I asked him again before I could stop myself.

I didn't know if it was the pleading in my voice or his exasperation, but he stopped in his tracks and turned around to look at me.

"Don't start again. You enjoyed that as much as I did, and I didn't cast a spell on you. Are you an idiot or have you lost your mind? If I had done a spell, wouldn't you have seen it? Also, before you say it, that's not how my natural power works. I can only feel what the other person is feeling. I can't make people do anything they don't want to do."

"But what about the time in the pub. When you made me so weak I couldn't even walk?"

I couldn't decide if I wanted to hear the answer or not. I was hoping I knew what was going on because if I didn't, it meant something completely different, and I didn't even know where to start with that.

I had never, ever felt anything for another man before, not even to experiment. Partly because my curse had been at play for most of my life, but also because it had just never crossed my mind. I'd never felt any urge to do anything with another man. If Caleb was telling the truth, what did that mean about me? Was I gay? Had I never been straight?

No! Sarah was real. There was a dead, rotting body to prove that. And my fucked-up feelings for her had also been real. Otherwise, she wouldn't be where she was today.

Did that mean I was bisexual? I was so confused, and the fact that I hadn't taken a crystal for the last twenty-four hours wasn't helping. It was what had started this whole mess in the first place. If I hadn't started feeling the cravings, the witch would never have succeeded in kissing me, and I wouldn't have kissed him back. Was the fact that he carried magic within him enough to make me high for him? Was it even possible to get high off a witch's natural power?

I wished I could put the chaos in my head in order. I wished I could categorize everything and file away what wasn't needed and deal with the rest at the right time. Now was not the time to deal with this bullshit. Not when we were being chased, and especially not when the mission to break my curse was underway.

"We need to go. We've got to get the rest of the ingredients," the witch said, and he climbed the stairs.

He was right of course. We had to get moving. We couldn't spend all day in the basement of a church.

A church?

How could a witch go into a church and not get hurt? It hadn't occurred to me when we'd come in because we were being chased and there had been no time to think about anything other than escaping, but now it occurred to me.

How could a witch withstand the holy power of the angels? He should have died from the effect of the angel force surrounding the church. That was strange. Certainly worth investigating when all of this was done and dealt with. Something told me there was more going on in the BLADE force than Director Marlowe let on. Spend enough time with a witch and things start not adding up. Was he purposefully lying to us?

I followed Caleb up to the ground floor and found him on the phone.

"I'm okay, sweetheart. I'm with Wade, remember him? The man you healed last night... He is okay too... I'll tell him that."

Tell me what? What did the little girl want him to say to me after everything that had happened?

I scanned the church and looked for any blind spots, but the coast was clear, and I would imagine so was the outside. I let him finish his call to his daughter and tried to find a way out of the church which seemed to be locked. It was definitely empty. Worst case scenario, the witch could use his lock-picking skills again and get us out of here.

"Nora has asked to give you her kisses. Do you want them now or do you want them later?"

Was he joking? After everything?

"You think this is funny?"

Caleb came closer to me and pinched his fingers in front of my eyes.

"Just a little bit," he said.

"You're an asshole."

"Tell me something I don't know. Now, have you found a door, or do you need me again?"

I rolled my eyes and ushered him to the nearest exit, where he got to his knees and started working on the lock.

He looked good there, down on his knees. In front of me. If only he turned around a few degrees, he'd be a sight to behold.

Fuck! What was wrong with me?

I knew what was wrong with me. I was spending way too much time with a witch. Maybe that's what happened with witches in churches. Maybe instead of dying, their powers became rampant and wild. That would explain a lot.

Caleb got up and announced that the door was open.

"Do you know where to get the other ingredients?" I asked him.

"Of course," he said with a purse of those sexy lips and a cute little shrug.

No. Not a cute shrug. Just a shrug. For fuck's sake. I needed to get out of here.

———

We came out of the church, and the winter cold of London bit into me like a motherfucking bitch. Caleb didn't seem to mind the weather, and the jacket he was wearing was lighter than my shirt.

As we walked down the street, and I followed behind him, my gaze dropped to his ass, where his round butt cheeks flexed with every movement.

What was I doing? I didn't like men. Why was I checking him out? Since when did I check out another man's ass? Something was really fucked up in all of this, yet I couldn't figure out what. I would have to endure it though. Until I could get my heart back.

I caught up with the witch and our shoulders brushed.

"Where are the other ingredients, then?" I asked him.

Caleb stopped walking and looked at me with sheepish eyes.

"The other ones are not as easy to retrieve. The good news is that they're both in the same place."

"What do you mean they're not easy to retrieve? Where are they?"

Caleb shoved his hands into his pockets and started walking again, watching the road in front of him. I stayed next to him, keeping my eyes on him and waiting for his response.

"I have a feeling...you're not going to like this," he said.

How could he possibly already know what I liked and didn't like?

"What is it?" I asked him.

"We have to..." he started and then mumbled something I couldn't understand.

"We have to what?"

"We have to sneak into a witch's house," he said when he finally looked into my eyes.

Had he said...? Did I hear right?

"Are you out of your mind?" I asked.

"Oh, now you care about the law? But when you kill witches it's all good, right? No fucks given."

What was he talking about? While he did have it right that we did kill witches and killing was against the law, we were also a secret government organization, so all of our killing was sanctioned by the British government. We did what we had to do for the common good. Besides...

"I don't care about stealing, I care about covering our tracks. Considering we've been attacked by everyone in the last twenty-four hours, I don't like putting my life at risk, again. Why can't we just ask for the ingredients?"

"We could, but then we would have to explain why we want illegal ingredients, and then we would have to explain why we want to do a transference spell, which wouldn't go down well with this particular witch. Oh, also, I hate his guts. That's why," he replied as if it was the most normal thing in the world.

"Okay, you've got a point. Where is his house?"

"Where else? North London, of course," he replied and turned around to continue walking.

"Of course. Why of course? Do all witches live in North London?" I said as I followed him.

"I'm not telling you that. But, where do you think posh people live?" he asked.

"And is this witch posh?"

He brought his thumb, index finger, and middle fingers together and rubbed them with a sly look on his face.

Okay. So that was a yes.

"How are we going to get in? Doesn't he have protection spells around the house?" I asked. "Also, how do you know he's not in his house?"

"I can bypass the protection spells. Also, I used to be his bodyguard, so I'm pretty familiar with his schedule."

I had a hard time picturing Caleb as a bodyguard for anyone. Not that he wouldn't be a good one because as far as I'd seen he was able to hold his own, but he lacked the muscle and build one would expect from a bodyguard. Maybe witches were less about the muscle and more about the magic. But it did add to the sense of mystery about this guy. Since I'd met him, he'd admitted that he'd been a vampire, that he had a kid that was not his kid, that he had died, that he had been a witch's bodyguard, and, from what I had gathered, had a broken heart.

He was a strange creature with so many layers. Layers I wanted to peel off one by one.

"Okay, I'm intrigued. Bodyguard?"

He laughed, but not in a mocking way. More like in a reminiscent way.

"Yeah, I've had my fair share of jobs for the high council. When they need a lackey to do something for them, I'm the first number on their list. But this particular job turned sour quite fast."

"And is that why you don't like this...witch?"

Caleb turned his head in my direction.

"You've gotta stop this, you know. I don't like it," he said.

"Stop what?"

"The way you seem to get queasy every time you say the word *witch*. I know you've grown up your entire life thinking we are evil, but do you have to feel sick every time you say it?" he asked. Before I could reply he raised his hand. "Also, we do have names."

He had a point. And it was true, but what he had to understand was that this was a temporary partnership, and we would go our separate ways once the spell had taken effect and our hearts had switched. Well, that was if I didn't end up killing him, which was a possibility. Especially if he tried to kill me first, like he'd mentioned to Annabel.

I didn't wanna be friends with him, or anything more as a matter of fact, and I would still go back to my witch-hunting ways after all this was over. Hopefully, with a big promotion and a generous pay rise.

"I'm still a witch hunter and you're still a witch."

I shouldn't have felt guilty saying it out loud, but

the look on Caleb's face made me feel like a monster. I didn't know what I could say to make it up and didn't know if it even mattered. We were together to do a job and that's what we were doing. We weren't friends. We were never going to be anything more than temporary partners in crime. So why the fuck did I feel so guilty talking like that?

Caleb got on a bus without another word and stayed silent throughout our short trip to St. John's Wood. Once we got there, we got off and navigated the streets of the community that felt more like a village in the middle of the country than an expensive gentrified area in London.

"We're almost there," he said after what felt like hours of the cold shoulder. "You just wait for me around the corner, and I will go and inspect the house. Make sure none of the security spells go off. Then I will give you a signal, 'kay?"

I gave a single nod, and he walked up and turned around the corner. The street was quiet, lined with large, detached houses that looked like they'd come right out of a magazine. A few of them were lit by uplighters as if they were mansions, and I was pretty sure a lot of them were, and others had their lights completely out, probably empty while their owners visited one of their many properties around the globe. Expensive cars that didn't belong in the city and that were worth more than three years of a normal person's salary lined the driveways and the pavements.

Caleb was working outside a house three doors down. I couldn't see exactly what he was doing, but I did see some dust going up, which meant he had used a spell.

There was so much valuable information to use when I returned to the force, finally uncursed, a free man, that was guaranteed to eliminate the pests that were making London an unsafe place.

The thought should have made me all giddy because it meant advancing in the ranks of my chosen profession, but it didn't. What was going on with me? Was the witch starting to get to me? He had already managed to infiltrate my mind with lies and different ideals.

"All clear." I heard the witch's whisper carry over to me. He was standing outside the house, looking casual as anything, and when I approached him, he smiled.

"He's out, just as I thought, so we've got the space to ourselves," Caleb said.

"What is it we're after and where? Maybe we can split up and get things faster before he returns."

I didn't like the idea of stealing from someone, although he was a witch, and everyone knows what they say about love and war.

"I don't think so. This guy is very particular about his things, and if you go rummaging through his stuff, he will notice. Besides, he should be gone for hours."

He walked up the steps to the front door and

asked me to stay on the lookout while he worked on the lock. I kept my eyes on the street. The last thing we needed was for someone to call the police and have to explain why we were trying to break into a very expensive house if not for money. I was sure the police would not believe that we were breaking in for a couple of herbs.

I heard a creak and turned around to see Caleb had opened the door and was inviting me in. I took the steps two at a time.

"Now what?" I whispered.

Caleb went digging in his pockets and retrieved his phone, lighting up the foyer with the torch.

"We need to get to the kitchen," he said in his normal voice, as if we hadn't just walked into a stranger's house. "Let's get the ingredients and get out of here."

He didn't need to tell me twice. I followed him into the back where a large kitchen with marble surfaces and a kitchen island were. Despite the ample space, the cupboards around the room were many, and some had a glass display allowing full view of the contents inside.

A round glass hatch glared in the middle of the kitchen and from the minimal light, I could see shelves upon shelves of wine, and a rotating staircase that led farther down into what I could only assume was the rest of the cellar.

"This guy has more money than he knows what to

do with, huh?" I said and turned to Caleb who was rummaging through the cupboards.

He didn't hear me. I approached him and inspected the labels on the jars he was looking through.

"What is it about this guy's collection that we couldn't get from the market or somewhere else?"

Caleb sighed and opened another cupboard.

"There are some ingredients that are illegal, and so finding them in the market would be almost impossible. And I stopped trading on the black-market ages ago, so stealing it from someone who has the money and doesn't care about the law was the next best option."

"I dunno how I feel about this. If the ingredients to make this spell are illegal, does that make the spell itself illegal?"

Whether it was illegal or not, everything else about it was. A witch hunter working with the enemy. Sneaking into someone's house to get the ingredients for a spell. Making a deal with the devil and saving his ass from my partners.

We'd already broken the law a hundred ways to Sunday. If it got me what I needed, I didn't care. I could always make it up to the BLADE force, but who would ever make it up to me? Who could ever help with my cursed heart other than a witch?

"Let's just say witches transferring their powers is frowned upon," Caleb replied.

"Is that what this spell does? Does it mean—"

Caleb shook his head and with absolute certainty told me, "Humans can't get natural powers from witches. Don't worry, hunter. You're not going to become a witch."

Before I could react to his words, I heard a laugh coming from somewhere really close. I pasted myself against the wall near the kitchen entrance and peaked into the hallway.

From the limited light outside, I could make out a blur of a shadow trying to unlock the door. A suited man stumbled through moments later with another suited guy on his arm, obviously inebriated if their unstoppable laughter and their lack of balance were anything to go by.

"We've got company," I whispered.

TEN
CALEB

"**G**otcha," I said and grabbed the two ingredients I was looking for when Wade whispered from behind me.

What on earth was Ash doing home already? Last time I'd checked, he still had the same work schedule. He should have been gone until morning.

This was bad. This was really, really bad. If he found me in his house, there would be no escape from Graham's wrath.

I was supposed to stay well away from Ashton Beauchamp, and if he found me in his house, that would only add fuel to his fire. While being the only one that could resist his pheromone manipulation powers long enough to actually fancy the guy for who he really was should have been a noteworthy accomplishment, Ash was also an ass about status, and anyone that didn't belong in his class was not good enough to share in his family fortune.

As he had reminded me on numerous occasions after our tête-à-têtes. He needed someone who was respected in the witch community and someone who could be a good trophy husband. So, he really hadn't appreciated having a vase thrown at his head and my abandoning his protective detail, leaving him vulnerable to the elves that had been after him.

"What do we do now?" Wade whispered.

I looked around the room, and the only point of interest seemed to be the key feature. The door to the wine cellar.

We tiptoed over to it and I opened it up. Wade approached and was the first to step in. Once he was sufficiently under cover, I descended the round steps of the cellar, making sure to leave the door a crack open so I could tell what was going on.

"Would you like some wine?" I heard Ash ask off the hallway, and I wanted to swear at the gods that were supposed to be keeping an eye on me but weren't.

All I needed was to get this fucking deal done and move on with my life. Why couldn't they give a little nudge to help the situation.

"Sure thing, sexy," I heard another man respond, and my insides twisted.

Had he really got over me this fast? Did he already have a booty call only weeks after we'd broken up? Had our thing been a joke to him, or had my status meant he'd never really felt anything for me?

I looked up and prayed to the gods for a little lenience. That was exactly why I needed this spell. To get rid of this clingy, needy Caleb that couldn't stop falling for the wrong guys, and who couldn't stop getting his heart broken.

Was that too much to ask? I was sure other people asked for a lot more. All I wanted was a little luck. That was it. The rest I'd do on my own, as always.

Wade pulled at the hem of my trousers and brought me back to the present situation.

"Now what?" he asked.

"Do you have a preference? I have all the wine you could ever need," Ash drawled.

Fuck off, Ash. No one needs wine. No one needs all the wine in the world, either.

I couldn't believe I'd ever fallen for his charms.

"That's it." A lightbulb lit up inside my head.

His wine cellar was far superior to any other. This booth we were trying to hide in was only the beginning.

"Keep going down," I said, and thankfully, Wade obeyed.

We descended into darkness, and darkness led to more darkness. The cylindrical part of the cellar was only for show. The real thing started at the bottom of the stairs.

It was like a catacomb of old shelves in massive

rows, storing wine more expensive than my entire house. The temperature was slightly cooler down here, which was to be expected. I took a moment to take it all in. I had known he'd loved his wine, and that he had a lot of it—he was known for it—but he'd never brought me down here, and I'd never left the bedroom long enough to explore.

The lights in the basement came on, and it sprang me to action. Wade and I ran to the end of the room and ducked behind the last row of wine shelves we could find, hoping he didn't need to come all the way down.

His footsteps click-clacked on the wooden staircase and echoed across the basement but didn't stop there. We heard his heels land on the ground and pace the room, the echo becoming louder and louder as he approached our aisle. He whistled a tune while browsing through his wine, and my mind got busy trying to identify the song instead of worrying about being found out.

There wasn't really anything I could do. I'd run out of any useful spells, and the ones I did have weren't any good for hiding or escaping. Our fate relied on the kindness of the gods. Now if they decided to be assholes, I'd have to deal with them later.

I saw his shadow growing bigger on the side of the wall, and from where we were sitting, it looked like his shadow was toying with me. It looked as if it had a mind of its own and it wanted to push us to the edge so we could surrender.

The whistling stopped, and I braced myself for impact, half-shutting my eyes as if that would soften the blow.

Only the impact never came. In its place, the whistling continued, and I saw the shadow disappearing into the second to last aisle. I heard Ash mutter "perfect" to himself and then he rushed out of the cellar and back up the stairs, closing the glass hatch behind him.

Wade crept up to the top of the aisle and peaked around the corner and then turned around to give me the thumbs up.

"That was close." I breathed a sigh of relief at seeing the hunter confirming Ash's departure.

"What the fuck, dude? You said he'd be gone for hours," he whispered.

"Yeah, so I thought."

"What are we going to do?" he asked.

"I've got the ingredients we need, but if we try to sneak out, it will be a risk. One I'm not willing to take. We'll have to wait him out."

"What if he doesn't leave the house for the next week? Are we going to stay down here till then?"

I huffed. "He's not staying in the house for the week. He's important. He'll be back out in no time. You'll see."

"If you say so," Wade muttered.

"Look, Ash is a busy man. We'll be out of here soon enough."

"Yeah, I heard that. Busy with another man," Wade said with a roll of his eyes.

It stung hearing it, especially from him, but I pretended it didn't faze me. Because it didn't. No siree.

"Well, unless the other man is a fucking incubus, they'll do the deed and be on their way," I told him. I sure hoped so anyway.

Wade's look at the word *deed* was so precious it made me forget about Ash with another man. It was the same face he'd had when I'd made the mistake of kissing him. The same apparent disgust at the mere mention of two men together, getting it on. But he had enjoyed our kiss more than he cared to admit, which only told me that his current reaction was a front.

"So...what do we do until they're...finished?" he asked.

"Nothing else we can do. We just wait."

And we did. We waited half an hour, then an hour, and then some more. From our vantage point down here we could hear all the laughter, the muffled sounds of their conversation, and the clinking glasses. We even had the pleasure of hearing them bang.

Although, if I was being honest, the sounds were a bit of a turn-on. Too bad the company was so repulsed by the idea of a good man-to-man fuck, or I would have been tempted to start something we'd both regret afterward. Had I been on my own, I'd most likely have rubbed one out.

As hot and steamy as it was listening to other people having sex, even if it was Ash I was listening to, I also hadn't slept for nearly forty-eight hours, and I was running on low. Wade told me he'd keep an ear out for them and allowed me some minutes of rest. Maybe those few moments alone would do him some good and make him realize that two consenting grown men could have a good time together without female company. Maybe it would make him realize that he also wanted to try something—or someone—new, and I'd have been more than happy to be his guinea pig.

When I woke up, I had no sense of time at all. I was so fuzzy and confused, like the times when you sleep for twelve hours straight and yet you still can't drag your ass out of bed. But my eyes popped open as if on instinct, and when they finally adjusted to the darkness and the situation I was in, trapped in a wine cellar with a hunky, deadly witch hunter, I sat up.

Wade had his back to me, hunched over something I couldn't see. Had he fallen asleep while on watch? Or had something happened and I'd missed the show?

I crawled behind him, not wanting to startle or rouse him if he was indeed sleeping and tried to assess if he was okay. Just as I was about to peep over his shoulder, he lifted his upper body with a big sigh of relief, stretching his shoulders.

On the floor in front of him was my bracer,

missing two spells, and a bottle of wine next to it. I could see traces of my missing spells around the ring of the bottle. It looked just like the dust residue spells left behind, but somewhat rougher, harder than usual.

I didn't know what he had done, but heat rose in my chest. I bit the inside of my lip to stop myself from shouting at him.

"What the fuck have you done?" I said. "Why did you take my bracer off?"

Wade turned around with slow movements and stared at me with bloodshot eyes.

"I had a little taste." He giggled.

Was he drunk? Had he drunk some of Ash's wine? Or had he lost his bloody mind?

I wanted answers, and I wanted them now, so I touched him.

Big mistake.

Adrenaline rushed to all of my extremities, my heart pounded in my chest, and my head went fuzzy as if I'd had the world's worst hangover. As if all that wasn't enough, my cock hardened and stretched at full mast within a second.

Nothing like a good spell to take the edge off, I heard him say.

Had he...had he just snorted up raw spell dust? Was that his vice?

Was that the reason why all the high council members I'd found dead had had no spells or spell-books on them?

I'd never known anyone who had taken up spell dust as a recreational drug, but it all made sense now. We had been finding witches without spellbooks for years. We just never knew what to make of it. The only reason why finding the high council victims without them was disconcerting was due to the strong, powerful, and very expensive spells they carried to protect themselves and others on a daily basis.

If they'd ended up in the wrong witch's hands, that could have meant destruction. I didn't know if I was thankful they'd instead ended up in someone's bloodstream or if I should be angry. I did know I was fucking furious he'd wasted two more spells. Two spells we could still need to help us. Not only was I running low, and that was always risky, especially in a dangerous situation like the one I was currently in, but they were also fucking expensive.

"Are you out of your mind? You have just used two very important spells. What's wrong with you," I whisper-shouted.

Wade smiled. Not a sexy smile. More of an I'm-five-and-just-had-my-first-lick-of-ice-cream kind of smile.

"I'm sure you'll replace them with better ones. Let me enjoy these ones," he said.

"You're an asshole," I told him and punched his big muscly arm.

"And you're not so bad yourself," he said, and he touched my fist with his hands.

But it wasn't an aggressive touch. It was soft, like a hint of a touch, but it was all it took for my powers to go awry.

This guy's so fucking cute. I wish I could fuck him from here on till tomorrow.

Just listening to his thoughts made my boner pulse harder in my jeans, and my need for him grew from moderate to desperate. Uh-oh. There was no stopping me now. When someone had such strong emotions, my empathy was my weakness.

My hand shot straight for his face, and I squeezed his cheeks together, bringing my mouth down to clash with his. Our last kiss might have been a stupid decision, but having our lips reunite was like my own version of a drug. It was crazy, and stupid, and exactly what I needed at the same time.

His tongue nudged for access, and I let him in, roaming free inside my mouth, like the reunion of two long-lost lovers.

That was the disturbing thing about my power. In times like this, I didn't know where my emotions started and the other person's ended. Everything melded into one, and all I could feel was an overwhelming heat of sensations.

I inserted my tongue into his mouth, creating a little wet dance between us, trying to take in every single piece of him and make it mine. I was like a wolf claiming what was rightfully his.

Fuck this is hot, I heard Wade in my head, and it

only made my desire stronger, if such a thing was even possible.

My other hand grabbed the nape of his neck and massaged it while I cozied up to him. His cock rested against my butthole, and my own erection rubbed on his stomach.

I haven't felt like this since Sarah.

What did I make of that? Was that good? Was it bad? Did I even care? Sarah had been the one he had killed, his girlfriend. The only person he had ever let into his cursed heart. The only person he had ever felt something close to love with. Did that mean he felt the same for me? Was he falling for me like I was falling for him? How was that even possible? He had a frozen heart. He could never fall in love.

I remembered our visit to Mother Red Cap and what he had told her. That he becomes a killer when love creeps in, and he was getting close to feeling it for me.

Grounding myself on his dick, I allowed myself to feel good about it. Yes, I was fully aware of who he was and the shit he'd done in his life, but I couldn't help myself. I could see he wasn't a bad person. He had grown up in the wrong world, with the wrong education, and that wasn't his fault.

Or at least that's what I was trying to convince myself so I didn't feel terrible for kissing the enemy. I could tell he wasn't afraid to fix himself. But maybe I could help him fix his mistakes also. Maybe erasing his memories wouldn't be good enough. Maybe that would only make him work harder to find us and kill us. Make him more aggressive, more lethal, more cruel. Maybe if I let him keep his memories, he could change and become an ally.

I wish this feeling could last forever.

His thoughts rang crystal clear in my head, and it only solidified my apprehension.

He wasn't all bad. He'd been dealt a shit hand, and I knew exactly what that was like. And perhaps that's why I was falling for him. That's why I was attracted to him. Because he reminded me of myself so much when I was younger. My life had been shitstorm after shitstorm and bad decisions after bad decisions.

It seemed I was still making them.

Wade's hands finally lifted off the floor and wrapped around my butt cheeks. He squeezed, and I swore I could have come to my undoing, but I didn't. Like Wade, I didn't want this to be over. And besides, we had so much time to kill.

A soft sob escaped my lips, but he drowned it with his tongue immediately.

His hands trailed up to my back, and once he had a good grip on me, he lifted me and turned me around so I was lying on the ground on my back. My legs wrapped around his waist and his bulge rubbed over my jeans where my balls were. I wanted him so badly, so desperately, that I could let him have me here in the middle of a robbery.

He rubbed himself on me, his lips never separating from mine, his hands free to roam my chest and arms.

The fuck am I doing? What is this fucking witch doing to me, taking advantage of me when I'm high? Why can't I stop? What sort of spell has he cast?

His thoughts shouted in my head as clear as the sky, accompanied by the frustration flaring in my chest. It made me pause and look at him. His face was red and looking him in the eyes only made it redder.

His hands came up to my neck and squeezed before I could react.

The witch needs to die. It's the only way to stop him. He needs to die.

The hatred infiltrated to my core, and I found myself fighting for my life.

The change in his emotion was so sudden it made me lose my grip on my powers. I struggled for a moment, but the more he squeezed, the angrier it made me, and the more it brought me back to my senses.

I pushed all of his fucked-up feelings back at him, put all my concentration into the act. I wasn't just trying to save myself. I was trying to save him from himself too.

His hands around my neck loosened, and without removing my skin from his, I grabbed his wrists and pushed him off me. It wasn't just hatred that was flaring up inside him.

My heart pinched and my breath quickened. He

was feeling shame. Shame that he couldn't control himself. Just like I did when I couldn't keep my powers under rein.

Wade collapsed on the floor, and I climbed on top of him, unwilling to let our skin contact end. I was going to stay there as long as it took him to feel normal again. His kind of normal. And his current state wasn't his normal.

"Are you sure you want to trade with me?" he cried under me. The tears trailed a path on his face just like they did on mine.

Don't let me go. I hate you, but don't let me go. Please, he begged.

I didn't know if he was conscious I could hear him, or if it was something he was telling himself, and at that moment, I didn't care.

"I'm not letting you go. 'kay?" I whispered in his ear.

Then don't stop kissing me.

I didn't even have the energy to comprehend how I could hear his thoughts so clear even though they weren't associated directly to any particular emotion. I usually could only hear the gist of the emotion. Most of the time, that was enough to tell me all I needed to know.

But my powers were out of control, and so was I. And so was Wade.

So, I did what I'd been asked. I brought my mouth back to his mouth, only this time I made sure to not let him have any control over his body. Just like he'd asked. He didn't want to hurt me, and he didn't want to hurt himself, and that was the only way it could be accomplished. By holding him prisoner of his own hate and need. And boy did I need him too.

ELEVEN
WADE

I wanted to kill him, but I didn't have the strength or power to do so. I had never felt like this before. Never before or since Sarah. And even with her, it had taken dating for three months before the urge to kill her had grown ravenous inside me. This was a whole new level of fucked up. I'd only known Caleb for forty-eight hours, and he was a man for fuck's sake, besides being a witch too.

I shouldn't have been feeling anything for him. But the hatred coursing through my veins was apparent. And I knew it wasn't my natural hatred towards witches. It was my curse playing up.

Was I falling for the witch? How the fuck could that be?

I couldn't even begin to process what those repercussions would be if I was truly falling for him. There was no fooling around with my curse, and my killer instinct had taken over my entire body.

But I needed him. Until he mended my frozen heart, there was nothing that I could—or wanted —to do.

There was no space for error on this mission until I got my end of the bargain. But it seemed I was getting more than that. When the witch reflected my hatred back to me, all I could feel was the shame and the guilt of being like this. An assassin. I had inadvertently become what I hated. My job. A killer of everything that was good and gracious in this world. And boy did Caleb feel like both those things right at that moment.

Caleb kept true to his word and didn't let me go. Suppressing any protest with his mouth, protecting me from myself. That felt better than I cared to admit. I'd never experienced anything like this before Sarah. No, scratch that. I'd never felt anything like this ever. Resisting him was an impossible feat, but my deadly instincts were an uncontrollable force. Had he not had the powers he did, he'd be dead already, and I would be none the wiser. But the more I stayed under his control, the more I realized I was in deep trouble.

I rested my hands on his upper body and massaged his torso before moving them to his back. Everywhere I touched seemed to blaze with passion into him, and his kisses became more intense. His tongue wilder in my mouth. His moans rowdier.

Hopefully, he'd remember we were still hiding from a dangerous witch.

It wasn't just my hands that roamed freely on his body. His also explored mine. From what I understood about his powers, as long as we were in constant contact, I would be fine, and I wouldn't be able to attack him. As long as his lips stayed locked with mine, we'd be fine. It wasn't a terrible situation to be in. Minus my killer instinct, of course.

I tried not to think about the fact that the kisses and the touches were coming from a man. I didn't need to think about that right now or the implications because we were in a dangerous position as it was. There was no time or space for me to question what the hell was going on with my sexuality and why I couldn't resist the touch of another man.

He ground on me like he knew all the spots that would make me come faster. Of course he knew. He knew everything about me. I had to remind myself to ask him how his powers worked. I didn't like that he could have complete control over me, but for now, I succumbed to it and let myself enjoy it. He rubbed the fabric of my trousers, my cock tight and swollen in my pants. It begged for its release, and I was only hoping he'd indulge me.

"Your wish, my command," he said and put his hand under my jeans, reaching for my raw erection waiting for him. A whimper vibrated through both of us, and Caleb lifted his mouth off mine to stare into my eyes. I bit my lip to tame the beast roaring inside, and he crawled down level with my crotch. He teased me with his teeth as he bit on the mound over the fabric. His teeth took hold of the zipper, and I watched him as he slowly pulled it down, each second feeling like an hour spent under this man's thumb. When he finally let go of the zipper, his fingers were already fiddling with the button, and before I could protest or approve, his mouth wrapped around my cock. Not that I would be crazy enough not to support his endeavor.

I did. I absolutely did.

I had never been allowed the freedom of being with someone so fully, so completely, when my curse was in full effect. Having Caleb take me, make me his while also keeping me intact felt wildly liberating.

With anyone else I'd slept with before, when my curse was starting to act up, a few handcuffs and ropes could do the trick. At least, for a little while. And that could tip me over the edge, I wasn't going to deny that. Sometimes, I wondered if I would have had the kinky side to me had I not been cursed, but it was a question I didn't tend to linger on. I guess having the curse removed would show me how much of *me* was left inside.

But for now, being a prisoner of someone without any physical restraints in a completely safe environment, sans the whole robbery thing, was making my dick ache with pleasure. Even if it meant that as soon as he removed his hands, I would go back to the killer I was, for now, I could just enjoy being free under his control.

His head bobbed up and down as he licked my length and sucked for dear life. My hands found their way to his hair. I pulled it, but it did very little to divide his attention from my erection. The closer he brought me to the edge, the more I pulled, and he didn't seem to mind. Hell, if I didn't know any better, I would say he was enjoying it.

Before I knew what was happening, I came all over his face, and my release made the beast inside, the one under Caleb's rule, go back to sleep.

Trying to keep watch over the happenings upstairs with Caleb asleep next to me had been the worst kind of torture. All those crystals in his spellbook there for the taking. I knew I shouldn't have done it, but I couldn't control myself, and once I'd snorted one, I needed more.

And if Caleb hadn't woken and caught me, I would have probably finished them all and died in the process. His spells were strong. I could feel it in the way they pulsed in my hands but also in the incredible high they gave me. If they hadn't been so strong, maybe the beast wouldn't have awoken inside.

"You can let me go now," I told him, and without removing his hands, he looked up, his eyes shiny and needy, still full of desire.

"Are you sure? I can keep going," he said.

I wasn't entirely sure if he meant keeping me a prisoner inside my own body or continuing his naughty work on my cock. And I wasn't sure I cared. I could tell from his voice that he needed his own release, so without a word, I grabbed his chin and brought his face to mine, and we were kissing again. I grabbed his back and butt, and I swung him over on the floor.

"I'm fine now, but if you feel safer, you can keep me in check."

"You don't have to do this. I know you want to, but you don't have to," he said.

"I want to, so I'm gonna." I released his cock from his trousers.

I wasn't surprised there was a ring at the base of his shaft, where it connected with the balls. It made me shiver. His dick was thick in my hand, although not as long as mine, which was probably for the best because I'd never done this before, and a smaller dick was probably a good place to start.

Trying to keep some of that fearlessness in me because I didn't know how to do this, I licked his glans and let my tongue taste every part of him, inch by inch, trying to assess his pleasure points. How hard could it be? I knew what I liked in a blow job, so I'm sure he was no different. I continued with the licking, still too scared to put it in my mouth as if it was going to bite me, but whatever it was I was doing seemed to be working because Caleb couldn't take his eyes off me. And the little gasps he let out every so often told me I was going in the right direction.

When it finally came to it, I took his tip in my mouth hard and stroked the rest of his length with my index finger and thumb linking around his circumference.

He grabbed my head and urged me on, moaning, asking for more. Which I was willing to give him.

I went faster, and he seemed to lose all control. So much so I had to take one hand and shut his mouth to stop him from screaming. That seemed to get him even more riled up.

Without warning, although I guess his orgasmic panting should have given me a clue, I was choked by the heat of his seed in my mouth, and before I knew what to do with it, I swallowed. It was equal parts salty and sweet, and I let myself indulge in his cum before I regretted it.

Caleb collapsed in a heap on the floor, and I came up for air, wiping the corners of my mouth where my drool had dried. We stared into each other's eyes for a few moments before he sat up, and I crawled next to him, our backs against the wine shelves, trying to come to grips with what had just happened.

"You know, for a first-time gay, you are fucking good," Caleb said and patted my thigh as if to say good job.

Which, it turns out, it was.

"Yeah, I don't know what came over me."

He squeezed my thigh and it made me look into his eyes.

"It's okay if you're regretting this. It was just the adrenaline mixed with the curse and a whole lot of other fucked emotions," he said.

"Strangely," I started, and I couldn't believe I was even saying this, "I'm not regretting this. I'm glad it happened."

Caleb grimaced and I stayed silent.

"I would have expected you to freak out and panic. But then again, your emotions say you enjoyed this more than anything ever before, so what do I know, hey?"

I chuckled if only to cover up for the awkwardness of the situation.

"So how do your powers work?" I asked him.

He looked at me, and I was sure he wasn't going to tell me anything, and I was about to dismiss my question. But then he opened his mouth.

"I would say that's none of your business and to stay the hell out of mine, but considering what we've just done, I think I owe it to you, believe it or not."

I didn't know about owing it to me, but I was definitely curious.

"I can feel people's emotions when I touch them, and I can hear their thoughts associated with those emotions, but unlike Mother Red Cap, I can't hear everything you're thinking. Only the strongest of thoughts that are associated with how you're feeling at the specific time that I'm touching you."

"And what about the rest? When you kept me down and I wasn't able to move. Like you did at the bar, and..." I looked to my right where we had just done the unspeakable and hoped my face said everything.

"Once I have access to someone's emotions, I can direct them back at them. Almost like a mental shield. It's like I can cut you off from the rest of the world and make you a prisoner of your own self."

It sounded eerily close to how it had felt being under his control. And while it had turned me on before, it was scaring me how much Caleb could do with just a little touch.

"What about those gloves you're wearing all the time? How do they help?" I asked and looked at them on the floor.

"They're spelled so that they block people's emotions when I shake their hand or touch them. It can all get really exhausting pretty quick, which is why I wear them all the time now."

"But when I touched you at the bar, you were still able to use your powers on me," I said, remembering what had happened when I'd tried to strangle him. He had overpowered me.

"My hands are the main channel of my power. With my hands, I can do the worst of the damage. But if anyone touches me anywhere else, it still gives me access. If anyone touches me anywhere else, I can still feel it all. But most people don't try to choke me and kiss me at the same time, so the gloves tend to do the job."

I ignored the comment about kissing. The more time passed, the more embarrassed I felt by what I'd just done.

"Is that why you want to swap with me? Because you want to shut the rest of the world off?"

I could understand being overwhelmed by everyone else's thoughts and emotions, but it still didn't help me understand why he would want to freeze his own heart so he could never feel love.

"Yes and no. It's a long story," he offered again, like last time I'd asked.

"We got time," I replied and looked at my watch. It was two in the morning, and I was way past my peak of exhaustion.

Which meant sleep would be the worst thing I could do right now.

"Okay," Caleb murmured with hesitation while massaging his arm. "I mean, I know why you want to get rid of it, it's only fair. Right?"

He sounded more as if he was trying to convince himself rather than me. Which was why I didn't say anything but let him process things in his mind.

"Yeah, no, it's fine," he said with a bit more confidence in his voice. "Here we go. When...when I first turned into a vampire I... I met this man. He was an incubus," he said, and he'd already lost me.

But that didn't prove a problem because he seemed to have picked up on my confusion as he turned around and explained.

"Incubi are Nightcrawlers that feed off sex energy. In mythology, they are demons that kill their victims through sex. In reality, that's not the case. They feed off the energy of sex, so why would they kill someone if they can get more from them?" he said, and I nodded my head as if I understood what he'd just said.

The only thing I could focus on was the fact that he had been with someone who's entire existence centered around sex. How could anyone compete with that?

Why did I care about competing with that? Caleb wasn't my boyfriend. He wasn't even my friend. And it's not like I wanted him to be either.

Did I?

"What happened?" I asked, both to find out more and to distract myself from the mess in my head.

"His ex happened." His voice broke and he turned away from me.

"He abandoned you for his ex? And you're still hung up over him?"

He shook his head.

"No. That's not it." He stared at something right in front of him instead of me. "His ex was involved with bad people. He was an elf, so...you know, moth, flame, the whole shebang. He couldn't help himself for being drawn to evil. Which is fine. To each his own and all. But the problem was when the elf was caught between a war of clans, he turned on Jin, and they went after him. Jin was my boyfriend by the way. If that wasn't clear.

"They came while I was at work. They smashed the door, got through my protection spells, and killed him dead. I..." his voice gave out and his head slumped.

On instinct, I put my arm around him, empathy and bullshit be damned.

"What happened to them? Did someone catch them? Were they punished?"

If they were still at large, I had half a mind to go find them myself for what they'd done to the witch and his boyfriend. No one deserved a fate like this.

The irony didn't fail to punch me right in the gut.

In the darkness, I caught a trace of a smirk on Caleb's face.

"You've become overly possessive of me all of a sudden. I can't decide if I like it or not," he said, ignoring my realization about my career choices. I removed my arm from him before he could go any further in that fucked-up head of mine.

"It's sweet of you to think it but wildly unnecessary. I've already taken care of it. I went dark for a while and tracked every single motherfucker down and killed them the same way they killed my Jin," he stated as if he was discussing his shopping list.

I felt a chill up my arms. This man, this ex-vampire and now witch was a lot more dangerous than I'd made him out to be.

"But the elf? The elf I left for last. And I enjoyed taking his life more than anything in the world. Even if it cost me."

We let the silence infiltrate the cellar between us while I absorbed what he'd just told me. But then, when the silence was starting to become suffocating and uncomfortable, it dawned on me what that cost had been.

"That's when you died. And Nora brought you back?"

Caleb nodded, and it all seemed to make sense at that point.

"So? Is that why you want to give up your heart? Didn't you see what happened? If you didn't have these—these powers of yours, I would have killed you. That's what happens with this curse. It won't bring you peace. It will only bring you more destruction. More pain. Are you sure that's what you want?"

"I am." His gaze remained unmoving from whatever had taken his focus, but it was like I could see what he was thinking. It was as if, at that moment, I had his powers and could delve into his mind.

"And what happens when one of these days Nora comes to you and gives you a kiss or a hug, and you feel all of her love. What happens when your love for her makes you want to kill her?"

I didn't know why I was trying to dissuade him from going through with this heart transference thingy, but if I told myself the truth, I couldn't let him go through with it. I couldn't bear the thought that I'd hurt people through him. People that, up until now, he loved.

"You sound like you're having second thoughts about this. Don't worry. You will be free to do and love whoever you want."

"And what about you? Who will you love after this?"

Caleb turned to look at me.

"No one," he simply said.

He must have loved this Jin guy a lot if he was willing to do this. It must still hurt him like hell. And while I could understand the pain, I couldn't understand why anyone would want to inflict this fate on themselves.

We heard a creak on the stairs and the thumping of feet.

"I can't believe I overslept."

Two sets of feet shuffled about in the room directly above us. The panic and chaos of getting ready while in a rush made their floor—our ceiling—grace us with dust and rubble. Then, before we could do anything, we heard the door click closed, and it was followed by absolute silence.

"I think the coast is clear," Caleb said, and he got up.

He fiddled with his zipper, and once he was proper again, he turned to look at me and then rushed for the stairs.

I dressed, too, and followed him quietly. His words, however, were ringing like a siren in my head.

No one.

He would never love anyone again? What about me?

TWELVE
CALEB

Ash left the house at the right time. I didn't know what else I would have shared if we'd stayed down there. And I still wanted to keep some things to myself, regardless of whether I erased his memories at the end or not.

Yes, after everything that had just happened, I wasn't sure erasing his memories would be any good. Not because I wanted him for myself. I wouldn't be able to love after today anyway.

It's because he was a good man that had been done wrong by a witch.

I couldn't say that everything he'd said about Nora didn't scare me a little, but I was confident I could handle it.

If not by using my powers on me, then definitely by ways of the many, countless spells that I had access to.

We made our way back to Camden, and yet again, I had to sacrifice a spell for access to Mother Red Cap's den.

I was seriously running low on spells, and even though I'd soon be able to go home and top up, I didn't like feeling weak and unprotected with so many Nightcrawlers, witch hunters, and other witches out there. Especially with one on the loose helping the hunters.

"You took your time," Mother Red Cap said as soon as we came into the clearing.

"We hit some snags," Wade replied, and she smiled.

Probably because she'd read his thoughts about what had happened down in that wine cellar. For fuck's sake. I didn't need her to know that and didn't need her criticizing me, but I knew she would. What witch wouldn't judge another for sleeping with the enemy?

"Can we just get on with this?" I asked and gave her the two ingredients from Ash's house. Wade passed the box with the mandrake root.

She pursed her lips and didn't comment on the inappropriate subject. Which was good, because if she kept going on like she'd done yesterday, reading every single one of Wade's thoughts, I'd have to intervene.

"This will take a while. Why don't you rest? You both must be beat. Running all night and everything," she said, and I saw Wade's cheeks turn bright red.

"You can have a lie here." She pointed to the middle of the room where the fire was burning with loads of cushions around it that seemed to be calling my name desperately.

"I'll work from the other room," she said and then disappeared with the ingredients at hand.

"Is she doing that because she doesn't want me to see how you witches create spells?" Wade asked, and for once, he didn't seem to say the word *witch* with spite and disdain. Hm...progress, maybe? Was I finally getting through his many, many walls?

"Even if you did see the process, you wouldn't understand it. She probably left to give us a chance to talk."

Wade crammed his hands into his pockets like an awkward teenage schoolboy and looked at me. I felt like I could see the million questions running through his head.

"Do you want to? Talk about it, I mean?" he asked.

"Do you? You are the one who's never been with a man before."

Wade's gaze wandered around the room for a few moments before turning back to me.

"I'm good. I'm not going to pretend I understand everything that happened tonight or that it didn't feel weird, but I don't think talking about it will help."

"We can talk about other things if you want." I slumped onto the cushions and felt the lick of the flames soothe the exhaustion that tensed my body. "Like why would a witch curse you and your brother?"

He sighed and also took a seat a few feet farther from me.

"I wish we knew. But we never found out. All we know is that our mother came home one day and announced we'd been cursed so we could never fall in love, and that was the end of it. We didn't know who that witch was or why she'd done that to us. We tried to get Mom to talk, but she shut herself off after that . She didn't talk much. She took a leave from the force."

"When did this happen? How old?"

It all sounded very strange. And it didn't make any sense why a witch would curse a witch hunter's kids. As much as we hated them, kids were off-limits.

"Eleven. I was just eleven. And Winston was eight. I think he got the short end of the stick because at least I remember some of my life with my full heart. He doesn't remember a life before this, you know, so it hasn't hit him as hard."

"What about your dad? Where is he in the picture."

"My dad abandoned us when we were babies. We never met him."

"Wow! That's rough," I said. I had first-hand experience of how much the lack of a parent could fuck you up for life. Hell, I was living proof of how much it could mess you about.

"And she never talked to you? What about now, after all these years?" I asked.

"She died when I was sixteen. Witch hunters don't have a long lifespan, on average. We lose way more in the field than we take...down."

I ignored the obvious remark about killing my kind off and focused on the topic at hand.

"I thought you said she took leave from the hunt."

Wade nodded.

"Yeah, she didn't die in the field. She took her own life. I think having us cursed made her miserable. She lost her sense of self. I can't say I blame her. It's not ideal when your kids try to kill you every other day."

I couldn't even begin to imagine what that must have felt like for her. Having her two kids loveless and turning against her because of the love they had once felt becoming pure hatred.

"After that, Winston and I kept our distance from each other."

"Wasn't he just thirteen?" I asked.

Wade's eyes lowered to the ground and the creases in his brows told me he didn't enjoy the subject.

"He was. But it was the better of two evils. I didn't want to kill him, and he didn't want to turn on me, so we kept a safe distance."

"That sucks, man," I said, and I meant it. I'd never had a sibling even though I'd always wished for one, but even I could imagine how tough it must have been for them both. And his brother, being abandoned at such a young age? What a number that must have done on him.

"So, yeah, I never got the chance to fight for my right to know. I never had the answers I wanted. If I'd had more time with her, or if I had been more persistent at the time, I don't know, maybe I would know the witch who cursed us and find help for my brother and me."

If only I could help both of them. No one deserved to have this fate inflicted on them without their consent. No wonder they'd both turned to a life of crime and murder. Even if they didn't know or see it that way.

"What about your family?" he asked.

"What about them?" My gaze darted up at him, and I stared into his eyes as his lips formed a sad smile.

"Where are they?" he said.

I shrugged.

"One is in Cambridge, the other is in Leyton, and most are in Croydon," I answered.

I didn't miss the confusion on his face.

"I don't know my real parents," I said. "I grew up in foster care."

"Oh, God. What was that like?"

My grimace must have given him the answer he was after because he continued with his next question.

"Did you, like, never look for your parents?"

"Of course I did. I did when I was a teenager, and then again when I became a witch. But even spells can't find people who don't want to be found. The only thing I know is that at least one of them was a witch. I would have given everything to come to my powers earlier in life, but I don't know if they knew they were witches, so that's a consolation.

"What do you mean? Why wouldn't they know?"

I wasn't sure if sharing the information with him was worth it. Would it help him understand witches and turn a new leaf in his life? I sure hoped so. If only I was a psychic as well, then I'd know what's right and what's wrong.

Heck, if I was a psychic, I wouldn't be in this situation today.

At the end of the day, he deserved to know the truth about me as much as I did about him. He had been more than forthcoming about his life. The least I could do while waiting for the spell was to do the same.

"Here is something they probably don't teach you at witch hunter school. Not all witches know they're witches. In order to get your powers and the ability to use spells, someone needs to ignite your dormant powers."

"How does that work? They have to set you on fire? I don't understand." Wade looked perplexed by my word usage, and there was a small pinch in my chest with how adorable I was finding his newness to the real witch world.

"Witches are unlike everyone else. They're human until they're not. Witches are born from other witches, but we're all born with dormant powers that can only be awakened by the igniting ritual. And if a human goes through it, they can die. That's why finding new witches and igniting their powers is an arduous job, and why the witch population is only a tenth of what it could be if we knew how to do this in a safe way."

"When you said you weren't a witch before, that's what you meant, isn't it?"

I made a gun with my fingers and pointed at him with a wink. "Bingo."

"You're right. They don't teach us these things at the BLADE force."

"I told ya." My yawn stretched out my jaw painfully, and Wade copied me. "I think we should get some rest," I suggested and cozied up on the cushions. Wade did the same, and before I knew it, I was back to sleep. I hoped I didn't wake up to find him sniffing my spells again.

———

"Wake up, sleepyheads," I heard from behind me.

I turned to see Mother Red Cap standing in the middle of the room. Wade was already awake and stretching his limbs. When he realized I was staring, he offered me an awkward half-smile before getting off the floor.

"Have I been out for long?" I asked.

"A few hours and then some," Mother Red Cap

said. "You needed it anyway. I told you this would take a while."

She moved behind a desk, holding something wrapped in a silky, red bundle.

I approached the desk, Wade beside me, waiting for the big reveal. The sage witch didn't disappoint. She set the bundle down in front of both of us and lifted the fabric's corners away from the center.

A large, black crystal, with sharp edges and many facets, rested proudly inside. I could sense the vibrations emanating from its magical core. My fingers instinctively tensed, pulled by its energy. I traced its shape and absorbed as much of it as possible.

This crystal, this spell, was a work of art.

"Is that it?" Wade asked.

Mother Red Cap nodded.

"How does it work?" he asked.

"He just has to say the words and the spell will be activated," she said. "Whenever you're ready, we're good to go."

I made a move to take the crystal, but Wade grabbed my wrist and looked at me.

"Are you sure you want to do this? Are you absolutely, one hundred percent sure you want to go ahead?"

It was sweet of him to check with me, again. It almost made me think he liked me, but that was impossible, wasn't it? He had a frozen heart. Yet he didn't act like it unless it was to kill me.

"I am sure," I reassured him, and he removed his hand from mine.

"What's the word?" I asked Mother Red Cap.

"*Oculo ad oculum.* An eye for an eye."

"That sounds ominous," Wade said.

I couldn't resist laughing. He was so naïve. It was sweet on him. Especially after I'd seen him hateful and murderous and pretending to be a know-it-all, having him appear sweet was...well, endearing. He was right of course, but I wasn't going to tell him that.

"Words for spells are just that. They're only meant to activate the spell. It doesn't have any effect on the actual result," I explained.

Wade put his hands up in surrender and approached the table with the crystal.

"Do we have to do anything, or do we stand there looking pretty while it works its hocus pocus?"

Mother Red Cap smiled.

"There's no need to be nervous. The spell won't hurt you. And no, you don't need to do anything. Just stand there looking pretty like you always do," she said with a wink, and I had to restrain myself from laughing.

Either Mother Red Cap hadn't been with a man for a while or she was messing with Wade. Or both. But I couldn't blame her, whichever the reason. Wade was a looker if nothing else.

I took my gloves off and grabbed the spell, then turned around so Wade and I could hold it together. I could sense his nervousness, and I made sure to give him an extra squeeze with my other hand.

"It's going to be okay," I whispered to him.

He gave me a side smile that didn't quite reach his eyes.

What if it doesn't work? What happens then? I heard him in my head.

Instead of delaying the inevitable and reassuring him about something I most certainly wasn't sure about, I said the words.

"*Oculo ad oculum.*"

The black crystal spurted, creating an iridescent dust storm that enveloped us so it was Wade and me and no one else. I felt a pull and a gentle squeeze over my heart, but it only lasted for a moment before the dust settled and placed us back in the room with Mother Red Cap.

"And...how do you feel?" Mother Red Cap asked.

I glanced at Wade and allowed myself access to his emotions.

"I feel...the same. Should I? Be feeling the same?" he asked.

It hadn't worked. I felt nothing different also. The spell hadn't worked.

"Nothing happened. Why?" I asked.

Mother Red Cap frowned and stood up and then walked around her desk.

"I-I don't know. It should have worked. This spell

was my best work in years. The transference should have..." She paused. "Unless..."

"Unless what?" I asked.

"Unless the curse is a craftier work than we thought."

"What does that mean?" I said.

"I'm thinking perhaps the witch that put the curse on you thought these things through and maybe put constraints on it. Or maybe your empathy is blocking the transference, although I've not heard of that happening before," she explained. "I'm afraid I've done my part. There's nothing else I can do until you figure out what's blocking the transference."

Wade turned from Mother Red Cap to me with pleading eyes. How could I resist those eyes? I felt like I could do anything they asked of me and that was what terrified me. At least before, I'd thought my time feeling like this for him was limited, that I wouldn't have to deal with these fucked-up emotions after the spell was cast. But now? Now I had to physically stop myself from doing something stupid.

"It's okay. It's better this way. You would have suffered with my curse," he said, and I knew he only half meant it. He wanted to be free. He wanted to fall in love with someone. And I'd promised to give him that. I'd failed my promise.

"We *will* figure this out. I promise. We'll try—"

"No. It's fine. Maybe it's a sign that things are meant to be as they are. I'm used to my curse, and I know how to handle it. You don't. You'd have struggled."

I was about to disagree. To tell him I needed this as much as he needed to be free. That I wasn't weak, and I could handle it. That he wasn't meant to be this way.

I didn't get the chance because my phone rang. I pulled it out of my pocket and checked the screen.

It was home. Probably Nora had made Annabel call me because she was worried about me. I had missed two bedtime stories, after all. Who could blame her?

This sucked. Working with Wade had pulled me from my family. The very reason I didn't like doing jobs for Graham anymore.

Not to say I wasn't grateful I'd met Wade. Even if he was a murderer.

No, Caleb. This is what gets you into trouble. You allow yourself to fall in love and you don't think about the consequences.

And boy would this have consequences if I went on. I didn't even want to begin to imagine how bad the repercussions would be.

I slid the button across the screen and answered the call.

"Annabel...I'm so sorry. I promise I'll make it up to —" I said but was cut short from the panic in Annabel's voice.

"Caleb, you need to come home. Now," she said.

"What happened?"

"Graham is here. And he's pissed off."

I'd known the bliss wouldn't last. Not that spending two days with a witch hunter being chased and attacked by everyone was bliss. I'd seen this a mile out. Of course Stef and her boyfriend had talked. And Grace had probably caught up with Graham about my adventures. If I knew Annabel, she had probably said what had happened the night before, although I really hoped she'd kept that to herself.

"I'll be right there," I said and hung up.

Annabel shouldn't have to put up with Graham. She was a troll, after all, and she didn't need the stupid witch politics on her plate. There was already enough on her plate.

"Everything okay?" Wade asked.

"I need to go home."

"I'm coming with you...if that's okay."

"No. You can't come with me. This is serious and—and I'm in trouble."

He didn't need to know that. Why did I tell him that?

"Then I'm definitely coming with you," he said.

See, this was the kind of thing that made me fall in love, and this man wasn't making it any easier for me.

The whole knight in shining armor crap was the worst thing one could pull on me. It was what had made me fall in love with Jin in the first place.

"Wade, no. Please. You can't come with me. I have to do this on my own."

"What the hell is going on? Is everything okay with Nora?"

I nodded.

"Then what?"

I gave up. I was dying to tell anyway. It concerned him too. If Graham was at the house, he knew about Wade.

"My high priest is at home, and he's probably pissed. No, scratch that. He *is* pissed."

Wade stepped closer with a determination I couldn't help but find all the more alluring.

"Then I'm definitely coming. I got you into this trouble, so I'll get you out of it."

THIRTEEN
WADE

I didn't know what to expect when we got to Caleb's house, but I was going to do whatever was necessary to protect him from the wrath of his high priest. I knew very little about what that title meant or how the witches' world worked, but I'd do my best, regardless, to help him.

Caleb had gone to great lengths to help me, even resorted to crime to help me with my curse. Although he didn't seem to mind the illegal stuff he'd had to do all that much.

It didn't matter to me that the transference spell hadn't worked. It was probably for the best anyway.

Yes, I was looking forward to the day that I could fall in love with someone and not worry about killing them, but at least I'd had more than half a lifetime to get used to it. If Caleb had taken on my curse, he'd have struggled. And I couldn't let him struggle.

He was a good man. Even if he was a witch.

This was crazy. Never in my life had I looked at another man and thought how handsome they looked. Never in my life had I dreamed of sleeping with one. But since our alone time in the basement, that was all I could think about. Sex with Caleb and how it would feel to be inside him, connect with him at a whole new level.

And as much as I tried to tell myself this was wrong and how this wasn't me, my mind wouldn't obey.

This new Wade didn't make sense. Was I attracted to Caleb because he was the only one that could tame me when I was having one of my rages? Was that reason enough to make me like him in that way?

That still didn't explain why I'd felt the same way I had with Sarah. How was it possible that I was having the same feelings for someone I'd known for two days that I'd had with someone I'd known for three months? None of this made sense. I wished something would make sense, but since I'd met Caleb, everything was making me question my sanity.

"I meant what I said back there. I will help you," Caleb said as he unlocked the front door to his house.

"Let's worry about that later. How bad is this going to be?" I asked him and stepped inside the hall-way, the floor of which I'd acquainted myself with intimately a couple nights before. None of my blood was there, which must have meant Annabel had cleared it, but the memories lingered.

"Pretty bad. Which is why I'd rather you stayed out here."

I shook my head before he could even finish his sentence.

"No. I'm definitely *not* doing that."

"You are very hotheaded, aren't you?" Caleb said, and I saw a trace of a smile on his face, despite the worry lines around his eyes making him look older.

We climbed upstairs, and he inserted the key into the second door, but he didn't get a chance to twist it, as the door flung open, Annabel standing behind it.

She looked pissed off, and I couldn't blame her. My collaboration with Caleb was what had got us into this mess, and she didn't need to pay the price for aiding and abetting.

"Where is he?" Caleb asked as soon as he walked through the door.

A man in his late forties with white hair and an equally white, abundant beard stood up from where he was sat on Caleb's couch.

The same one I'd bled all over only two nights ago. It was oddly unscathed from the mess I'd made, although I didn't know how odd it actually was considering I was in a house with two witches, a troll, and a phoenix.

Of all the things I'd expected a high priest to be wearing, it wasn't skinny blue jeans and a red silky shirt. Not that I'd expected him to be wearing a robe and holding a staff, but...yes, no. That was exactly what I had expected.

"Is that him?" he shouted as soon as he laid eyes on me.

"Keep your voice down, Graham. Nora's having her afternoon nap," Annabel shouted back at him.

He glared at her, and when I thought I'd have to intervene, he held his hand up in apology.

Dear Lord. If a high priest was scared of Annabel, she must be one hell of a Nightcrawler species.

"Apologies, Annabel. I'll take care of that," he said and looked at his watch.

He picked the tiniest crystal and rested it on the center of his palm. He mumbled something and the crystal shot out of his hands and onto Nora's bedroom door where it pulsed and the dust floated in front of it.

"That should do it," he said and turned around to look at me again. "Is this the hunter?" he shouted as if Annabel's interruption had never happened.

"Hi, sir. I'm—" I raised my hand, but it was as if I wasn't even in the room.

"I wasn't talking to you, witch hunter," he growled and glared at Caleb.

"It is him. But, Graham, I can explain—" Caleb said, but Graham interrupted him.

"Explain why you're working with a witch hunter? I'd love to know the answer to that. I've got witches and Nightcrawlers coming to me and asking me why a witch is attacking them and protecting a hunter. I don't know what to tell them, Caleb. I don't know... you...you had a mission. The high council—"

Caleb raised his voice. "That's what I'm doing. If you let me explain, then you'd know."

"And working with a hunter is part of your mission, is it? Pray, do tell, have you found out why they're killing high council members?"

Caleb pursed his lips and looked down.

"No. We've been busy. But he knows there's a witch working for their director. And he wants to help." Caleb pointed at me.

"Then why isn't he? And what could be more important than finding the mole who's leaking names to Christian?"

Wait... how did he know Marlowe's name?

"You-you know Director Marlowe?" I asked.

The high priest's eyes burned with hatred, looking at me.

"Yes, we've crossed paths before," he said.

"I was going to get him undercover to identify the witch," Caleb said, "but he got made, so the witch hunters are after him too. So, we've been working hard to get around this little problem. Don't act like I don't care about the high council members."

I surely hoped his high priest couldn't read minds like Mother Red Cap.

"If you did care, Raphael would still be alive," Graham said.

Caleb's gaze shot up to his priest, the worry and confusion as recognizable as his physical features.

"Raphael's dead?" he asked.

"Yes, he is. Same MO as the others. Has your friend helped you with that?".

Caleb turned to me with pursed lips and shook his head.

"If you're talking about the new ritual, I can tell you what it is," I told the high priest, who looked at me with disgust.

"I'm listening," he drawled.

"Director Marlowe said that it's a new ritual to make sure the witches' souls are extinguished completely. He's been studying some of the angelic scripts, and he made discoveries that could help elimi- nate witches' souls for good. I've been the only one trialing it. He told me if it was successful, it'd be rolled out to the rest of the force as standard practice."

Graham laughed. "Angelic rituals, ha? Nice one," he said. "Is that what he's made you believe? That he's an angel?"

His laughter was making me sick, and I felt the urge to punch him.

"He's not an angel. He's been studying the angel blood properties all his life, though."

"Does this look like angels to you?" Graham shouted and thrust a picture at me. A male in his forties lay on top of a pentacle, his front completely drenched in blood."

"Winston," I whispered.

"What are you talking about? His name is Raphael," Caleb said and stood next to me, inspecting the picture.

He placed his hand on mine. His touch was comforting despite all it could do to me. I just hoped he couldn't read all my fucked-up thoughts until I was clear on what I felt.

I didn't mind he was using his power on me. I'd have told them anyway, but if he preferred to get the truth out of me with his power, he could.

"Your brother did this? How do you know?" Caleb asked.

I didn't fail to see the look on his high priest's face when Caleb removed his hand. He obviously didn't like Caleb touching me. If I had a mirror, I'd have looked at myself in it to see what he was seeing, what was making him cringe. But I didn't, and all I could do was straighten my face as much as possible and hope I didn't give anything away.

"I know his style. It's the way he draws the pentacle. The top corner is always stretched, longer than the rest. And he does like the chest area. He usually cuts the symbol of a cross in the front."

I'd never felt more ashamed by my profession than now. I'd been doing the angels' work. That's what I'd been told all my life. But looking at the brutality in the picture now, I wasn't so sure there was anything angelic about it.

"It's a family business, then? How charming," Graham said.

Christian had given Winston the trial run. Winston was equally as good as me out in the field, although he had a thing for blood that I didn't care for. But he was also a lot more careless, which meant we didn't have much time before the next victim.

The fact that I considered the witches victims, now the tables had turned, didn't escape me.

"Who is this Christian and why do you know him? Do you have any suspicions on who could be turning their backs on us?" Caleb asked his high priest.

"No, no suspicions yet. The department we leaked the information to is quite large, so I don't know who it could be. That was your job, Caleb. That's why I sent you. And instead, you start frolicking with a witch hunter," he said, and I felt my chest about to explode.

How dare he speak to Caleb like that when he was only trying to help. And how dare I feel so protective of him when he was nothing to me. Because he was nothing to me. Right?

"Hold up, Graham. I'm doing what you asked me to do. If I deemed it necessary to work with a witch hunter to accomplish that, that's none of your business. You send me for results, and that's what you're gonna get."

"Then stop fucking about and get to it. Show me your head is still in the game," Graham spat.

Caleb didn't seem fazed by it. I decided to stay out

of it until I understood more of the dynamics of their relationship.

"Where was Raphael found?"

"Arnold Circus." Graham glowered.

"Shoreditch? But he doesn't live anywhere near there...now that I think about it." Caleb turned to address me. "What's up with the locations? They were all found miles away from where they live."

"Marlowe never said. He just said those places had a high concentration of angel energy, which would help absorb the witches' souls and destroy them for good," I said, feeling slightly evil. Caleb's eyes pierced into me, and I wished I could make up for all the hurt I'd caused.

What was happening to me? Two days in the presence of a witch and I was growing a soft spot for witches? What the hell?

Graham swallowed so hard all three of us heard it and turned to him.

"Did you say absorb?" he mumbled.

I nodded.

He staggered back onto the couch and clasped his heart.

"No, it can't be. It's just a myth," he breathed out, the color washing off his face.

"What's just a myth?" Caleb asked.

Graham didn't seem to have heard Caleb.

"How does he even know? And if it's not a myth, then..."

Caleb sat down next to Graham and snapped his boss's attention back to the room.

"Graham, what's going on? Why are you acting like this?"

The high priest shook his head like a maniac as if trying to deny something that was a fact.

"I should have seen the signs. How does he know about it? And how does the witch know about it? No one knows about it," he mumbled on and on.

I was starting to think this guy belonged in an institute.

"Graham!" Caleb shouted. "Take deep breaths and tell me what the *hell* you're talking about."

That seemed to bring Graham out of his panic mode and back into the room.

"If he is really doing this, th-then you need to know," he said. His gaze traveled from the coffee table he'd been blankly staring at to Caleb and then to me. "You both need to know."

"Know what?" I asked.

"The truth about Christian."

What on earth did he mean? What truth? And what was there to know about Marlowe, and why could that high priest offer me any enlightenment on the subject?

"I'll make you some tea, Graham," Annabel said and rushed to the kitchen to turn the kettle on.

"I think we'll all need one, Annabel."

She nodded and turned back to the countertop to retrieve three more cups from the cupboard.

"If you're going to understand what I'm about to say, I need to start from the beginning," the high priest said as soon as we'd all sat down with a cup of tea in our hands.

A sip of the drink told me this was no ordinary tea.

"Witch hunters have been notoriously bad at tracking witches for centuries. Look at all the witch hunts that have happened throughout history. Most of the victims weren't real witches. So, the high council never considered witch hunters a real threat. Not here or anywhere around the world. We've tried to stop them, but it's become impossible. We'd bring one station down and another two would pop up with twice the recruits.

"However, someone came along a few years ago, and he had a personal vendetta against witches. He tried for decades to defeat us and destroy the high council, but we were always able to stop him. Until he took control of the BLADE force."

Was he talking about Marlowe? Why did Marlowe have a personal vendetta against witches?

"That person was a vampire. But, by the time he took control of the force, he'd turned into something else. Something...different. Something that hasn't existed for years. Centuries even. He became a dhampir."

"A dhampir? What the hell is that?" Caleb asked before I got the chance.

"A dhampir is a vampire who's outgrown their hunger for blood. The only thing that can quench their thirst is energy," Graham explained.

"Magic?" Caleb asked.

Graham nodded.

"Yes. Dhampirs feed on magic. And this particular one decided to take control of the BLADE force and change their methods. Over the years, he'd discovered and perfected blood magic, and he used it to feed off the pure energy of witches.

"The problem is, the more he fed, the hungrier he became. And the hungrier he became, the more witches had to die. He had to be stopped. So we sent a very powerful witch to him, undercover, to get her to stop him. But she didn't last long. And she got made."

"He killed her?" I asked.

Graham ignored me.

"Before he managed to get his hands on her, she performed a very potent ritual to bind him to a single crystal. His entire life force trapped inside the stone."

"You can do that?" I turned to Caleb who shrugged at my question, unable to take his eyes off Graham.

"It's a very powerful spell, and one performed in only the most extreme circumstances, but it was our only hope. He was growing uncontrollable."

"But you stopped him, right? You got the crystal

and you destroyed him?" I asked. I'd never heard anyone in the BLADE force referring to any vampire incidents. But then again, I'd never heard of vampires before I met Caleb. Surely if there had been such a big incident, we'd have heard about it at HQ.

"Unfortunately, he got to her before she could return to us. He killed her and took the stone. He couldn't destroy it without risking doing some harm to himself, so he kept it safe and continued to control the witch hunters. No matter what we tried, he always defeated us. and he got hungrier and hungrier. There's a reason why dhampirs don't last long once they turn, and it's because there's only so much energy they can consume before they starve and die."

"Who is this guy? What are you talking about?" I asked him.

He was suggesting that the force was under a vampire's control, and I wasn't going to sit there and listen to him making stupid, ludicrous accusations. If there was a vampire in the force, we'd know about it.

"What kind of question is that? Your director of course. Christian Marlowe." Graham paused for effect.

I didn't believe him. There was no way Marlowe was a vampire, or dhampir, or whatever. He was the most admired witch hunter in the history of the force. He'd made us powerful and strong. Who we were today. He'd increased our retrieval and disposal rate.

He'd made us the most successful BLADE force around the globe. He wasn't a vampire.

"You're lying." I huffed and shook my head in disbelief.

I couldn't believe we'd let this guy waste our time with fairy tales like that.

Graham shook his head slowly.

"This can't be true," I said. "Marlowe is a respected hunter in the force. He's not a vampire, and he doesn't control us. He directs us."

"You know those pentacles you draw on witches when you kill them? They feed Christian. They don't trap the witch's soul or whatever lies he's made you believe. They just feed their energy, their magic, to him."

"No, no, no. Christian has been in the force for years. We would have noticed if he was drinking blood."

"That's what I'm trying to tell you," Graham bit back and tapped his hand on the table impatiently. "He doesn't drink blood. He drinks energy. And all these years you've been feeding him and making him stronger with your swords and your pentacles. He doesn't lace your blades with angel blood. He crafts them with vampire blood to perform blood magic."

"Even if that was true"—it wasn't—"how has the force not discovered him? We have authorities. We have other directors and other departments. The government performs audits on us all the time. So does the military. How would he have avoided them for so long?"

"Lesson number one, witch hunter. You do *not* work for the government. You work for a sadistic prick. Lesson number two, Christian is a man of power. And he will stop at nothing to get what he wants. I wouldn't be surprised if the other directors, the audits, all those people you'd met over the years were his minions. I don't know why he's not been made, but what I'm telling you is the truth."

"What do the high council witches have to do with this whole thing?" Caleb asked. "Is their magic making him stronger? Is that why it's so critical to stop him? Why do I only find out about this now after all these years?"

I snapped my eyes to him and glared. Was he actually believing this bullshit? Was he believing those lies? As if I'd have spent my entire life killing witches to feed a vampire and not known it.

"There is a myth. If he's doing what I think, he's trying to do something that hasn't ever been done. Tapping into the ley lines and feeding on the energy aligned underneath."

"Fu-uck," Caleb said and placed both hands to his mouth, whether to stop himself from cursing further or because of the shock, I didn't know.

"The what lines?" I asked.

"Ley lines," he mumbled and cleared his mouth so he could be heard. "They are geographical locations that align to create a single straight line. There are various ley lines running throughout the world, and the places where they intersect are fueled with unlimited energy. But that's just a myth. All we've ever been able to prove is that there is a higher concentration of magic in those locations, but no one's been able to tap into them." Caleb turned to Graham for confirmation.

The high priest nodded.

"There's a myth that if you release enough energy in these locations, you can access the magic underneath," he explained.

I was so lost. I didn't know what was going on.

Caleb stood up. "If someone was able to have access to that much magic...all hell would break loose." He jumped away from the table to grab a seat in front of his desktop.

He went on the internet and Graham, Annabel, and I followed him to see what had got his ass on fire.

There was a map open on his browser, and he began by marking locations in London. Places I'd been recently.

Fleet Street, that had been victim number one. Charterhouse in Barbican, victim number two. Christ Church in Southwark had been Camille. And lastly, Arnold Circus where Winston had killed the witch called Raphael.

Once he'd marked them all, he connected the dots with straight lines, and when he was done the shape of a pentagram was superimposed on the map.

"This is creepy. The four locations are intersections of the ley lines. And there is one more," Caleb said and pointed at the map.

I leaned in and read the location. "Tower of London."

"I'll have people staked out there and ambush their attempt," Graham said.

"Or I can go after my brother and stop him," I told them. "If Christian has assigned Winston my case, I can get through to him."

"I won't let you do this on your own," Caleb said, turning to look at me.

"You two have done enough. Now we'll take over. I can't have a witch hunter on the loose with one of my best witches," Graham said.

"With all due respect, you're not my boss. And since you're implying that my actual boss is an evil monster, I will do what I need to, to prove you wrong and protect my brother. If you're right, he's as much a victim in all this as the witches he's killing. So am I."

Of course Marlowe wasn't an evil vampire. I wasn't going to let this high priest get my brother killed because of a lie.

"And I'll help," Caleb added.

He got up from his desk and walked to his bookcase. He pulled a book out and opened it. Inside it, there was a selection of small shiny crystals.

"You're going to sit your ass down and do as you're

told. I might not be his boss, but I am yours," Graham said.

Caleb glared at his high priest and the silence that followed could have been translated into an entire book.

Graham's face was full of fear and Caleb's full of curiosity, and the more they looked at each other, the more confident Caleb got, and the less Graham's back kept straight.

"What are you not telling me?" Caleb asked him, finally, after what felt like ages.

"Nothing," Graham mumbled.

Caleb took a step towards his high priest and repeated his question.

"Graham, I swear to the God and Goddess, I'm going to punch you if you don't tell me. What is it? What are you keeping from me?"

"You can't go after Christian. That's not your job. You were only supposed to find the witch working with him," Graham said, trying to straighten his back, but any attempts to change the dynamic in the room failed.

Caleb raised his voice. "Why can't I go after Christian?"

"Because he's innocent," I said.

Caleb raised his hand in my direction, his eyes never fleeing Graham, and pointed his index finger at me as if to say, "If you say another word, I'm going to punch you too."

"I'm gonna go after whoever is trying to hurt witches, and I'm gonna stop them," Caleb said. "Do you wanna waste more time while another witch's life is at risk?"

Graham took a deep breath and swallowed. Hard. His eyes dropped, and he took a step back.

"If you're going to go after him, you need to know the truth."

"What truth?" both Caleb and I said at the same time.

"There's more?" Caleb shouted. "What the fuck are you waiting for? The apocalypse?"

"It's about time you told him," Annabel said and got up from the table, clearing our cups of tea.

"Tell me what?" Caleb turned to her.

"What happened on the year you can't remember," Graham replied.

Caleb glared at his high priest and then back at Annabel.

"You know? How do you know? And why haven't you told me?" he asked her.

"What year?" I asked.

"There is a year in my life, after Jin's death, that I can't remember what happened to me. I woke up one day and a year had passed. Nora was two years old, and I had no idea what had happened to me. No one did," Caleb explained before he addressed Annabel again. "You know? And how do you know? I met you after?" The last two questions were meant for Graham.

Annabel came up to Caleb and took his hands. I saw a flicker on Caleb's face as she let him look inside her mind and he read her emotions.

"I don't know what happened to you. I just know he sent you on a mission," Annabel said and looked at Graham.

"How?" Caleb said, taking his hands off Annabel.

"I will tell you. But, Caleb, you need to promise to stay calm. And you need to listen to me. Try to understand what happened and why we had to do what we did."

"Who's we?" I asked as Caleb crossed his arms and stood in front of Graham, waiting for his answers.

Once again, I found the high priest ignoring me as if I wasn't even in the room.

"After our failed attempt to defeat Christian, we didn't give up. The high council came up with numerous plans to take him down, but we didn't know how to get the upper hand on him. He could predict every single move, every single tactic we tried. There was just no stopping him.

"And then I met you. You weren't like any other witch that hadn't been ignited yet. You knew about the Nightcrawler world, and you'd been a vampire. You were the perfect person to infiltrate the force and get the intel we needed on Christian. So, before I ignited your powers, you agreed to go undercover for us, as a witch hunter."

"No, he didn't," I shouted. "I'd remember Caleb if I'd seen him at the department."

I didn't know what the high priest was talking about, but I'd never seen Caleb before in my life. I was sure someone like him would have made an impression on me. This whole thing was starting to resemble a very bad and tasteless charade. And boy was I starting to crave the spells in the priest's hands. Perhaps if I had another hit, all this bullshit would make sense.

"He was meant to stay in the shadows. Take the easy hits. We'd meet him where he was and trick-feed Christian with the help of spells. He wasn't supposed to kill any more witches. He was there to get Christian's attention," Graham said.

"You sent me to seduce him," Caleb said, and the image of Christian falling for Caleb's charms dominated my mind. I didn't want to think of the two of them together. I didn't like the image. It was a lie.

Why did I care anyway? I couldn't fall in love, and if I could, I wouldn't fall for Caleb. He was a man for crying out loud. Our stars weren't aligned. They were never meant to be. We would never be together. Because I wasn't gay. And I couldn't fall in love with anyone even if I was.

Ugh! Why is this happening to me? This is torture.

"Y-yes," Graham answered. "And you were successful. We wanted you to get into his bed, find out where he's hiding his crystal, then steal it."

"I'm not dead, which means—"

"That he didn't succeed," I said. "Haha, this has been a very entertaining hour, but if you don't mind, I've got better things to do than listen to wild fabrications, from a witch, nonetheless," I said and made a move for the door.

"You did. You stole the crystal."

I paused and turned around to look at the high priest.

Was he being serious? And why was Caleb believing all this bullshit? He'd lost a year of his life, and conveniently, it was all linked to our current situation?

Yeah, not buying this crap.

"I sense a but coming," Caleb said.

"He came after you just like he'd done with Tania. But you managed to disappear before he could get to you."

"So where is the crystal?" Caleb asked.

I was starting to lose track of what was going on. So, Caleb had infiltrated the BLADE force, somehow, without ever being seen by me, stolen the crystal that kept Christian's life force trapped inside, but Caleb couldn't remember any of it?

"We don't know," Graham said. "You ran away and took a potion to erase your memories so the hunters or Christian couldn't get the information out of you."

"So what? All the things I remember about you, meeting you and igniting my powers, that was all a year after I actually met you and agreed to work for you? Why didn't you restore my memories?"

"Because it was safer that way. Christian went ballistic after he lost it. He had his hunters on constant alert, torturing all the witches they could find until they talked. As much as we wanted to stop him, there were certain risks involved in unlocking your memories, and even if we got the crystal, we still didn't know the spellword to cast it."

"I thought you wanted to stop him," I said. "It sounds like you made things worse. How was that helping?" I didn't know why I was even playing along with the guy's game. Not only did I never remember Caleb being a witch hunter, but I also didn't remember a period where we'd captured witches and tortured them. We'd only ever tracked and killed.

"We did, and we had to stop the senseless killing. In order to do so, we met with Christian and...we... made a deal," Graham said, his gaze darting to the ground.

"You made a deal with the devil?" Caleb asked. "What kind of deal, Graham?"

Graham didn't look up when he answered. It was obvious he wasn't proud of whatever he was about to say. And after he revealed why, I couldn't blame him.

"We-uhm-would feed him a specific number of witches a month, and he would leave the rest of us alone."

Caleb's eyes shot open, his face turning red in an instant.

"What? What kind of witches?" he shouted.

Graham didn't dare lift his gaze.

"Fledgling witches. We would take the ones...the ones...witches that didn't have much potential...and give their names to him."

"You are disgusting," Annabel hissed. "You are responsible for these people. Your job is to find them and help them come to their powers, and you send them to the fucking slaughterhouse?"

My stomach growled and the bile climbed my throat, burning everything in its path. Had I heard right? He was supposed to protect and guide younger witches but instead was using them to feed a vampire? What kind of vile creature was he?

"I am not proud of it—no one is—but we did what we had to do to protect the rest of us."

"No!" Caleb screamed so loud as if he was about to explode. In a way, he was. "You did this to protect your own asses. You were my teacher, Graham. You are the teacher of any new witch that comes into the coven. You are the one that ignites their powers and trains them on how to control them. And you are sacrificing them to feed a fucking monster?"

"Wow. That is a whole new level of evil," I said.

If he was telling the truth, and I was now starting to think he was because who in their right mind would ever admit to such a heinous act, I had been a pawn my entire life. Not only had I killed innocent young witches, their coven was sacrificing those people so they could feed a dhampir and keep their more powerful witches safe.

I didn't know how to feel about any of this. It was disgusting and gross, and an absolute disgrace. I'd been a puppet in this whole charade. Had my mom been a puppet also? Had Christian fooled her too?

What was I talking about? Of course he had. He'd fooled everyone.

"I want my memories back," Caleb hissed.

"Caleb, it's dangerous. You don't know the spell-word to destroy Christian's stone." Graham pleaded with him.

"I don't care. And how do you know? You took my memories. Maybe I found out."

"No one could know the word, Caleb. Not even Christian. If you get the crystal and he gets his hands on it, then all hope is lost."

"And what about now? You think there is hope now? He's opening up the ley lines. He's going to feed off the raw magic that is running underneath our very feet. And if he does, there will be no stopping him, ever, no matter if we find out the word or not. All hope is lost already. For you and the high council. You can no longer tell me what to do. You don't have the right. I call the shots now, and I want my memories back. The high council is not allowed to get involved in this. Wade and I will stop Christian."

Graham turned to me with disgust on his face.

"The witch hunter will help you?"

I opened my mouth to reply, but Caleb did it for me.

"You mean the witch hunter you helped make? Don't forget, he's only been killing the witches you gave to him. Don't act all high and mighty. Your time is up, old man."

Graham looked as if he was about to break down in tears. Not that I cared. He didn't deserve any sympathy.

"What are you waiting for, asshole? Give him his memories back," I shouted with all the authority and hatred I could muster in my voice.

"Okay. Okay. I-I just need access to your kitchen," he murmured.

"This way. I'll keep an eye on him," Annabel said and pushed Graham towards the open-plan kitchen. She followed every single one of his movements. He wasn't doing anything dodgy under her watch. That much was obvious.

"How do you feel?" Caleb asked and stepped in front of me, short of a hug, and gazed into my eyes.

"How do *you* feel?"

The red in his cheeks strengthened, and his breathing became heavy.

"How do I feel? Angry. Confused. Ashamed. You? You can't be faring any better. You just found out that not only have you been killing innocent witches, but you've also been killing them for a magic-thirsty dhampir."

He was right. I was all of those things.

"I need time to process all this," I said.

"You don't have to do this with me, you know. It's going to be dangerous."

"Are you kidding me? I was born dangerous," I said, and he cracked a smile. It was a picture to behold, especially after everything that had just happened. I didn't know what was going on inside my head, but whatever it was Caleb made me feel was a million times better than finding out the truth. And that I could live with. "Besides, I'm not letting you go after that asshole on your own. We're gonna take him down. Together."

I was ready for it. It was time to do the proper work of the angels and stop this dangerous monster, one of the many, as it had proven tonight, that had been in power for far too long.

FOURTEEN
CALEB

G raham passed me the crystal he'd whipped up, and I held it in my hands. A purple stone that resembled an amethyst trembled with power. If he could make a spell to restore my memories, it must have meant he'd also made the potion to erase them.

I couldn't believe he'd lied to me all these years.

"The word?" I asked him.

I didn't care for Graham anymore. What he'd just admitted to was beyond revolting. He was worse than Wade and what he'd done throughout his witch hunting career. I couldn't believe that the man I had trusted and looked up to had agreed to such a terrible thing.

"Memories," he replied, and I grimaced.

He shrugged.

"What? I didn't have time to be fancy."

I raised an eyebrow at him but let it go. Instead, I focused on the spell in my hands. The spell that could give me back everything I'd lost.

I repeated the spellword with clarity, and the crystal exploded in my hands, suffocating me with its dust.

Everything around me disappeared. There was just darkness. The voices and presence of Annabel, Graham, or Wade had faded, and I was standing in nothingness. But nothing else happened.

Had Graham tried to fool me? Did he think I wouldn't know or notice? Or maybe he was trying to buy himself some time so he could warn the high council. I was about to take a step forward and put an end to this spell when it hit me.

"Hi, my name is Graham, and I'm a witch." I saw a slightly younger version of Graham smile at me. He extended his hand, and I shook it. Then everything rippled, and when it stopped, I was with Graham again, but in a different place.

"It's going to be dangerous, but I have faith in you. You can do it. Your time as a vampire gives you leverage. You need to get close to him and give us a leverage too," Graham said.

The world around me rippled again, and I found myself in the BLADE force headquarters. For a moment, I didn't know how I knew, but then I realized. I remembered. I remembered walking in there and being given the address. I remembered everything that had led up to that moment. My meet up with Graham, his explanation of the witch world. Asking me to do this mission before he ignited my powers.

I remembered everything.

"You need to impress him. That should get his attention," Graham said. "Then, it will be up to you to get the job done."

"So, you're counting on my whoring skills," I replied.

It was good to know I'd still been myself.

I got flashes of my time at the force. I remembered making a couple of friendships. I remembered going to missions where Graham would meet me, and we'd save the witches and offer a spell to Christian instead.

I even caught a glimpse of Wade, but we never ran in the same teams. Was that why I had those fucked-up feelings about him? Was it because I'd seen him before even if I didn't know it until now?

I saw the face of a man, his eyes were hazel, and his hair blond and sleek. His skin was whiter than any skin should be.

Christian Marlowe.

"I've heard the best, Stones," he told me and the present me laughed. What a dig. Coming up with a fake identity had all been part of the plan, of course, but the name itself? That had been my baby. Stones came from my anticipation to use spells like a real witch. The first name was Tristan. Just because. "The guys in Manchester can't stop praising you. Your results here have been equally fantastic. What's your secret?" he asked me.

Everything about him told me I needed to run away as fast as possible. I could tell he was a vampire when I was sitting opposite him, and I could tell he was a vampire remembering these moments now. It was clear as daylight.

Everything rippled and it picked up on another moment.

"Great job, Stones. Are you gonna go out and celebrate?" he asked me.

I should have run when I'd had the chance. Instead, I went straight into his arms.

"I was hoping we could celebrate together," I told him and ran a finger from his neck down to his chest.

He looked at me, his eyes burning with desire.

It had taken me two months to get under his sheets. His resistance had been strong. He didn't want to mix work with pleasure even though he had a thing for foxy little men like me, and even though I knew who he was and what he was, I found myself enjoying the challenge. Enjoying the mission more than I should.

It hadn't been an accident why Graham had chosen me. I was picked for various reasons. My vampire history was one. My love life was the second. But the third, and perhaps most important, was my appearance. I ticked all of Christian's boxes.

I was just hoping I hadn't fallen for the vampire. It

wouldn't have been the first time I had fallen for the wrong person.

"You need to stop teasing me like this," Christian whispered in my ear, and his warm breath did things to my neck. I got goosebumps.

"Then stop resisting me," I told him.

There was a knock on the door and a man walked in.

Dear gods, it wasn't just any man. It was Wade.

Christian pushed me off him and scolded Wade, and after Wade reported whatever crap he had to report, he left the room.

When I climbed back onto Christian and he got his boner back, all I could think about was Wade, not Christian.

Holy fuck.

We had met before. I could see why I didn't remember him, but why could he not remember me?

My memories jumped back to the time when Christian first kissed me. Two months after I'd started, and after I'd fed him with more trick magic with Graham's help, he was so impressed with me, he'd called me into his office. I played my success up, and he ended up kissing me.

"Why are you so irresistible?" he'd said in my ear.

The memories lapsed again, and I was in a van with Wade, staking out our next "hit."

Christian had given me a promotion and paired me with Wade, one of his best men.

I knew then I should have hated him for killing people like me, but I couldn't stop looking into his beautiful blue eyes that hid so much sorrow and misery.

"So, you and the boss are close, huh?" he said to me while eating a doughnut.

I shrugged it off. Christian was work. I couldn't care less for him.

"Yeah, I guess. Why? Are you jealous, Rawthorne? There's enough of me to go around, you know," I told him, and he choked.

I leaned forward to pat his back, and he pushed my hand away.

"I'm not a fag, thanks. Even if I was, I don't think you'd be my type."

I made a sizzling sound with my teeth and backed off.

"Okay, buddy, message received."

Again, the memories jumped forward, taking me through different events. I didn't need to watch everything that had happened that year to remember. The spell was showing me the highlights, and my brain filled in the gaps.

I saw Christian and me in bed, and I saw us fucking in his office behind closed doors. He was slowly getting under my rule. If I waved a finger, he'd be there, begging like a puppy.

And at the same time, Wade and I got closer. We became very close partners, and with Graham's help, we managed to fool him into thinking he was killing witches when in fact he was helping them.

Wade was sweet and naïve back then as well, if not more so. Of course he was. He was a twenty-five-year-old who thought he knew everything about the world, and I challenged every single one of his perceptions.

It took us a few months for him to open up to me about his curse, but he did, and my crush for him became stronger. But he was off-limits, and I had a mission to do.

The closer I got to Christian, the closer I got with Wade. We were buds. He'd tell me about his latest sexual conquest and brag about his prowess, only to be brought down by me. He'd tell me when he felt the urge to kill those who got too close, and I hated seeing him in pain.

"I just want to be myself again, you know? I want to have someone," he told me when we were on a witch's tail.

I caressed his head before I could stop myself, but he didn't flinch. He should have, but he didn't. Instead, he turned to look into my eyes, and before I knew what the hell was going on, he leaned in for a kiss. It was the same kind of kiss he'd given me now. Angry and passionate, but also sweet.

Before I had a chance to understand what the hell was going on and enjoy it, he pulled away.

"I'm-I'm sorry. I don't know what's wrong with me. I'm not even gay," he said.

I tried to catch my breath, but he'd stolen it. He stole everything I had with one damn kiss.

"Who gives a shit?" I replied and kissed him again.

This time he didn't pull back. It took him some time to work through what he felt for me, but eventually, his need for me and my need for him won over.

Our first night together had turned into the kind of disaster we'd had in Ash's cellar. Despite the fact he'd tried to kill me, I could hold my own, and with the help of a sturdy pair of handcuffs, we could both enjoy each other's bodies.

This was so fucked up. We'd met before, and we'd been with each other before. Were the gods playing a joke on us or had this all been orchestrated by someone more human?

While Wade was turning from a friendship into more, Graham kept harassing me about Christian. I had to keep a straight face and my affair with Wade secret, especially from Christian.

It took months to get Christian to open up to me even more and admit to me that he wasn't human at all.

"You must hate me. Don't you?" I remembered him asking me in bed when he finally told me the truth. We'd been sleeping together for seven months now, and I'd been with Wade for a little under that. It'd been nine months since I'd started this mission, and I was finally breaking through him.

I remembered missing home. And thinking I was

the worst person for leaving Nora on her own. Even if she had Annabel and Graham to look after her.

But I also remembered being crazy infatuated with the man that had stolen my heart now. I knew Wade wasn't evil—he was anything but—and I knew this wasn't meant to last. But that didn't stop me from falling for him.

"I hate seeing you, knowing you're with him," Wade had told me after another night of hot sex.

"I can't, okay. I can't explain."

It was killing me not being able to tell him. That I knew he worked for a monster, but I couldn't do anything about it.

"If you love him then you should be with him. I'm unlovable anyway. I could never feel the same for you as you do for me."

I rolled my eyes and gave him a deep kiss.

"You know that's bullshit. You haven't had an incident in months. Maybe it's faded. You don't know that. And even if not, I still love you," I told him.

"Then let him go," he begged.

"I can't, baby. I wish I could, but I can't."

Wade turned his back to me and sulked.

"I'm sorry," I told him.

"I'd rather you left me alone, then. I'm only going to bring you trouble anyway."

I grabbed his chest and spooned him.

"Have you had another one of *those* incidents?"

"Yeah," he murmured. "When I finished my shift

yesterday. I was leaving HQ and then all of a sudden, I was in bed this morning."

I squeezed my hand and rubbed it on his skin.

"We'll figure it out, baby. I swear. We'll figure out the curse and the memory losses. Everything. Okay?"

Wade responded with a shrug.

The memories rippled and showed me Christian again. I immediately missed Wade's face. I wanted to see more of him and me, together. Even if I now remembered it all, I still wanted to live through it. It made me feel less stupid for falling for him again. It was because my heart had never forgotten about him. I might not have known who he was, but my heart did.

"Why won't you tell me what's wrong? I don't understand," I remembered begging Christian.

He wouldn't tell me. As much as he trusted me, and I'd sucked his cock way more times than I cared about to get there, he loved his power more.

My memories flashed forward again.

"What's taking you so long, Caleb. Your head is no longer in the game. Have you got bored?" Graham asked me in one of our catch-ups.

"It's not that, Graham. I can't get closer without making him suspect something is off. I have to be careful."

And it was true.

So was the next memory.

"Maybe this is the way to get to him. Maybe if I stay in the force, I can help save more witch's lives.

Maybe we can get more of us undercover and turn the force on its head," I told Graham.

"What the hell are you talking about. They're the enemy," Graham said.

"Only because he's made them believe we are."

"Witch hunters hated witches long before Christian. What's going on with you? Have you fallen in love with that monster?" he yelled.

He didn't know about Wade. And I didn't care to enlighten him.

"Find that crystal and get out of there. Now!"

The memories rippled and showed Wade and me again. This time, after I'd told him the truth about Christian and the force.

It'd taken a lot of guts to do so, but I trusted him, and he trusted me. Despite his curse, I could tell he cared about me, and I wanted to help him. I wanted to help him with his memory lapses and the curse itself. It would just have to wait until Graham ignited my powers and I could use spells.

"He must keep it in his office. He's always there. That's the only place I can think of," Wade said.

"Are you sure about this?"

Wade grabbed me by the neck and inserted his tongue in my mouth. That was answer enough.

The memories rippled, and I found myself inside Christian's office.

I'd emptied his entire bookcase looking for a secret room or a hidden safe but yielded no results.

I'd put everything back where it had been when he came in and took me by surprise. Thankfully, evidence of my snooping was long gone. I only needed to put one last book back.

"What are you doing in here?"

He'd caught me, but Wade was supposed to keep watch. Where was he? Had he betrayed me, or had Christian done something to him?

"I was just looking for a good book to read. Which angel should I read about next?" I asked him, playing up my sex appeal.

"The one about Ezekiel is a great one," he told me, and I only saw a sliver of doubt in his face.

When I saw Wade next, he had no memory of seeing Christian pass through him.

Fast forward to another day when I decided to use Wade's help to look through Christian's office.

Christian had been distant and kept busy. He hadn't asked to see me since he'd caught me in his office, which he now kept locked at all times.

Christian was called out to a meeting one evening, and I picked the lock. I ignored the bookcase and scanned the room. The paintings had nothing behind them. The fireplace, no secret stashes.

His desk was a no-go zone, and the floor was a non-starter. Nothing in the room gave away his secret. It even made me doubt the story Graham had told me about the dhampir.

Or maybe he'd been smarter and hidden it some-where where it couldn't be found.

Whichever the case, I'd given up and turned to open the oak doors when something caught my attention.

The wood carving of mythical creatures and angels was an intricate work that I'd never spent any time admiring. But now, I noticed one of the angels holding something over their heads. It looked to be sunlight carved into the wood. But in the center, something dark glistened. Initially, I thought it was darker varnished wood patch, but when I looked at it closer, I realized it was the stone.

I took it, and as I came out, I saw Christian beating Wade inside the training room.

I wanted to help him. I didn't want to leave him. But I had a chance to destroy this asshole for good.

Without a second thought, I went over to the training room and grabbed a sword on my way in.

"Hey, wanker. Leave him alone," I shouted, and Christian turned to look at me.

"Tristan, don't. Run," Wade managed to growl.

"Shut up," Christian told him and then said to me, "I should have known you'd betray me. But to betray me for this?" He pointed at Wade as if he was anything less than human.

Look who the fuck was talking. A monster of a vampire.

"Let him go," I said, but Christian laughed.

"Or what?" he said.

I showed him his crystal, and his laughter was cut short.

"What do you think you're doing with this?" he asked.

"You think I don't know what it is?" It was my turn to laugh. "Let him go or..."

I put the stone on the floor and swung the sword over my head.

"You don't know anything, foolish hunter. Stop this stupidity now, and I might spare your life," he shouted.

"Not a chance," I said and struck the crystal with the sword.

I knew it wasn't going to stop him, but I hoped it would give me the distraction I needed to save Wade.

And it happened.

The crystal pulsed and spurted black lightning bolts that blasted Christian across the room. Wade jumped up off the floor, and I picked up the crystal again. We both started running.

"Stop," Christian shouted, but I kept going.

When I looked beside me, though, Wade wasn't there. I turned and looked at him. He was standing by the door to the training room and shaking his head.

"Go, Tristan. Run," Wade begged me, and I had no idea why he couldn't join me. What was stopping him?

I wanted to go back and get him. I made a move to, but he shook his head.

So, I did what I had to do. I ran with Christian's life force in my hand. I had to. It was the only way to stop him. Even if I hated myself for doing it and leaving Wade behind.

I ran.

I had to get the crystal back to Graham, but I knew Christian would send his hunters after me, and I couldn't lead them back to the high council. There was no way of escaping with the stone and my life. I had to hide. Both of us.

The memories rippled around me.

I was at Southbank, and I was up against three hunters. Three friends. Well, ex-friends now. I fought them off with my sword. And by that, I meant I killed them. It was the only thing I could do, and it hurt, but I had to protect myself and our one shot at bringing this asshole down.

Then I found myself at the Shakespeare's Globe with another five witch hunters who wouldn't let go. I was desperate, and I definitely couldn't lead them back to the coven or Nora.

When my memory jumped again, I was out of breath and about to collapse when I reached the Tower of London. By that point, I'd lost all hope of ever making it back to Graham so he could save me.

A raven swept in and, in a flash of smoke, turned into a man.

"If you've pissed off the witch hunters for them to hunt you for so many miles, you're doing something right," he said.

"Who are you?" I asked him.

"I'm one of the ravens of the Tower of London. My name's Hew, and I protect the spells that everyone knows as the Crown Jewels. Why are the witch hunters after you?"

The idea formed in my head before I had the time to think it through.

"You protect spells? Can you protect one more?" I asked him.

I remembered explaining to him in brief detail what the crystal was before I revealed it to him.

It felt foolish to trust a complete stranger, and present-me would never have done anything like that, but past-me was desperate. And as much as I wanted to save Wade, I had to save myself too.

Hew took it in his hands, turned back into a raven, and flew inside the tower.

Then I ran. I ran as far away from there as possible because I needed to cover my tracks before I did what I was about to do next. Graham had given it to me for an emergency. To protect my friends and family.

I didn't want to do it. It meant forgetting Wade. Even if only for a few days. But I didn't know what other options I had. I got as far as Whitechapel and stepped into a supermarket. I grabbed hair bleach and paid for it before ducking inside a bar, going into the disabled bathroom and shutting myself inside. I let my hair go white and washed it in the sink.

I joined the dancers at the bar and ordered myself a drink. If I was going to do this, I might as well do it in style.

Bottoms up!

When Graham found me, weeks later, he barely recognized me. He got me back home to Annabel and told me about my fate as a witch before igniting my powers. In reality, it was payment for services rendered, even if my mission was incomplete.

The darkness that enveloped me dropped to the floor and turned into sand, and I found myself back at home. I took long, deep breaths. Wade was there, next to me, keeping a watchful eye on me. Like he'd done all those years ago when I'd betrayed him and left him behind to suffer under Christian. But why didn't he remember any of it?

"Are you okay? Take it slow," he said.

I nodded when all I wanted to do was take him in my arms and make him remember what we'd had.

"You've just had a year's worth of memories come back to you. You need to take it easy," Graham said. "Listen to your...friend." I didn't miss the way he pronounced the word *friend*.

After everything he'd done, he had no right to criticize my choices. He didn't know.

"Why did you never tell me? Why did you put my life at risk?" I asked him.

Graham bit his lip and shook his head.

"My dear boy, why do you think I gave you the job at the cafe? Why did I introduce you to Lorelai? She's supposed to protect you," he said.

"Lorelai knows?" I asked, but I already knew the answer. Graham wouldn't have risked anyone knowing what had happened, especially if I could sense it when I touched them. "And you chose to leave me without my memories. You were willing to let the crystal stay hidden and Christian to be at large. Why?"

He didn't answer. It didn't make sense.

I knew why I'd changed my appearance—to lose the hunters' tracks until Graham could find me and give my memories back. I'd never expected to lose them for good.

"Answer me!" I shouted at him. "Why would you not give me my memories back so we could stop him? Why did you choose to make a shit deal with him instead?"

"Because I didn't know what you'd gotten yourself into!" he shouted back. "You wanted to stay at the force, Caleb. You were getting too close to Christian, and it was showing. I didn't know what you'd do if you remembered and found the crystal. I still don't know. Are you going to take it to him? Or are you going to give it to us so we can finish him once and for all?"

"Are-are you fucking stupid? Why would I have stolen it in the first place? I was counting on you. And you left me hanging. For five damn years. And no, I wasn't in love with Christian, you idiot. I was in love with him," I said and pointed to Wade.

"What?" everyone said, and I could feel their eyes burning me with their glares.

"What do you mean you were in love with me?" Wade asked.

I did the thing I'd wanted to do since I'd remembered. I touched him. Took his hands in mine and looked him in the eyes.

"We've met before. I don't know why you don't remember me, but we used to be partners. And we fell in love. I told you the truth then, and you tried to help me. But I betrayed you. I left you behind, with Christian. I left you to die," I said.

My voice broke. I knew now why I couldn't stop myself falling for Wade, and I knew now I wasn't stupid.

"What are you talking about? My partner from five years ago died. He died in the training center when I accidentally stabbed him during practice. His name was…" he said and then paused. "His name was…"

"Tristan. Tristan Stones," I said.

Wade shook his head.

"No. That doesn't ring a bell. Besides, he was taller than you and dark. He looked nothing like you," he said.

I didn't know what the fuck was going on, but I knew where to start.

"Look, you used to have memory lapses when we

were together, and we were trying to figure it out.
Together. I promised you back then that if I got the
crystal back to my coven, we'd be able to stop Christian, and I'd be able to use my powers to help you. And
that's what I've done again. I don't know what the
fuck is going on or why you can't remember our time
together, but I know we need to take that motherfucker down before he hurts anyone else. I know
where the crystal is."

"Where is it?" Graham asked.

"I'm not telling you," I said. "You need to leave
now. And I'm not going to ask twice."

Graham nodded, and he slowly got up and wiped
his hands on his thighs.

"Are you sure—" he started saying but I cut
him off.

"Yes. Go."

He thanked Annabel for the tea even though she
looked ready to murder him, and he opened the door.
As he did, he turned around and looked at me.

"I just want you to know, Caleb, I did everything
with the best intentions, but I know what I did was
wrong. I know what we all did was wrong. I hope you
can forgive me one day. Be careful out there," he said,
and he left my house. Finally.

I wrapped myself around Wade before I remembered he wasn't there yet and pulled my hands back.
He'd get there. If he could love me once, he could love
me again. Curse or not.

"I'm sorry," I said. "It's just too much. But by finding my memories, I found you again."

"You mean, you were saying the truth? We've met before?"

I nodded.

"I've got so much to tell you. We can get Mother Red Cap to restore your memories. But first—"

"First we need to get this asshole. Got it," he replied. "Where are we going?"

"Tower of London. Where the last ley line location is. What are the chances, right? I hid the stone with the Crown Jewels," I said. I needed to get dressed, and I'd top up my bracers with spells. It was such a shame Graham was a bastard because I could really use his help and the spells he could create for me, but I didn't want anything to do with him.

"I hope you know what you're getting yourself into," Annabel said, and I looked at her for the first time that night.

She had been there for me from the beginning. Even before we got Nora, she had been a constant in my life even if she preferred to keep out of my business. Which was for the best because that's what kept her and Nora safe.

"Annabel, thank you for everything you do. I'm sorry I'm such an ass."

She rolled her eyes in her signature way, and I went in for a hug.

"You're an ass, but I do love you, idiot. Now you

better be careful because I'm not answering Nora's million questions about what happened to Daddy and his friend," she said.

"She was talking about me?" Wade asked, a glimmer in his eyes.

"Non-stop," Annabel said.

A smile formed on his lips. One that I could easily kiss for the rest of the night. But we had work to do.

A ringtone broke out in the room, and Wade patted his pockets and retrieved his phone.

"I've got to take this," he said and answered the call. "Hello! I can't hear. Hello..." He moved around the room, trying to get better reception. "I'm gonna take this outside," he whispered and proceeded to leave the room and walk downstairs.

"Ann, would you mind calling Lorelai and telling her I won't make it to work again tomorrow," I asked. "Tell her I'll owe her loads."

I felt guilty that she was left with all the heavy lifting of running the cafe and the spell shop in the back. But Lorelai was a friend. Hopefully, she would understand and soon I would be able to make it up to her.

"She'll be fine. Take care of this Christian fella," Annabel said, and as I attempted to give her another hug, Wade rushed in and slammed the door behind him.

"We need to go. Now," he said.

"What happened?" I asked.

"That was a friend from the force. My brother got the next witch," he said. "We don't have much time before Marlowe finishes his ritual and taps into the ley lines."

We didn't waste any time. Before long, we were on our way to the Tower of London. I was hoping for longer to scavenge some good spells that I could use, but there hadn't been enough time. I'd grabbed whatever I could find. I'd also been hoping to see Nora for a few moments before I'd left, but she still hadn't woken up from her afternoon nap, which might have had something to do with Graham's spell. That bastard.

"What if we talk to your brother? Won't he understand? I interacted with him before. He was reasonable," I said, unable to believe the words I'd just said.

Only a few hours ago, I'd had no clue about any of this.

"Only if there is proof. Winston doesn't do chats. He does action," Wade explained.

"Which means he'll keep on doing Christian's bidding until we prove he's evil. Gotcha," I said, and Wade gave me one of those smiles. The ones I hadn't been able to resist then, and which I was powerless to do now.

I stepped into his personal space, lifted my hand to his nape, and locked lips with him.

I was expecting him to push me back, or panic about the people around us, but he did none of that. Instead, he kissed me back, just like old times. Maybe he was remembering. There was a reason I was attracted to him. Maybe he was attracted to me for the same reason. Because his heart remembered.

"I don't know what any of this means yet. But what I do know is what I'm feeling for you is easier than the rest of the mess in my life. But I've never been with someone... like you before," he said, and I wanted to reassure him.

"You have. And it took you time back then too. But I understand if you don't want to be with me. Or you need your time."

"Just promise me you will protect yourself. When the killer comes out of me and tries to hurt you," he whispered. "Because I can feel it happening."

"I promise."

I was more than capable of holding my own. And now that I had my powers, I didn't even need the ropes. Unless he liked them.

By the time we got to the tower, the sun had set, and the castle was closing down. We got a ticket, despite objections from the ticket seller, and ran inside.

We made our way to the entrance of the Crown Jewels, and I saw a familiar face. A face I wouldn't have known was familiar until today.

"Hew," I called out.

He was hunched over, holding his stomach, his hand covered in blood.

He looked up and his hazel bright eyes met mine.

"Caleb, is that you?" He groaned.

Wade supported him, and I had a look at his wound.

"It's been, what? Five years? Is it finally time?" he asked.

"Yes, Hew. It's time. What happened here?"

"Disaster. That's what happened," he said, curling in pain.

I removed a crystal from my spellbook and placed it over his wound.

"This won't heal it completely, but it will help stop the bleeding," I told him and activated the spell. Thick dust covered the wound and it turned into a patch that merged with his skin.

"How does that feel?"

He nodded.

"The crystal. Where is it?" Wade asked.

"That's why I'm fucking annoyed. This guy walks in and steals it. As if that's not bad enough, it turns out he's my fucking mate, isn't he," he said.

"You've found your mate? So, the man who attacked you was a witch?"

Was it the witch who was working with Christian, or had Graham warned the high council? That wasn't possible. I hadn't told him where the crystal was.

Hew answered with a sigh.

"No. He's a witch hunter. And tell me, Caleb, how is that even possible? How does a familiar mate with a fucking human?" he asked.

"I don't understand what's happening," Wade said.

"I don't blame you," I said. "Hew is a familiar—"

"Half familiar. The other half is a witch, thank you very much," he said, pointing a finger at me.

"Hew is half-familiar, half-witch. Familiars are shifters. He's a raven of the Tower of London," I said.

"What does this have to do with mating?" Wade asked.

"Familiars are a witch's soulmate. When a familiar and a witch mate, they mate for life, and they're destined to protect each other for the rest of their lives. But it only works between a witch and a familiar. Humans don't mate," I said.

Hew made himself stand straight and looked at Wade. His face went white.

"He looked a lot like you. Wait a minute. You're a witch hunter too."

Hew turned to me with questioning eyes.

"Hew, I can explain. Wade is trying to help," I said.

"The hunter. You said he looks like me. What did he look like?" Wade asked him.

"Tall, handsome, deadly. Everything happened too fast. He had the same blue eyes like you, though."

"Winston!" Wade and I exclaimed in unison.

"Who the fuck is Winston?" Hew asked.

"He's my brother," Wade said.

Hew cursed and looked to the sky.

"Fuck! So not only did I mate with a hunter, I

can't even hate him because everything inside me wants to protect him. What am I supposed to protect him from when he's the one who attacked me?"

"He attacked you? How did he if you've bonded?" I asked him.

"He tried but he couldn't deliver a blow. And I couldn't hurt him either, but somehow, he managed to get one on me. I don't know. He-he looked possessed," Hew explained.

"We need to get to him. Can you find him before he gets to Christian?" I asked.

"He won't have gone far. Remember the ley lines. If he's planning on tapping into them, he must be close," Wade said.

Hew nodded and stumbled a little. Wade helped him despite Hew's protest.

"Are you going to be okay?" Wade asked him.

"Of course. I've got a whole artillery in there," Hew said and pointed to the building behind him.

"Wait a minute, you can use those?" I asked him.

"If it's to protect people from a dhampir, yes-yes I can."

Hew entered the building where the Crown Jewels were kept, and he came out five minutes later after I'd tried to explain to Wade a bit more about the familiar bonding.

"So, once they bond, that's it? You can never undo it? You can never fall in love with anyone else?" Wade asked.

"That's the principle, yes. And once you bond, you have this connection, a connection that no one can break. You can sense each other. Feel each other when you're in danger."

Wade looked away and took a moment to recollect.

"And-and every witch gets a mate?" he asked.

I bit my lip when I stepped in front of him and forced him to look back at me.

"No. Some witches don't," I said.

"How do you know if you do?" he asked.

I could see he was trying to keep a straight face, pretending he didn't care, and it was melting my heart.

"You don't. It either happens or it doesn't. Some say every witch has a soulmate in a familiar. But not everyone gets to meet them."

"So there's a chance you—" he started, but I placed my fingers on his lips. It was eerie. The familiarity of me touching him. As if I'd never stopped doing it. And despite the fact he was still coming to terms with his sexuality and accepting his feelings for me, I couldn't resist getting close to him.

"I don't give a shit. I've fallen for you twice. I'll fall for you again. No familiar or mating can come between us, you hear me? And I know this sounds fucking weird when you've only known me for three days, but it will all make sense when we get you your memories back."

Before he had the chance to say anything, Hew appeared again, now wearing a belt spellbook filled to the brim with spells. Spells that I could sense were dangerous. More dangerous than anything.

"I'm gonna go track him. He can't be far. Follow me on foot," he said, and with a bang, a flash, and smoke, he turned into a raven. A raven larger than life. Looking at his familiar form, I could see there was no mystery why the seven ravens of the Tower of London were so famous with humans across the world. Humans didn't know what they were. They just thought their connection to the tower made them different. If only they knew the truth.

"Okay, are you ready?" I asked Wade when Hew took flight, and I turned around to look at him, but his fist made contact with my face. Everything spun around me until it all went black.

Had Wade just betrayed me?

FIFTEEN
WADE

I didn't know why I punched Caleb. What I did know was that I was no longer in control of my own body. One moment I was standing there, contemplating what Caleb had said about familiars and worrying that he'd one day meet his familiar and bond with him and have their happy ever after, and the next my hand impacted with his face, knocking him out.

Swinging him over my shoulder, I carried him across the gravel. I didn't know where I was taking him, and at the same time, it was clear in my head. It was like having a word on the tip of your tongue but which you couldn't get quite right.

Instead of a word, it was my memories, however.

I remembered going out to take the call on my phone when we were still at Caleb's house, and I remembered hearing Christian's voice on the other end, telling me something, but I couldn't remember exactly what it was.

What happened to me? Why was I doing this to Caleb? I didn't want to do any of this.

How was Winston involved in this? He couldn't possibly know the truth about Christian, which meant he was probably perverting the truth to get Winston to do his bidding. I'd have done the same, wouldn't I? If it was a few days ago, I'd have followed Christian anywhere, done anything he asked of me.

What had he asked of Winston? Was he okay? The thought of Winston mating with a man for life was impossible. I didn't know what to make of it. He'd always been a hardcore straight guy, and while his killer instinct wasn't as strong as mine, he hadn't killed anyone because of it. He worked his way around the ladies. Which was why I was finding it hard picturing him with Hew.

It was all very confusing and was made even more so by the situation I was currently in. Carrying Caleb to somewhere I knew, but which I had no idea at the same time.

Yeah. Fucked up.

I walked across the field, approached the White Tower in the center, and climbed the steps two at a time. A yeoman was standing at the entrance and he let me in without so much a word, then closed it behind him. While my destination was both a mystery and not to me, I took all the stairs all the way to the rooftop.

My chest was pounding, and my stomach inflated and deflated. I was so out of breath I wanted to collapse, but I couldn't. It was as if I wasn't in control of myself anymore, and no matter what condition I was in, I had to keep going.

When I approached the center of the rooftop, I saw Director Marlowe.

He was smiling.

He rubbed his knuckles. Two rings with black obsidian were visible in his fingers. I'd never seen him wearing those before.

Winston was there also. His sword was drawn and glistening with what I'd always thought had been angel lacing, but which I now knew was vampire blood.

I wanted to open my mouth and shout at Christian. I wanted to tell Winston what was going on, but I couldn't do either of those things.

"Put him down," Marlowe said, and my arms obeyed him.

"Wake him up," Marlowe said, and, without meaning to, I slapped Caleb. He didn't rouse.

"Again," Marlowe shouted, and I slapped Caleb again.

He opened his eyes and looked around him. He tried to move, but Marlowe spoke again.

"For crying out loud, Rawthorne. I thought I told you to remove his spellbooks. Do it now," he said, and again, I obeyed him. I unclipped his bracers and removed them before he could do anything.

"What's going on? Wait, what are you doing?" Caleb shouted.

"Tristan, long time no see," Director Marlowe said.

Caleb looked up and saw Christian. His face changed.

"Restrain him," Marlowe ordered me, and I took both his hands and pinned them behind his back.

Help me. Help. I can't control myself.

I was hoping he'd get it. That he'd understand me. That he wasn't too distracted by my apparent betrayal and he'd hear me. I knew he'd said he could only feel emotions and thoughts connected to those, but I was hoping my desperation and confusion were enough to tell him that I needed his help.

"Hello, Christian. Long time no see indeed. I hear you've become quite the murderous little vamp since I last saw you," Caleb told him.

Can you hear me? Please help me. I didn't betray you. I don't know what's going on.

I kept begging, hoping he would do something to release me. I had no idea what that was, but hopefully, he did.

"Me? Murderous? I never kill anyone. It's been a few decades since I did," Marlowe said.

"Oh yeah, sorry. I forgot. You got your witch hunters doing all the dirty work. How could I forget?" Caleb replied.

Christian Marlowe cackled. It took me by surprise just as much as it made sense. There had always been something in the back of my mind telling me he was evil, but I'd never witnessed him in that light before. Now I could see him in his true form, it was all becoming crystal clear.

"You think you can feed off the ley lines without destroying yourself?" Caleb said.

"Oh, I know I can. And there's nothing you can do to stop me," he said and opened his hands to reveal a crystal hanging around his neck. It was dark and shiny, just like the one we'd used for the transference spell, although smaller.

"Thanks for that by the way. I've missed it over the last five years. And I've had my men search high and low for it," he said. "And for you, of course."

"What? You've had witch hunters looking for your crystal? That's rich."

"The witch hunters are not the only ones under my control." He smirked.

"Really? Could have fooled me," Caleb said and looked behind right at me.

Don't. Please. It's not like that, I said and hoped he could hear it.

"Aw, do you like my puppets? I've worked on them for so many years. They're very faithful," Christian said, and I wanted to go up there and kill him with my bare hands. Who had he called a puppet?

"A puppet?" Caleb asked. "Is that what they are?

Because they do your bidding? What? Did you have him pretend that he wanted to stop the murder of the high council witches and that he needed to break his curse?"

He must have known I was trapped. Those were all the questions I had in my mind. Otherwise, why would he be asking them?

"Have you not noticed he can't remember you? Tell me, is it fun? Was it painful that your lover didn't know you from Adam?" Christian asked, and he approached with small, measured steps.

So, Caleb was right. We had met before. And for some reason, I didn't remember him.

"You had your witch erase his memories and replace them with lies. So. Fucking—" Marlowe tutted and waved a finger at Caleb. "What?"

"Try again," he said.

"He couldn't have faked it. I could sense his cursed heart and his pain. I know he doesn't remember me," Caleb said.

"Oh, this crap with the cursed heart. It won you over the first time too. I should have done away with it when I had the chance," Christian spat.

What did he mean do away with the curse? How would he?

"They never had cursed hearts, did they?" Caleb asked him. "It was a lie."

"What do you think?" Christian said.

Caleb flicked his hair away from his eyes and continued to stare into Christian's.

"You were always a sadistic asshole," he said.

Christian stretched his hands and did a little bow.

"I do like my toys," he said.

"Toys? Now your witch hunters are your toys? You do realize they are people, right?"

"You don't understand me, Tristan," Marlowe said, and he came a breath away from Caleb.

He touched his cheek and then placed the back of his hand on my face. The rough texture of his rings catching my beard.

"These two are my toys. I can do whatever I want with them," he whispered to Caleb.

How?

"How? What are you talking about?" Caleb asked.

"Blood. Magic," Marlowe hissed.

Caleb clenched my shirt and leaned back.

"You mean the one you've infused all the swords with? That's not how this works, is it?" he asked, the fear in his voice breaking out.

"There's an ancient ritual only dhampirs can use. I just put it to good use. And what do you know? It worked. I have two of my best hunters under my control," Marlowe replied, and his face twisted like a psychopathic clown.

What did he mean ancient ritual? What had he done to us? What was he talking about?

"So you bound them to your will?" Caleb said.

Marlowe smiled.

"This one required consent. And their mother gladly gave it to me. How splendid is that?"

Our mom had given what to Director Marlowe? Consent for what? I didn't understand. And what did Caleb mean Marlowe'd bound us to his will? Surely we'd know if he was controlling us.

What, like he was doing now and making me hold Caleb prisoner without my permission?

"What do you mean she gave it to you? Why would she let you control her kids?"

There was no way Caleb couldn't hear me. He was asking all the right questions.

Caleb, if you can hear me, we've got to stop him. You've got to stop him.

"Oh, she didn't know I'd be controlling them. You see, she was stupid enough to fall in love with a witch, and he hurt her so badly, she wanted to protect her kids. So, she came to me and asked me if I knew a way to keep them from falling for the wrong people. If I knew a way to stop her kids falling for the charms of witches. And before you know it, I had an eleven-year-old and an eight-year-old under my rule. All I had to do was use the crystals binding their souls," he said and looked at his rings, "and they do whatever I want them to."

So my curse wasn't real? What about the killer instinct? What about all the times I couldn't feel any love? What was that all about?

"So they were never cursed, but you made them think they were. Clever. But what did you do with them? To make them think they would turn into killers if they ever started feeling love?"

"It took attention to detail, you see. I couldn't have them suspecting anything or anyone else for that matter. Although if these two asked the wrong kinds of questions, I could always erase their memories and start over.

"That's the beauty of this binding magic. I can order them to do whatever I want, even if it shouldn't physically be possible. Lust, hatred—" Marlowe listed.

"Addiction," Caleb added.

Marlowe laughed. "You've seen him when he's high? Isn't he the most amusing thing you've seen?"

I wanted to kill him. Not the person he controlled. I, the real Wade, wanted to terminate him.

"Why go to all this trouble? Why make them think they turn to killers when they start to fall in love and that they have to turn to drugs to heal the pain?" Caleb asked.

"Isn't it obvious? To make it more convincing of course. I wanted them to think they had cursed hearts," Marlowe replied.

"Is that why you made him kill Sarah?"

Marlowe took a step back and looked at me with surprise.

"You know about her? Well, color me shocked. He's been hiding this secret for years. The guilt he felt when he killed her. But yes, of course I made him kill her. He had to believe his curse was real, and he was starting to have his doubts. Especially after he met you."

"So you tortured him by letting him have a few moments of bliss with her before killing her?"

"Of course." Marlowe replied. "How else would I have some fun?"

"You are sick," Caleb said. "Just because I fell in love with him doesn't mean he has to suffer."

Marlowe's face turned sour and his eyes narrowed.

"He had to pay the price for sleeping with what's mine," Christian said.

Caleb tried to free himself, but I was stronger and didn't budge.

"You fool. I was his before I made you think I was yours," he said.

"Wrong!" Marlowe shouted. He crept back to Caleb and leaned into his ear, piercing me with his eyes. "You will always be mine." He smirked and turned around to Winston. "Start the ritual."

Winston sprang to motion, and his blade crackled against the tarmac ground as he got to work, drawing a pentacle.

"When did you find out about me? Was it the witch who works for you who told you? Or did you connect the dots when Wade came to you when I ambushed him?" Caleb asked.

"Danielle only gave me your new fake name. She'd

never seen you before so she couldn't provide a picture," Marlowe said. "But when Wade came into my office asking how I got my information, I had him tell me everything that happened between you. And it was as if I could draw your picture. Of course, I didn't know why you didn't remember him and had no idea you were now a witch, but that's why I had him. To get me all that information."

Caleb nodded in understanding. "So you made him forget your conversation and come running to me. Genius."

Marlowe grabbed the collar of Caleb's shirt and shouted in his face. If I'd been in control of my own reflexes, I'd have jumped away from him. All I did as a reaction was take a step back.

"I needed my crystal, Tristan. You took it from me, the only thing that can stop me. However, all of this will become irrelevant after tonight. Once the ritual is complete, no one, not even the crystal, can stop me."

Winston was still drawing the pentacle. As usual, his top corner was stretchier than the rest. It always bugged me, and I'd wanted to correct him. If I was trapped in my own body, he must be too. He had no idea what was happening. I needed to find a way to get to him. We had to escape this maniac.

We'd never been cursed. And Sarah was never my fault. I didn't know what to make of the revelation.

And what about Caleb? How did he know I was starting to feel things for him again? How did he know to order me to kill him? Had he planted a seed in my mind when he found out who Caleb was?

Marlowe watched Winston, and I could detect sadness in his eyes. He placed a hand on Caleb's chest, and I felt the pressure of it on my own.

"You were the only one that got through, you know that?" Marlowe said and gazed at Caleb. "Together, we'd be unstoppable. I would even let you share."

"You'd never share your power, Christian. You know that," was Caleb's reply.

"You're right. You had your chance, and you blew it," Marlowe said and removed his hand from Caleb.

When he did, it felt like a weight lifted off my shoulder. I didn't like him touching Caleb. I wish I knew why I was so possessive over him when I couldn't remember our first run together. If I fell for him once, I could fall for him again, right? Christian had made me forget Caleb and everything about him. If it'd happened before, surely that meant my feelings now weren't entirely alien to my body. They'd been through these motions before. And if I got over my hang-ups then, I could get over them now.

"What do you see in him anyway?" he asked and glanced at me.

Caleb didn't reply.

"Hold him tighter," Marlowe ordered one of his rings, and I felt my hands squeeze tighter around Caleb.

"He has a heart, unlike you." Caleb wailed in pain and it coursed through my body.

"After everything I've just told you, you think he has a heart? You are a hopeless case after all."

Winston approached Marlowe and stood to attention in front of him.

"The pentacle is complete," he said in a monotonous voice.

That definitely wasn't Winston. That was a puppet. Marlowe's puppet just like me.

Marlowe turned around to look at me.

"Kill him," he ordered me, and I could see him enjoying the words taking effect on me.

I dragged Caleb to the middle of the pentacle and pushed him to the ground. When we separated, any little composure I had left abandoned me. If Caleb didn't stop me now, I was going to kill him.

"What the hell are you waiting for? Kill him now!" Marlowe screeched behind me, and I sprang to action.

SIXTEEN

CALEB

I rolled away from the edge of his blade and was quick on my feet. I knew Wade couldn't control himself, but I also didn't know how to stop him.

It made sense now why the transference spell hadn't worked. Because Wade was never cursed. He was just under the rule of this asshole that had killed way too many witches to feed his ego.

I'd heard everything Wade was telling me telepathically. It'd never happened to me that I could hear anyone's thoughts in such a big, intense capacity. I didn't know if it was because of our connection, or because my powers were expanding, something that was always a possibility, but that I'd never cared enough to explore.

What I did know was that I had to stop Christian. The only way to get to him was to go through Wade. But I didn't want to kill Wade. I couldn't kill him. Not only because I was short a spellbook or two but because he, along with his brother, was a victim in all this, and I was in love with him.

"Even in my last moments, you can't do the dirty work?" I shouted at Christian who stood outside the pentacle.

"Of course not, darling. I don't get my hands dirty. You should know that by now."

"You haven't changed one single bit," I said and avoided another swing from Wade's sword.

I looked around for my spellbooks, but they had been discarded and lay at Winston's feet. There was no way of retrieving them. And without my spells, I couldn't protect myself for long. Wade could kill me before I managed to even make the effort.

"I thought you needed powerful witches to tap into the ley lines. You think sacrificing me will help? I'm not even a member of the high council."

It wasn't much of a plan, but it was all I could try. If I convinced him that I wasn't powerful enough to help him achieve his goal, perhaps he wouldn't kill me straight away. I just needed time. More time to come up with a plan.

"From what Wade has told me, you're plenty powerful. I'm sure it will do the trick," Christian answered, and all the hopes that had manifested inside me were squelched.

Wade zoomed closer and took another shot at me, but for every step he took, I took two. I wasn't staying still, but this plan wasn't going to work for much longer. Sooner or later, he'd get me, and it'd be game over.

A blur of someone from the corner of my eye took my attention, and I turned to look at who that was, almost risking a cut to my throat.

It was a brunette woman with red lipstick and a simple red dress who stepped forward, wearing a beautiful necklace with an incredible arrangement of spells.

She was the witch. The witch that had betrayed us all. It had to be. What had Christian called her? Danielle?

"Help me. Absolve yourself and help me," I shouted at her. She stood opposite Christian, on the other side of the pentacle, and watched the events unfold.

"Why would I help you?"

"Because you are a witch. And so am I. Witches help each other," I told her as I rolled away from Wade.

"Do we now? Not in my experience."

"Danielle has no faith in witches. She wants to see that high council of yours rot and burn," Christian shouted.

I turned to look at him and saw a glow in his eyes. The same glow he'd had all those years ago when I'd slept with him. The thought of it now made me sick.

"I see you still trust witches. After everything? I have to say I'm surprised. I thought you were smarter than that," I said and noticed a shadow on the ground in front of me. The shadow of Wade and his sword behind me, and I moved to avoid it.

I needed to find something, anything that I could protect myself with. Wade was on top of me again when I spotted a broken pipe at the edge of the pentacle where Winston stood.

I made a small prayer to the Goddess in charge of me tonight and made a move for it. It was a risk, but it was one I was willing to take. Christian was a sadist. He wouldn't turn Winston against me. He hadn't been the one to fall for me.

No, it'd have to be Wade. He'd want to see his face afterward, before he erased his memories again and took what we had away. Again.

"I trust the right witches, for the right reasons. Danielle and I have an agreement. I know I like a good deal just as much as she does," Christian said.

I grabbed the pipe and twisted around just in time to stop Wade's blade digging into me. I pushed him back with the pipe and hoped it lasted long enough.

"You believe him? You think that cutting a deal with the devil will help you? He will destroy the witch world as we know it. If he taps into the ley lines—"

"Let them burn," she said, the hatred in her voice cutting through the air.

I wondered who she was. Who had made her lose faith in the witch community? I'd never seen her before, but the coven was so big, and the high council so large, there was no way of knowing all of them. If I knew what had happened to her, if I managed to get close to her and touch her, I could use her knowledge to my advantage. But it was impossible with Wade out for blood.

He sparred with me, and I managed to block all his attacks with the pipe, but judging from the cuts it was obtaining, it would soon be fragments on the floor.

"Help me, Caleb," Wade begged, and it reminded me of the time at the basement when he'd wanted to kill me, and I wouldn't let him.

Wait a minute.

Back at Ash's cellar, I'd taken control of Wade, and he'd been unable to do anything to hurt me. When I'd directed all his feelings and emotions back at him, he'd become my prisoner instead of Christian's. At the time, I'd thought it was the curse that I'd been keeping in check. But it wasn't. It was Christian's hold over him that I'd somehow managed to subdue. I hadn't known. But now, after everything Christian had revealed, it was perhaps my only solution.

I bend backward just in time to avoid a slash from Wade's sword, and the pipe shattered on the ground beside me. It had been good while it lasted, but now I had a plan.

I needed to get close to Wade and give him back some control. But in order to do that, I'd have to get through his blade.

How did I do that without hurting myself? If I died and Wade had no control of himself, then that'd be the end. No one to stop Christian or give Winston and Wade back their freedom. It'd be the end of the witch world as we knew it, and Christian would be at large and unstoppable.

Surely there was something I could do. A way to get close to him without sacrificing everything.

But I'd tried that already, and I'd failed him. I'd promised to help him and be there for him, and he'd promised the same. And when it came to it, I'd run and left him in Christian's grasp.

I owed it to him. To give him a chance at freedom even at the cost of my life.

"Wade, you don't want to do this, you need to stop," I told him.

Outside the pentacle, Christian laughed.

"Do you not understand how mind control works? Are you stupid? What happened to you since I last saw you? Since you became a witch?" Christian said.

I knew that would do nothing to liberate Wade, but I could help him understand what I wanted to do.

"Remember the cellar? When you tried to attack me? And I stopped you. Remember that?" His face didn't change, but his eyes blinked.

He could hear me.

"Remember how you asked me to help you? To not let you hurt me?"

Another blink as he tried to slash my neck, and I rolled over on my back to avoid it, getting away with a scratch on my shoulder.

"You can do this. I have faith in you. You can take control back the same way," I told him.

Blink. Understood.

"Why don't you just give up and die?" the witch outside the pentacle said to me.

"Who hurt you?" I turned to her for a moment. "Tell me, and I will stop them."

"I can fight my own battles."

When I looked back at Wade, I realized I was standing in the middle of the pentacle and Wade? Wade was charging at me.

It was now or never.

"Wade, you can stop this. I can't stop your brother, or Christian, but I can stop you. Do you understand?" I said.

He blinked and a tear ran down the middle of his cheek. He didn't want to do this any more than I did. But he could at least get a chance at saving himself and his brother.

Everything slowed down. I could hear my heart-beat pounding in my chest with every step Wade took. Each step was one closer to my ending.

The blade of his sword cut through my clothing and pierced my stomach, taking my breath away. I gasped, fighting for breath, but there was no time for such trivialities. I grabbed Wade's face with one hand, wrapped the other one around his nape, and pulled him onto me for a kiss. It wasn't passionate or roman-tic. It was a messy, bloody affair. Before I choked him with my blood, I removed my lips. It felt like a worse death than the one I was experiencing, but at least we were still touching. Touch alone was enough.

Caleb, hang in there. Please don't leave me.

The fear made me shiver. The loss of blood made me cold and shaky.

I can't lose you. Not now that I've found you.

"Take control and kill him," I told him with all the strength I could muster.

My empathy didn't need words, and thankfully, I was still strong enough to push all of his emotions back at him.

I'll do my best. I won't disappoint you.

"You could never disappoint me," I said. I put all my energy into my hands and channeled it at Wade. I'd never tried this before, but I hoped it would work and buy him some extra time because he'd need all the help he could get.

I'd always pushed people's emotions back at them. I'd never channeled my own to anyone. Not only because I didn't want to give anyone access to my soul but also because there'd never been a need for it before. But now it was a life or death situation, and Wade needed as much leverage as he could get.

I channeled everything at him. My frustration, my fear, my agony.

I gave him my pain and my heartbreak. And I gave him my love. Everything I had ever felt for anyone. Nora, Jin, Annabel, all my other lovers. And him. I

gave it all to him. I knew Christian had kept him prisoner for years, and he no longer knew what was real
and what was fake, but I hoped having a piece of me
inside him would give him the strength to overpower
the bastard.

I didn't let go until he was ready. Every second
made him more powerful and me weaker. And it was
okay because as soon as he let go, he'd be fighting for
control over his own mind and body against Christian.

"Show him what you're made of, baby," I told him,
and he lowered me to the ground, removing the blade
from my stomach. My hand dropped to the side as he
got back up and looked away from me.

He was on his own.

SEVENTEEN

WADE

I didn't have any time to feel sorry for Caleb. To hold him and try to get him some help. Just because I'd got his message, it didn't mean I liked it at all.

Caleb was sacrificing his life to get close to me and give me back control. The worst part was, I didn't know if I could stop Marlowe. I'd never been up against a vampire before. I didn't know anything about them. At least with witches I knew what to expect. I didn't know if vampires were super-fast and super-strong like in the films, or if they were entirely different. Which was beside the fact that Christian was already a different kind of vampire. I knew nothing else. Just that he fed off energy and that was about it. Oh, also, he was a grade-A douche.

I glanced at Caleb down on the ground one more time. Struggling with his breath and trying not to choke on his own blood. I said a prayer for him, to keep him alive long enough until we could get out of this, and then turned my attention to Marlowe.

He looked at me defiantly, and when I took another step forward, he spoke to Winston.

"Kill your brother. It's about time," he said, and Winston jumped into the middle of the pentagram.

He swung his sword, and I raised mine to block it. Sparks flew where our blades met.

"Brother, you have to step away," I told him as I pushed him back, but it was no good.

He was as strong as me, and whenever we'd sparred at the training room, we'd always lasted the same, fighting to the very end.

There was no way I could defeat him. Not with the limited time ahead before Marlowe gained back control of me.

Winston pulled back, pursing his lips and furrowing his brows before bringing his sword back down on me. He was at war with himself, too, and there was no way I could help him. No way other than getting the rings from Marlowe.

As I avoided Winston's attack, a bird appeared at the corner of my vision.

A raven.

It shot down at Winston, and before he could react, the raven's beak gnawed at his face.

Winston stepped back and shook his head in confusion. I looked at Christian Marlowe, who had no idea what was happening. There was a flash and smoke and Hew appeared midair in the middle of the pentacle. His legs collided with Winston's chest and my brother fell on the ground, Hew on top of him.

"Don't worry. I've got him," Hew said and took a crystal out of his belt.

"Took you long enough," I said.

"I had to understand what was going on. For a minute there you looked like the enemy," he said and made the spell in his hand explode in front of Winston.

"Don't hurt him."

"I couldn't even if I wanted to," he said.

I nodded and turned to run towards Christian, determination coursing through my body.

An evil grin shaped his face as I approached him.

"You think you can stop me? What part of unstoppable did you not understand?" he said.

I waved my sword at him, but he stepped back, avoiding my hacks.

"Stop it," he shouted at one of the rings.

I felt an energy pulsing inside me. An energy that wanted to take over and make me obey his order. But I still had some control left inside, and I wasn't about to give up.

"Whatever it is he's done to you, you are running out of time. And then you will be back under my control, none the wiser," Marlowe hissed.

"Shut up. I always hated the sound of your voice. Now I know why," I shouted at him.

He laughed.

He laughed so loud he had to lean back, and it echoed off the buildings around us. It felt like the darkness itself was laughing.

When he lowered his head, I made the introduction of his face to my fist. He fell down, and I climbed on top of him, my sword ready to attack.

"Stop this madness. Obey your master," he slurred.

I could see in his eyes a sliver of fear that I could do some damage. I also felt the energy growing stronger inside me. Caleb's power was wearing off, and with that, my control was dwindling. I needed to take those rings before it was too late.

"It's working, isn't it? Stop. It," he shouted.

I could feel my hands shaking, needing to listen to him, but my mind was still warding him off.

He attempted to reciprocate the punch, but I ducked and avoided it. Before I could find my balance, I found myself on the floor, my face pressed against the tarmac, and Christian's arm around my neck, holding me in place.

"You know, I never thought of taking advantage of you, but I have to admit, this position is turning me on," he slurred in my ear, and I felt sick.

I could tell his control was breaking in through my barriers. The barriers that Caleb had sacrificed himself for. And I was going to let him down. I didn't want to let him down. He'd given everything for me, to help me. And I was about to let it all go to waste.

A thought crossed my mind. Worst case scenario, I died, too, and Caleb and I could be free from this perv for good.

I lifted my blade and tried to push myself to my knees. I'd never practiced this, but it'd be a technique I'd thought about if push ever came to shove. Well, it just had. If it didn't kill me, it could give me the upper hand again. Whatever happened, I had to try.

I pierced the blade through my own stomach, making sure to curve the blade upwards as I slit it through myself. The curve at the tip of the blade should do the rest.

Pain throbbed in my entire body. I let out a cry before I could stop myself. Marlowe's grip weakened. A gasp escaped his lips. The tip of the blade must have cut through something important. And even though it wouldn't hurt him, it would weaken him. I'd hoped it would, at least.

Before he could do anything, heal himself, or whatever it was he did that made him unstoppable, I grabbed his hand and forced the two rings off him. Then I retracted the blade into its hilt, and I was finally free of Christian, his body, and his control.

While I could still walk, I turned around and grabbed his necklace. The crystal that bound him. The crystal that could destroy him.

"You might have control back, but not for long.

You better enjoy it while it lasts," he said.

I kicked him in the face and then ran to the middle of the pentacle, where Winston and Hew were fighting. The witch in the red dress was staying out of it. Watching, observing, smiling. I didn't know what was wrong with her.

I spoke to the rings in my hands and hoped that it worked.

"Winston, stop fighting," I shouted.

Winston dropped his blade, and Hew grabbed him before he collapsed.

"We gotta get out of here," Hew shouted at me.

"How?" I asked him.

"I've got a spell." He helped Winston get on the floor.

I stepped closer to the center of the pentacle where Caleb was lying. I dropped to my knees and looked at him. The light was going out of his eyes, and his wound had colored the ground red.

"Caleb, how can I help you? Tell me," I asked.

He struggled to open his mouth, and when the word came out, it was nothing but a whisper.

"Home," he said.

I nodded and placed one hand under his knees and the other under his neck. When I tried to pick him up, I felt a kick in my back. I tumbled to the ground and Caleb ended up on top of me.

"Before you go, I'll have that," the witch said and forced my fist open, taking the crystal necklace off me.

I was powerless to do anything. The weight of Caleb on top of me and the fear of hurting him more by moving rapidly stopped me from doing anything.

"Thank you, Danielle. I'll have that back," Marlowe said and approached her.

The witch looked at Christian and smirked.

"Change of plans, darling," she said.

Christian smiled, although it didn't quite reach his eyes.

"You stupid witch. You think you can use that? Even if you take it, there's no way you can stop me without knowing the spellword," he said.

"Oh, I know the word," the witch said.

I wanted to keep up with the events, but Caleb dying on top of me kept me distracted.

I don't have much time left. I heard his thoughts in my head.

That hadn't happened before. How had he done that? That meant he still had some life left in him. And we were losing precious time.

"You do, do you?" Christian said. I could tell he was trying to keep his cool, but the fear glistening in his eyes told the truth.

"Let me tell you a story, Mr. Marlowe," she said.

No, not a story. We didn't have time for stories. We needed to get out of here immediately. I looked to Hew and Winston and tried to carry my thoughts across to them. Let's get out of here while they're distracted. But Hew's attention was taken by Danielle.

"Once upon a time there was a witch named Tania, and she got close to you. She managed to convince you she was on your side, and then—" Danielle said.

"And then she created this crystal." He completed her sentence. "So what? I told you that story."

"No, you didn't. I already knew it. Because that witch was my girlfriend. And I don't know if you can recall, I know old age can be a bitch with dhampirs, but you murdered her," she shouted.

"She was? She never mentioned it when she climbed in bed with me." Christian grinned.

"You think I'm going to be jealous? You think I'm going to cry and beg for your forgiveness because you slept with my girlfriend? It was all part of her mission. I knew she hated you. I knew she despised you."

"That's a very good story, but she never got the chance to tell anyone the crystal's spellword. I killed her before she had the chance. So, if you want to save your life, I'll have it back now," he said, his voice coming out rushed and raspy.

He was most certainly worried. He didn't want to die. I'd have felt sorry for the guy if he wasn't such a monster. I'd have felt sorry for him if this had happened three days ago when I'd still thought he was my beloved director.

"See, that's where you're wrong, Mr. Marlowe. She might not have notified the high council, but she told me. Long before she even made the crystal. She made the spellword the name of the one she loved most."

I turned to look at Christian, and whatever blood was left in his body seemed to wash off his face. It was obvious Danielle was getting to him.

"You are lying. You don't—" he started, sounding shrill and pathetic, but the witch lifted the crystal in her hand.

"Really? You want to try me?" she laughed.

She opened her mouth. "Da—" she started, but before any of us knew what was happening, Winston jumped at her and knocked her off her feet.

"What are you doing?" Hew shouted at him.

The stone rolled in front of us, and I grabbed it before Winston or Danielle grab it.

"I—I don't know. She was trying to hurt Marlowe," Winston said, but he looked more confused than anything.

"Give me that stone," Danielle shouted at me.

I wanted to. She knew the spellword and could cast the spell to wipe Christian off the face of the earth, for good. But how could I trust her after she stood there watching me hurt Caleb without stepping in to help us?

It didn't matter what I thought of her. Christian jumped at her in two big leaps and knocked her to the ground.

"So, everything was a lie, huh?" he asked her when he had her pinned. "Why? Why would you help kill the witches if you only wanted to destroy me?"

Danielle spat in his face.

"Because those witches were the ones who came up with this brilliant plan to place Tania with you. And that came to her undoing," she screamed.

Christian took a big breath and opened his mouth. "You're going to pay for this."

He leaned into her face, and I thought he was going to kiss her, but instead, he sucked in and a white stream of energy poured out of her.

"You're killing her," Hew shouted.

Christian didn't react.

If he kills her on the pentacle, the ley lines will open, Caleb said inside my head. *We've got to stop him.*

How? I can't exactly cast spells, I replied.

I looked at him and a tear dropped from his eye to my cheek.

Give it to me. I don't have much time left, but I can cast one last spell.

"No," I shouted at him. *If you do this, you will die.*

Yes, but so will Christian. And he has to be stopped.

I didn't want to accept that he had a point because he couldn't sacrifice himself. He'd already done so, and he was dying in my arms as a result. If I gave him that spell to cast it, he would die, and that was certain.

But Christian Marlowe had to be stopped. We both knew that. If he didn't, God only knew what more damage he could cause, to witches and humans alike.

Ok, I finally gave in and placed the crystal in his palm.

The spellword is the name of the one she loved most, I heard Caleb in my head.

"Her girlfriend," I said.

I hope so. It better be.

Caleb opened his mouth and barely a croak came out. Danielle was screeching on the floor the more Christian drained her of her magic and the force that kept her alive.

"Danielle," he said, barely a word. More like a whisper.

The crystal burst between us into a million pieces. Christian groaned and pulled back from the witch, grabbing his chest. Blood came out of his mouth, followed by his nose and his ears. His eyes turned blood red, and before he could even take another step, he collapsed on the ground, dead before his face touched it.

"Help us," I begged her as I felt Caleb collapse over me at the same time as Christian took his last breath.

Danielle turned to look at me, but before she could say anything she fainted with a pained grimace on her face.

Hew and Winston were both staring at us.

"You said you can get us out of here?" I shouted at Hew across the pentacle. "We need to get to Caleb's home."

Hew helped Winston get to his feet, and they came towards us.

"Do you know where he lives?" Hew asked.

"I do."

"Then think of it. Now," Hew said and retrieved a crystal from his belt.

He said the spellword aloud, but it was in a language I didn't know, and a dust storm surrounded us. My memories went back to Caleb and his home, and of Nora and Annabel and our meeting with Graham and Brick Lane.

Like a tornado, the dust storm lifted us off the rooftop, and within seconds we were let go. Once the storm cleared, I recognized Caleb's living room.

"My God," I heard Annabel scream.

I looked at Caleb, whose head was resting on my chest, still and unmoving. His only hope now was Nora. Carefully, I placed him on the carpet next to me and caressed his cheek. He didn't respond. Of course he didn't.

Caleb, are you still in there? Please tell me you are, I pushed my thoughts on him, hoping he could still hear me. But nothing happened.

"What's going on?" Annabel screeched. She looked Winston and Hew. "Who are you? What happened to him?"

"Annabel, please calm down. We went up against Christian and we killed him, but Caleb sacrificed himself," I shouted at her, and that's when my adrenaline rushed out of my body.

I'd also been wounded, and in my worry for Caleb, my own safety had taken a back seat. I fell apart on the floor next to Caleb, looking up at the ceiling and trying to take deep breaths. The blood that was gushing out of my stomach made its presence known to me again and everything spun around me.

"Nora. I've got to get Nora," Annabel cried, and she disappeared from my field of vision.

"Wade, what the fuck is going on? What have you gotten yourself into?" Winston asked.

"Winston, little bro, I'll explain everything, but now is not the time," I said, and something cold touched my face. Nora appeared at my side, and she smiled.

"Are you crazy? Take the kid away from this bloodbath," Hew shouted.

"It's okay," Nora said and turned to look at Hew. She stretched his hand and he took it for a moment. "I can help."

She let go of his hand and turned her attention to me.

"Are you okay, Wade? You don't seem okay," she said.

I twisted my head to where Caleb lay beside me.

"Your daddy was hurt. You need to help him," I told her.

"I know," she said with a serious face that didn't belong to a six-year-old. "I can't feel Daddy's presence."

That was all it took to make me lose hope. If Caleb was dead, there was nothing she could do. Could she?

"Can you still help him?" Surely, she could. She had done that once before. When he had been a vampire and died. I prayed that she could do the same now.

"Of course. But first let me fix you."

She placed her hand over me, and hot fire burned my wound.

Hew gasped. "A phoenix? I thought they were a myth."

I grabbed her hand before she could continue and begged her.

"No, help your daddy first."

Nora shook her head.

"If I help him first, I won't be able to help you. Now let me do what I do best," she said with the wisdom and the words of an adult, and I let go of her hand.

It caught fire again, and the lullaby I'd heard only two nights ago infiltrated my ears. I tried to tell the lyrics apart, distinguish the noise, hoping to under-stand what it was she was singing. But I couldn't. It was a language unknown to me, and probably unknown to most humans. If even witches thought phoenices were a myth, I'd be surprised if anyone knew how Nora's powers worked or what language her lullaby was in.

As I was starting to relax under her soothing song, I was enveloped in flames, and I couldn't see anything or anyone other than Nora.

Then, only moments after, the song stopped, the flames went out, and when I looked at my stomach, the blood was still there, but the cut was gone and so was the excruciating pain.

Nora fell backward, her little fingers turning into ashes as she tried to touch her temples.

"Nora, sweetheart, you need to take it slow," Annabel said to her as she bent down to help her up.

"I don't have much time. Daddy's aura might have gone, but his spirit is still here. If I wait, Daddy will be gone for good.".

"But, Nora, honey, if you heal Daddy, you will die," Annabel said.

"What the fuck did she just say?" I heard Winston, and I was about to tell him to shove a sock in it when Nora spoke again. Only it wasn't six-year-old Nora talking. It wasn't her sweet, innocent, cheeky voice. It was that of an adult. No, scratch that. Not an adult. Of many adults.

"My dear Annabel, you've looked after me for so long. Dear friend, don't feel sorry for me. I live and I die over and over. There's no end for me. Only many new beginnings," she said and then her voice dropped back to six-year-old Nora. "If I don't help Daddy, he will never live again."

She gave Annabel a warm smile. Annabel gave her a hug, her eyes full of tears.

"I'll always take care of you, my friend. No matter what happens," Annabel said.

Nora went on all fours and crawled in front of Caleb where she took a moment before speaking again.

"Before I do this, I need you to promise me something," she said.

"Anything. What is it?" Annabel asked.

Nora shook her head. "Not you." She turned to me and looked me straight in the eyes. "You," she said.

"Promise? Promise what?"

I seriously didn't know what promise I could make to a six-year old ancient phoenix. And why couldn't this wait until Caleb was breathing again? We were losing precious time. But then again, what kind of promise can I make little Nora after she sacrifices her current life for her daddy.

"Promise you will help Daddy take care of me when I return."

Her words took me by surprise. I'd never expected her to ask me this. I was expecting her to ask me to stay away from her, her daddy, and her entire family. I expected her to ask me to never hurt anyone else again. But instead, she was asking me this.

Caleb and I had just met.

No. We hadn't. We'd been together before. Before Christian had erased it all and played with my life. Regardless, could we really do this? I didn't want to have to decide now with Caleb's limp body next to me. He needed Nora's healing. Before it was too late.

"My daddy needs you just as much as you need him. He's spent his entire life looking for love only to have it taken from him over and over again. You've been searching for the ability to love, and he gave it to you. He gave it to you once before, and he can give it to you now. You need each other."

"What? Since when are you gay?" Winston asked from the side. Always focusing on the important shit, as usual.

"Why don't we go outside and get some air?" Hew said and touched Winston's chest.

Winston raised his eyebrow at the raven's touch and didn't budge.

"I don't wanna miss this," he said.

"Neither do I, but you're being very inappropriate," Hew whispered at him.

Winston huffed and pushed Hew's hand away but continued to stand where he was and shut his mouth.

This whole fated-mates thing might actually work for him. I didn't know how he felt about the whole situation, and I didn't have the energy to ask him right now. But if Hew could shut him up, then half the battle was won already.

I turned my attention to Nora. Her hands were settled over Caleb's body, her head focused on me. Her gaze waiting.

"I don't know if he wants to be with me. I can't make you this promise."

"Is it so hard to believe that someone can love you?" Annabel asked.

"I killed him. Why would he ever love me? I've killed dozens of witches and fed them to a vampire."

"And he has killed dozens of Nightcrawlers. But Nightcrawlers still come to him and ask him for help. He can't help himself. He's an empath. And if Nora thinks he loves you, then he does," Annabel said.

I didn't know what to believe or what to do. The fact that I'd never had a cursed heart was too big a subject to even begin to comprehend. I didn't know what it meant for who I was today. And did it even matter when Caleb's life was hanging on by a thread?

Did it matter whether I was a creation of Christian or my own self? I didn't know. Had I ever truly loved Sarah? Did I truly have feelings for Caleb? Or had everything been fabricated by Christian. All my life I'd wanted to be free of the curse. I'd had no control over my body, actions, and mind. And I was free of all of them. I'd wanted this for years. To be free and to be able to fall in love without hurting anyone or killing anyone. Now I finally had what I wanted. So why couldn't I make this simple promise to the girl so she could save Caleb?

"I promise. I'll help your daddy take care of you," I told her.

It was time to put the fear aside and take control of my own life.

EIGHTEEN
CALEB

I opened my eyes and had to blink before everything came into focus. Hew and Winston were sitting at the dining table eating pizza, and Annabel was sitting at the other end, sipping the tea she so loved.

Where was I?

I was at home, but why was everyone else here? What'd happened?

It took a second for everything to come rushing back. The trip to the Tower of London. Wade's apparent betrayal. Standing on the rooftop with Christian, and Wade and Winston under his control. Sacrificing myself to give Wade a chance to stop Christian. Me casting the spell to kill Christian. It all gave me a headache before I could even get off the couch.

I turned to the side, and once my vision cleared, I saw Wade illuminated by the sunlight of the windows.

He was holding something in his arms, and his smile was wide. I tried to push my upper body off the sofa, but it made my headache worse.

"Good morning," Wade said.

"What happened," I asked. Then, I noticed the bundle in his hands was a baby.

"Nora!" I shouted and jumped off the couch.

Big mistake. My head spun even faster, and I tumbled back on my ass.

"No. What happened?" I asked.

Wade took a seat beside me and allowed me to have a look at Nora.

"She wanted to save her daddy. And that's what she did," Wade replied, and I looked at the baby.

Her beautiful green eyes stared right into mine, and she greeted me with a smile and a giggle. I leaned forward and gave her my finger, which she wrapped her tiny little hand around.

"Oh, my dear sweet Nora. I'm so sorry," I whispered to her.

Her feelings of joy and happiness overwhelmed me. My dear Nora had given her life for mine.

"She wanted to help you," Wade said.

"I know she did. She always does. And I always take advantage of her. But this stops now," I said and made a mental promise to myself. No more using Nora. If I was given another chance to be her father, I was going to do this right.

"I'm so sorry," I whispered to her. "Never again."

Annabel came into my peripheral vision and offered me a cup of tea.

"Drink this. It's gonna help with the headache."

I knew it would. I took the cup from her hands obediently and tried to assess her mood by grazing her with my touch.

Her anger buzzed in my head.

Of course she was angry. Her friend had sacrificed herself, again, to save my ass. I felt angry with myself too.

"What happened last night?" I asked.

Annabel took baby Nora from Wade and disappeared into Nora's bedroom, leaving us boys alone. Wade helped me to the dining table where we sat down opposite Hew and Winston. I took a sip of the tea Annabel had offered, and the headache cleared in an instant. Then, I listened to them retelling the story to me because, as it turned out, I had some gaps of the events. Especially from the moment Wade stabbed me onwards.

"And then Hew teleported us back here."

I turned to Hew, and his hazel eyes warmed my heart. I hoped we'd be able to finally be friends after he'd kept my secret for so many years without so much as a price or return. Hew was an amazing guy, and I didn't need to know him from Adam to know that.

"Won't you get into trouble for using such powerful spells from the Crown Jewels?" I asked him.

I knew he'd said that he could do it as long as he

was saving people, but that didn't mean it was true. The Crown Jewels were being protected for a reason. Because they were deadly and powerful.

"Not your fight, my friend. I'll deal with that myself," Hew said, and he turned to Winston who held his gaze for a moment before Winston talked to me.

"So, you're the witch that took my bro's heart," he said.

I didn't answer, but instead, I held his gaze for a few moments, trying to gauge his reaction. We'd been introduced before, but neither he nor Wade could remember. He hadn't liked me then, either.

"So, you're the hunter who bonded with a familiar," I finally said, and his cheeks reddened. "I'm Caleb," I said.

"Winston," he offered me with a simple nod.

"I know. We've met before. But Christian erased all memories of me. Probably so you wouldn't make Wade challenge his own sanity."

Winston's stare deepened, and he blinked several times.

"He...what?"

I looked at Wade. Had he not told him? Had no one explained to him what had happened to him?

Wade shrugged and bit his lower lip.

"He's still trying to wrap his head around it all. As am I," he said.

My gaze fell on the pizza box again, and my

stomach rumbled. I guess it was better to focus on the hunger and the trauma than ponder Winston's question for too long. I had no idea how long it would take to get my Wade back, the one I'd been with before.

"Can I have some of that?" I asked.

Wade slid the box across the table and opened it for me. I'd missed not just the memory of him being attentive like that to me, but also him. With me. In the same room, sharing something unique.

"How are you two feeling?" I asked them, cutting a slice.

"It's a lot to take in," Winston admitted.

"I don't know what to think, to be honest. I know we were under his control, but I don't know what was him, and what was me," Wade said, and it took balls to do so in front of the others.

"I can only imagine. But I hope I can help with that. Where are the stones?" I asked.

Hew put his hand in his pocket and retrieved two rings, which he placed in the middle of the table without a word.

"Nothing is over until these stones are destroyed. Whoever has them can still control you," I said.

Hew nodded. "I was waiting for you to get it done."

I nodded at him.

"Before I destroy them, you two have a choice. I can make you remember everything." I looked at Wade. "Our time together, our first kiss. Our first...

everything. But that will also make you remember everything Christian ever asked you to do for him. And it may not be pretty."

Wade pursed his lips and considered my words. I wanted him to remember me the way I remembered him. We could pick up where we'd left off as if not even a day had gone by, instead of starting from scratch.

"I don't think I want to remember," he said.

A punch in the gut. I shouldn't have felt like that, but I did, and there was little I could do to change that.

"I hope..." he said and took my hand. "I hope you don't mind. I might have met you before, but I've met you again now, and I've fallen for you, against all odds. Again. That's all I want. I don't think I can go through everything Christian made me do. I..."

He stopped as if he couldn't breathe anymore. I felt how hard it was for him to do this. To say no to his life. To turn down a chance to know everything. But the guilt and shame he felt were equally strong.

I might never come back from it, he said inside my head.

I gave his hand a gentle squeeze and my smile of approval.

"You can help me remember everything. We can recreate everything," Wade added.

Yes, we could. He didn't have to remember what we'd once had and how it was taken from us by force.

We could start over. The new us. A better us. Yes, that was fine. That was enough.

"I'd love to," I said.

This was for the best.

"I want to remember," Winston said, and we all looked at him.

His face was tense, and his knuckles red from how hard he squeezed his fists.

"Are you—" Hew started to say, but Winston cut him off.

"I want to know everything that bastard made me do. I wanna make things right. I can't if I don't know all the disaster I've caused."

I gazed at Wade who was staring at his brother with a pained smile.

You're stronger than I am, little brother, his thoughts offered me.

I knew he probably wasn't ready yet, but I was hoping one day he'd be able to tell his brother out loud.

Hew took one of the rings and held it in his hand, and with one last look of uncertainty at Winston, who nodded once, Hew spoke to the ring.

"Remember everything Christian made you do. Remember everything he's made you forget," he said.

We watched Winston become wrought with emotions, and it took all my strength not to approach him and share some of the load with him. He didn't deserve this. No one deserved this. But he had Hew to look after him. Or so I hoped. I didn't know what was going on between them, and now was not the right time to ask.

When Winston came to, his eyes looked glazed. Empty almost.

Hew tried to touch him, but he raised his hand. Not in an aggressive manner. More in an attempt to say he was good, and he needed his space.

"I think that leaves one last thing to do," I said, trying to take the burden of attention off Winston. "The rings."

"I've got a lot of spells, but nothing that can destroy these rings. Blood magic is not something I'm versed in," Hew said.

I scanned the room and tried to go through my mental checklist of all the spells I had in store.

"I might have something," I said and got up.

Wade stood to help me find my balance even though I didn't need it. Ann's tea was magic, and it worked like it too.

"I like you looking after me again," I told him, uncaring that we were in company and Wade was still getting used to me.

He blushed but didn't say a word, only helped me walk to the bookcase where I retrieved a book and opened it to reveal the crystals hiding inside.

I grabbed a white one and closed the book, leaving Wade to put it back. I walked to the table and opened my hand to show everyone.

"This is a very rare spell. It brings other spells back to their original form and destroys them."

"That doesn't sound like anything I've ever heard of. Where did you find it?" Hew asked.

"A friend made it," was all I offered. I didn't know if Graham was still a friend. I couldn't imagine how, but it was his spell.

"You want to do the honors?" I asked Hew.

He shook his head and crossed his arms.

"I think this is all yours, my friend," he said and gave me the ring that had once controlled Winston.

I took both rings in my hand, and only then did Winston flinch. I placed Graham's spell in the same palm and closed my fingers around everything.

"Wait!" Wade said before I cast the spell.

All eyes turned on him.

"There—there's something you can help with," he said, and his gaze dropped to his hands.

I wasn't sure what he meant, and he looked like he wasn't willing to share it with everyone. With my free hand, I touched his.

My addiction. He said it was amusing. It was his way of torturing me. Which means it wasn't real, right?

I nodded.

"Then take it away. Please. I don't want him to control me in any way ever again," he spoke out loud, and I could tell the other two were confused.

I stepped away from Wade and picked up the ring that could control him. Making myself familiar with the spell and its intricate workings was a struggle, so while I searched for the right word, the right phrasing so as not to hurt him any further, Wade explained to Hew and Winston, his face red, and his eyes constantly blinking.

"Christian turned me into an addict. I used to collect witches' spells hoping I could find something to reverse the curse, but instead, he turned my obsession with breaking it into an addiction," he said.

"What do you mean? You can't cast spells," Hew said and turned to Winston who didn't say anything but looked at his brother hesitantly.

"You showed me those spells. After you lost Caleb, you showed me your collection. He'd made you go crazy for a while as revenge so in one of your desperate frenzies you took me home and told me everything. I—I told him about them. And he decided to make you into... whatever it was he wanted to make you into," Winston said, his words barely a whisper.

I looked at Wade, but his gaze was focused on his brother.

The words to erase his addiction climbed to my throat. I was ready. But I needed to wait for him.

"It's not your fault, brother. We were both doing his bidding. If you hadn't told him, I probably would have. Don—don't beat yourself over it."

No matter what he'd said, it looked as if Winston *was* going to beat himself over it. And that would be part of his journey to coming to terms with himself. Thankfully, he had Hew to help him out. If he let him.

"I'm ready," I said.

Wade gave me a dejected smile that nearly broke my heart. This had all been because of me. Because Christian wanted to torture him for falling for me.

No. It wasn't my fault I never went back for Wade. Graham and the High Council had taken that choice away from me.

"You're no longer to be addicted to spells. The pain that drove you to them is healed and so are you," I said clearly and with purpose, and then I watched Wade's face change. He closed his eyes for a moment, and when he opened them again, there was glow in them. He smiled and his whole face lit up. If I wasn't so happy, I would have cried at all the reasons this was heartbreaking.

"How do you feel?" I asked.

"You've done it," was all he offered me, but that was enough. I knew it had worked. I could see it. "Now, destroy those motherfuckers for good."

I wanted to beg him to allow me to give his memories back. Make one last plea. But he was at peace with his choice, and I needed to be too. I couldn't force his hand. Not after everything Christian made him do since he was just a child. I put his ring back in my other fist with Winston's crystal and the one with Graham's spell and closed my fist around them all.

"Destroy," I uttered.

White smoke erupted from my fist, and dark blood oozed from where the rings were. All eyes burned me with their stares, but I waited until the spell was complete.

The blood evaporated before it stained the table or anything else, and anything that was left in my hand became a heap of sand.

"It's done. You're free," I said and gazed at Wade who looked back at me with tears in his eyes.

"That's worth a celebration. Don't you think?" he said.

"I'd be up for that," Hew said. "Winston?"

Winston blinked as if he'd just been roused from a slumber and looked at Hew as if he was unsure what had been said. Before he could repeat his question, Winston nodded, and I didn't fail to notice the worry on Hew's face.

We left the apartment and went to the first bar we could find.

Whether or not Winston was up for it, it was time for us to celebrate victory.

———

"Do you want to come back to my place?" Wade asked me when Hew had to carry Winston home.

Poor thing had decided to drown his misery in alcohol, and none of us could blame him. I only hoped he'd let Hew help him figure it out because they still had so much crap to sort out, like their supernatural bond, the whole same-sex relationship that seemed to terrify him more than it did Wade, and the whole new world of creatures they hadn't known existed.

Yeah, no. That dude deserved his drink.

"Why? What do you have in mind?" I asked Wade once we were alone.

Wade bit his lower lip and looked away from me, digging his hands farther into the pockets of his jeans.

"You know, talk…and things," he said, and it was almost as if I could feel his cheeks getting warmer and full of color.

It was a different side to him; one I hadn't seen since the first time I'd met him.

My mind was so confused because that first time was five years ago, and while it felt like it, I also remembered every detail, every feeling, every touch as if it was yesterday because it had been yesterday when I'd been given access to my lost memories.

And to think I almost didn't get any of it back, that I'd almost lost him a second time because I'd been living inside my head too much.

I couldn't believe only a few days ago I'd wanted to erase all my love. How stupid and foolish had I been? I had living proof in front of me of what happened when you couldn't feel love. Or so I'd thought anyway.

It didn't matter that his heart had never really been cursed. As far as I'd known, he could never feel love. And I'd wanted that. Despite the deadly instincts that could have awakened at any time, the disconnect from the rest of the world, the lack of control.

Thinking back to Caleb from three days ago, I could swear I had been so close to fucking it all up. If the curse had been real...

But it hadn't been. It had been something much, much worse. And yet, Wade was still standing strong opposite me. It wasn't like his entire life had changed. He didn't look like a man who'd killed so many people in vain. He didn't look like a man who didn't know what part of him was true and what had been a fabrication.

I knew better. He was good at hiding it, but one touch, just a graze, a stroke of the cheek, could give me access to all the layers underneath.

I'd been running from love all my life, and he had been running towards it.

Had we been doomed from the start?

"I'd love to see your place," I told him. I was curious to see if he still lived in the same digs.

I desperately wanted to take his hand and wrap myself in his arms, but I held back. This was his decision to make, and he could take it as slow or as fast as he wanted. I might have all our shared moments, but he didn't, and he still had to come to grips with everything.

"I'll call us a cab," he said and stepped aside, pulling his phone out and getting busy ordering a taxi.

Ten minutes later, we traveled across to Kensington and jumped out of the cab and into a block of flats. Wade tapped a fob at the entrance, and it opened the door with a bleep. When we got into the lift, he pressed number sixteen, and I raised my eyebrow his way. This was definitely not the same apartment.

"Witch hunting pays well, huh?" I teased.

My comment didn't have the desired effect. Instead of lightening the mood, Wade sighed, and his head dropped.

"No, don't do this to yourself," I said and came closer to him, but I didn't touch him.

"How can I not?"

I tried to meet his gaze, but it was impossible without touching him, and this was the worst time to forget my gloves.

"Can I touch you?" I asked him.

He raised his eyes to meet mine, confusion written across his face.

"Why on earth are you asking that?"

"Because I don't want to intrude on your privacy."

I was fully aware this was quite ironic, considering our first encounter at the bar, but everything had changed since then. Three days? More like three lifetimes.

"Of course you can touch me," he breathed, and I didn't need to be told twice.

I placed my fingers under his chin and commandeered the emotions that infiltrated me.

Who am I? What even am I?

His thoughts hit me crystal clear. And so did the whirlwind that had broken inside. The feeling of loss and betrayal. The guilt. The pain.

And most of all, the desire. Desire that pulsed between us both. I let him feel mine. It was an interesting and different experience. Allowing someone to feel what I felt. Before, when we were together, I hadn't had my powers to connect us. Now?

Our mouths collided. Words were wildly inadequate and unnecessary. When our skins touched, that was all we needed. His tongue explored my mouth, his hands wrapped around me, a warm embrace that brought chills to my spine.

He tightened his grip, and I pulled him closer, feeling his erection growing against mine. For a moment, that was enough. In each other's arms, allowing our emotions to flow freely between us.

But then, Wade trailed his fingers down the middle of my back onto my waist, making me lose my shit. I shouldn't have been surprised that he knew my weakness. That was the whole point of sharing without hesitation. But it still made my knees buckle. Before I could collapse, he grabbed me by the ass and lifted me, my legs folding around his hips.

The doors of the lift slid open and someone cleared their throat. We both turned to find a prim and proper elderly lady, wearing a blue suit jacket, dress, and fascinator, staring at us with her hands linked in front of her.

"Hi, Mrs. Weatherby," Wade mumbled, and I felt his embarrassment by the tingle on my fingers.

"Hello, Wade," she responded and entered the lift.

Wade carried me outside it, smiling at the elderly lady until the doors closed on her. Just as they did and his relief washed over me, Mrs. Weatherby spoke.

"Nice boy toy."

And just like that, she was gone, on her way to the ground floor.

Wade's amusement combined with mine made us laugh out loud.

"Interesting character," I said when I managed to get my breath back, fully aware that my feet were still in the air.

"Doesn't hold a candle to you," he growled and took my air back with his intoxicating kiss.

He carried me to his door and unlocked it, clumsily. When we got inside, he slammed the door with his foot and carried me to his bed. There would be time to see what kind of accommodation he'd moved into later. I guessed it made sense that he'd moved. Christian hadn't known I'd lost my memories and didn't want me finding him. I wouldn't be surprised if Wade had only moved house five years ago.

He put me down gently, my back stretching over the comfiness of the mattress. Once he was sure I was secure, he lifted himself off me and planted kisses down my front. He suckled on my neck until it stung before he released me, then tried it again.

I want to claim you. Make you mine.

He spoke right through me, continuing his work until he was sure his love bites would stay.

I brought my hands to his hair and sniffed, taking in his musk. It served to make my cock pulse harder in my jeans, begging for release.

Wade crawled down to obey my indirect orders.

We've all the time in the world for me to tease you. Now, I give you what you want.

Then fuck me, I said, and I knew he'd heard me because he chuckled.

He unbuttoned my jeans and let my cock free of its confines. He'd been good when he'd sucked me off in the basement, but now, with the connection between us, I could teach him how to do it right. Again. Maybe I could bring him back up to speed with the old Wade. I did like a challenge after all.

Whatever I thought of, he did it. It didn't matter how complicated it might have sounded in my head. It was as if we were finally speaking the same language. We were in sync. So much so that he almost brought me to my climax. But I didn't want to come yet. The night was still young, and he had more to do to me.

You're sinful, you know that? he said.

So I've been told.

He climbed back up to me and pulled me hard to his mouth for a kiss.

Do that again, I told him, and his hand tightened on the nape of my neck. *I want you inside me.*

Wade's lips curved into a smile, and he hoisted himself off me. He grabbed my forearm and forced me to my front in one swift, dizzying motion before bringing his lips to the back of my neck and planting more kisses where he knew they'd have the most effect.

I lifted my ass and rubbed it against his hardened dick. This was killing me. I'd never felt so impatient to be fucked before. I'd missed him inside me. I hadn't known, but I missed him. And I knew he missed me. Regardless if he remembered or not.

His lips trailed down my body, and when he got to the small of my back, he used his fingers to trace circles on my pimpling skin, and his tongue to lick my flavor. I'd given him my weak spot, and now I'd have to sit under him and suffer.

And boy did I suffer. With every trace, I lost my breath. Every lick made my heart beat faster. There was no escaping him. I didn't want to escape him. I was under his control just as much as he was under mine.

We were equals.

Stop toying with me and fuck me.

I couldn't shout my thoughts, but that's what it felt like.

It didn't matter. Because next thing I knew, he had dismounted me, and when I tried to turn around to check what he was doing, he forced my head back on the mattress.

You gave me a command, and I'm obeying.

His hand lifted off me, and I waited patiently,

resisting the strong urge to look at what he was doing. Drawers opened and closed. Zippers went flying down. Clothes shuffling. I was inundated by sounds and while I didn't like it, it also made me hornier, hungrier for Wade's cock.

When his length massaged between my butt cheeks and he climbed on top of me, bare skin to bare skin, I came close to exploding. But he didn't mess with me more.

His hardness pushed against my hole, demanding access, and I eased myself to let his sleek, lubed cock in.

A moan, the first loud thing that had been shared between us since we'd walked into his house, released from my very core, and my hands searched for his head. I wanted to feel his hot breath on my neck while he eased inside me.

Wade lowered onto me and bit my earlobe, growling like a wild animal. His hands wrapped around my neck, and he squeezed gently, just enough to hurt my carotid, but more than enough to make my orgasm build up inside me, trying to claw its way out.

It had always been hard to find someone who enjoyed a little bit of kink with their sex, men that weren't fully into BDSM but enjoyed tight situations, and more than enough times I'd left whoever's house I'd slept in feeling like I was still missing something. But Wade could read me, and not just because I let him.

It hadn't been like this before. We'd been intimate,

but the fear of being found out had kept me from revealing my true self. That's why maybe it was better that he chose to not remember. We were starting over the right way. With honesty and truth between us. No lies.

When I looked into his emotions, he didn't feel bad about whatever it was I had him do to me. If anything, he enjoyed it just as much as I did. I could tell he wanted to go harder, pound me faster, squeeze my neck just a little more. And I let him.

I already couldn't wait for the countless nights of passion between us where we could let our raw sides out in the open. There was so much room for growth and development. And we had all the time in the world.

Fuck the witch hunters and fuck the high council. That was a worry for another day. They too would have to be dealt with eventually. But that was a different battle. And considering the last one had cost me my life, I wasn't looking forward to making sense of the disaster the two opposing sides had created.

Stop thinking about them. I've got you now, Wade said and tightened his grip around my neck.

I know you do. And so do I, I said back, as I tried to catch my breath.

Wade's cock rubbed on my prostate and with one last push, he came hard, and so did I. He didn't even need to touch my cock to have me spoiling his sheets.

"Oh. My. Goddess," I said when he collapsed in a heap next to me.

He looked drained, but I didn't miss the grin on his face.

"That was…" Wade panted.

"Different?"

"You can say that again."

I curled up into his arms and tickled his lips with my fingers.

"So, Mr. Rawthorne. How was your first anal experience?" I asked him.

He looked at me with a face that burned like sin.

"It was all right." He shrugged.

"Asshole," I said and slapped his bare chest. His nipples were still hard.

"Stop it, or we'll be having round two sooner rather than later," he said.

Instead of an answer, I slapped his chest again.

"I'm so happy I met you," he said when he'd mounted me again and tried to pin me down.

I let him put my hands over my head, and I looked at him.

"Me too," I said.

"I hope you can be patient with me while I relearn everything," he said.

"Always," I whispered.

He came down for a kiss, and as promised, round two started.

———

Later that night, and after a late Chinese takeaway, we slept in his bed, finally letting the exhaustion of the last few days knock us out.

A sparkle coursed through my veins. I was fine until then. And then I wasn't. The sparkle running through my body didn't wake me, but it worked to get me out of my dreamless sleep. And it grew into a pulse, which in turn became an explosion inside me.

I shot out of bed and massaged my temples while I tried to make sense of what was going on.

Wade screamed in agony, and I looked at him. He touched his head, wailing in pain.

And then, as if someone had flicked a switch, the energy faded, and my body was back to normal.

"What the hell was that?" Wade shouted.

I looked outside his floor-to-ceiling windows into the early morning skyline of London. It was nothing the bare eye could see, but we'd felt it. And so had the rest of London.

"That..." I started and turned to look into Wade's scared, pained eyes, "was trouble."

———

Killer Heart might be over, but the adventures of reformed witch hunter Wade and his beautiful empath Caleb are far from over.

What was the spark they both felt? What is next for the two troubled men and their relationship? And who will stand in the way?

Find out in Demon Heart, Book 2 of the Cursed Heart series!

A Letter from Rhys

First of all, thank you so much for reading Killer Heart. I truly hope you enjoyed reading it as much as I loved writing it.

If you take 2 minutes of your time to post a review on Amazon, thirteen familiars will arrive at your doorstep so you can take your chance on mating for life. I swear to God this is true.

The idea for Caleb and Wade has been brewing for quite a while, and it holds a special place in my heart. Three years ago, you see, after a trip to NYC with my new boyfriend (now husband) for an author signing, I was hospitalized. I had left myself untreated for far too long—not entirely my doing—but it left me trapped in a bed surrounded by sickness, sadness and loneliness.

And I needed an escape. Stat.

That was when I looked over my notebook full of

ideas and found three words that sparked something inside me. I'd been keeping a record of any story, regardless how small the idea was, since I was twelve, so there was quite a volume of them. Those three words were given to me by a friend so I could write a short story about them.

Blade, rain, dust.

Well, I never wrote a short, but things started to fall into place. I had spent a long time writing my previous book, stressing about the next one, agonizing over their success that I felt liberated when a seedling was born that was pure fantasy.

I only stayed in the hospital for two weeks—although it felt like eight hundred—but it gave me so much while I was there. And I was determined to finish it, to change my life around and to put my health and happiness first.

Well, if you've ever made any resolutions, you know how the next part goes.

It all fizzled out. My health was okay again despite the many treatments I needed, my life went back to normal, and the story wasn't quite working. There was something missing. So back to routine I was.

Since then, I've written three drafts that will never see the light of day, reworked the structure, the plot, even the names, bemoaned to friends and family about my story idea that won't conform and behave and despaired at the thought it will never be finished. Just like everything else I've started.

But then something magical happened.

It all finally clicked. I wish I could remember how, but all I know is that one moment I had one writing plan for my year and the next, it had all changed completely and I was telling everyone about my urban fantasy mm romance that would be out in late 2019.

And what do you know? It did happen. And it made me the happiest man alive writing it. Giving Wade his heart back. Making Caleb believe in love again. Having Nora put her faith and trust in her daddy again.

Of course, I couldn't have done it without some very special people in my life.

My husband, Alex, for putting up with me writing all the time.

My author bud, Ana, who is always there to listen to my frustrations and crack the whip when I'm not doing any work.

My alpha readers, Becki, Sandi and Xochitl, who looked at the bare bones and told me exactly what was on their mind.

My beta readers, Maria, Tiffany and Crystal, who didn't hold back and gave me the most valuable feedback so that the story made sense.

My editors for keeping me in check and consistent.

And my Everlies for helping me push through whenever I thought this book was never going to happen.

Lastly, you, dear reader. You picked up this book and read it from start to finish. Whether you loved it, liked it, or hated it, you're as important as the rest of the people who helped put this book together.

I hope you're ready for the rest because I have at least two more books coming out with Caleb and Wade over the next two months, and so many more ideas to explore.

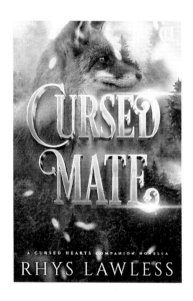

If you haven't done so yet, you can check out my short story, Cursed Mate, which I wrote as an introduction to the world of Cursed Hearts, and which explores the relationship between witches and their familiars in a little more detail. You might see some familiar faces so it's definitely worth checking out.

If you're looking forward to the next book,

Demon Heart is out and ready for your consumption. You won't believe the things I have in store for the two boys. The cast is getting bigger, the stakes higher and the love stronger.

If you'd like to get exclusive material as and when it's written, as well as advance cover reveals and a view into my life, you can join my Facebook Group **Rhys Everly After** where I share everything.

https://www.facebook.com/groups/everlyafter/

See you soon in another adventure.

Thank you,
Rhys Lawless, November 2019

Audiobooks

My books are coming in audio. For an up-to-date list visit my website at rhyswritesromance.com/audio

Rhys Lawless

Killer romance. One spell at a time.

Cursed Hearts Series:
Narrated by John York

Killer Heart, Book 1

Roman & Jude Series:
Narrated by John York

Elven Duty, Book 1

Elven Game, Book 2

Elven Heir, Book 3

———

Rhys Everly

Sexy romance with all the feels

A Proper Education Series
Narrated by John York

Teach for Treat

Beau Pair

Me Three

Your Only Fan

Missing Linc

CEDARWOOD BEACH SERIES

NARRATED BY NICK HUDSON

Fresh Start, Book 1

About the Author

Rhys Everly-Lawless is a hopeless romantic who loves happily-ever-afters.

Which would explain why he loves writing them.

When he's not passionately typing out his next book, you can find him cuddling his dog, feeding his husband, or taking long walks letting those plot bunnies breed ferociously in his head.

He writes contemporary gay romances as Rhys Everly and LGBTQ+ urban fantasy and paranormal romances as Rhys Lawless.

You can find out more about him and his works-in-progress by joining his Facebook group or visiting his website rhyswritesromance.com

INDEX

Blade - a witch hunter's sword. Also slang term for a witch hunter.

BLADE force - the task force of witch hunters whose sole purpose is to find and eliminate witches.

Coven - a group of witches, usually based on geographical location.

Crown Jewels - Powerful spells kept in the Tower of London and guarded by the seven raven familiars under the Queen's command.

Cyclops - A Nightcrawler species descended from giants.

Dhampir - A very rare Nightcrawler species. Energy vampires.

Dust - The effect of a spell being cast which in turn turns to residue. It fades off after a certain time, depending on the strength of the spell.

Empathy - the ability to feel the emotions of others.

Familiar - a shifter. Protectors of witches. They bond and mate for life with witches who they are destined to protect.

Green Mile - A pub where humans aware of the paranormal world meet and mingle with Nightcrawlers.

High Council - the governing body of a coven.

High Priest/ess - a member of the high council.

Ignition - The process of awakening a witch's powers, including their natural power and their spell casting abilities.

Incubus - A Nightcrawler species that feeds off sex. If you get an Incubus to fall for you, then you've found a partner for life. Plus, great sex forever. A female incubus is called succubus.

Lacing - the process of mixing energy with a physical object.

Mated App - An app for Nightcrawlers. Primarily used for familiars to find their mates, but also used for hook-ups.

Natural power - a witch's inherent power that does not require the use of a spell.

Nightcrawler - Paranormal creatures.

Phoenix - a rare and immortal Nightcrawler species that regenerates from their own ashes. They can also heal others by sacrificing part or all of themselves.

Potion - Lesser common use of magic. Usually in liquid form.

Spell - a crystal of various sizes and colours created by alchemy that can be used by witches to perform magical tasks. A spell can be cast by a word or phrase called a spellword.

Spellword - a word or phrase that casts a spell.

Tower of London - Primarily a safe place for powerful spells. Secondarily, a ley line intersection.

Troll - Earth Nightcrawlers with immense strength. They are a secretive species and not much is known about them other than they are the strongest species of Nightcrawlers.

Vampire - A Nightcrawler species that feeds off blood.

Made in United States
North Haven, CT
05 March 2023

33416023R00202